Linda Jaivin is a novelist, translator, essayist and playwright. She lives in Sydney.

Also by Linda Jaivin

FICTION
Eat Me
Rock 'n' Roll Babes from Outer Space
Miles Walker, You're Dead
Dead Sexy

NON-FICTION
New Ghosts, Old Dreams: Chinese Rebel Voices
   (co-edited with Geremie Barmé)
Confessions of an S&M Virgin
The Monkey and the Dragon

The Infernal Optimist
Linda Jaivin

FOURTH ESTATE • *London, New York, Sydney* and *Auckland*

The writing of this project has been assisted by the Commonwealth Government through the Australia Council, its arts funding and advisory body.

The Infernal Optimist is a work of fiction. The characters and events described in this book are entirely imaginary. Any perceived parallels with any real people or situations are, therefore, purely coincidental.

'I'm Fair Dinkum', written by John Williamson. Reproduced with the kind permission of Emusic Pty Ltd.

Fourth Estate
An imprint of HarperCollins*Publishers*, Australia

First published in Australia in 2006
by HarperCollins*Publishers* Australia Pty Limited
ABN 36 009 913 517
www.harpercollins.com.au

Copyright © Linda Jaivin 2006

The right of Linda Jaivin to be identified as the author of this work has been asserted by her under the *Copyright Amendment (Moral Rights) Act 2000*.

This work is copyright.
Apart from any use as permitted under the *Copyright Act 1968*, no part may be reproduced, copied, scanned, stored in a retrieval system, recorded, or transmitted, in any form or by any means, without the prior written permission of the publisher.

HarperCollins*Publishers*
25 Ryde Road, Pymble, Sydney NSW 2073, Australia
31 View Road, Glenfield, Auckland 10, New Zealand
77–85 Fulham Palace Road, London W6 8JB, United Kingdom
2 Bloor Street East, 20th floor, Toronto, Ontario M4W 1A8, Canada
10 East 53rd Street, New York NY 10022, USA

National Library of Australia Cataloguing-in-publication data:

Jaivin, Linda
  The infernal optimist.
  ISBN 0 7322 8275 6.
  ISBN 9780 7322 8275 2.
  I. Title.
A823.3

Cover design by Geeza Designs
Cover images courtesy of Getty Images and Stuart Horton-Stephens
Typeset in Bembo 11.5/16 by Helen Beard, ECJ Australia Pty Limited
Printed and bound in Australia by Griffin Press on 70gsm Bulky Ivory

6 5 4 3 2   06 07 08 09

> I'm fair dinkum,
> bloody oath I am
>
> I've loved the smell of gum leaves,
> since I was in a pram
>
> Some places may be greener,
> but I don't give a damn
>
> 'cause I'm fair dinkum,
> bloody oath I am
>
> John Williamson, 'I'm Fair Dinkum'

Part I

One

When I walked outta them gates, I coulda sung for joy. There she was, waiting for me — Marlena, me own little Version a Heaven. She Who I Love, Honour and Try to Obey. She Who Supports Me Through Thick and Thin. She Who I Call She Who For Short, what she is, being even shorter than me. She was sitting in the car, tapping them cute little fingers on the wheel. She got out when she saw me coming. 'Babydoll,' I said, opening me arms wide. 'Give your man a kiss in the Free World.' What she did.

I'd just thrown me swag in the boot and climbed into the passenger side when she informed me, in no unswerving terms, that it better be the last time she had to collect me from prison. She looked hard at me as she turned the key in the ignition. 'No more schemes, Zeki. No more deals. No more stealing stuff that doesn't belong to you.'

I gave her a little poke in the ribs with me elbow. 'No more getting caught, anyway.'

'Zeki!' She turned off the motor and crossed her arms over her chest.

'Only joking, darl.' Marlena's like the Gym of Accusation, I swear. She gets me guilt muscles fully pumped. I swore to her that it was just a joke. I swore that from then on in I was travelling the straight and narrow. I swore it all the way home. I swore it in through the door. I swore it on me knees. I swore it on me grandmother. I swore it on the extra-large pizza I got her to order us for dinner that night.

It was hard work. Finally, She Who believed me and let me do what a man's gotta do when he gets outta the nick, and that is *relax*. I settled onto the sofa with me woman by me side, the remote in one hand and a stubbie in the other, and switched on the telly. Now, I don't know much about world politics, and I don't have no particular feelings for or against the US of A, except I is very keen on Tupac and J-Lo and Snoop Dogg and Tommy Hilfiger what come from there. But when I saw them towers fall, me eyes nearly popped outta me head. I was detonated. What got to me most was the sight a them people falling outta those windows. I'm something of a window specialist meself, and I know all about getting in and outta them. You don't wanna be doing it from that high off the ground. I looked over at Marlena. Her big eyes were filling with tears.

'The world's too scary,' she said, after we finally managed to stop watching and switched off the telly. 'I want you here with me. You really, really, really gotta be good from now on, Zek.'

It was time to lighten the mood. The world was fucked — pardon me French — but it didn't have nuffin to do with us.

'I am good, darl.' I patted her on the arse and winked. 'And I'm gonna show you just how good I is. I'm planning on being good all night long.'

She gave me one a them looks what she and me mum both do perfect, what says they don't think I be listening to anything they been saying. 'Zeki.'

'Darl, I promised you I was going straight. I mean it.' I winked again. 'Straight to the bedroom.'

She tried not to smile.

I was doing me best to keep that promise. I got me a nine-to-five as a storeman in a warehouse and everything. But I'm not gonna lie to you, I wasn't making that much in the warehouse. And you gotta be realistic. You can't expect a man to get rid of all his bad habits at once. Life don't work like that. Besides, I wasn't making that much in the warehouse. I had to sublimate me income somehow. It was only for the short term, I swear.

The trouble began about a month later, one night in October. That night, me and Marlena, we was due at me folks' for dinner. Me dad had called and said Mum needed cheering up, what Marlena always did for her. Me mum had been pretty stressed since September Eleven. See, it didn't matter that most Muslims — especially Aussie Mossies like us — were horrorfied by what happened in New York. Every time me mum picked up the phone at the Community Centre where she worked, she got abuse in her ear. Like she done it herself. Like me mum was Osama bin Laden. I mean, she's starting to grow a few hairs on her chin, but that's where the resemblance stops. Someone threw some stones through the window a me brother's shop, too. And me cousin Tulip, what wears the veil like me mum, she got spat on when she was out shopping. Maaan. I don't wanna sound like no hippy, or be in labour with the point, but I don't see why we can't all get along. Me, I don't care whether you're a Chinaman or a Paki or Eye-tie or any other sort a wog — we can all be friends. She Who is a Christian, by the way.

That afternoon, I phoned Marlena and told her to meet me at the station at six. That gave me enough time, I reckoned, to meet a man about a dog first. It wasn't really about a dog, but you know what I mean. I was doing the deal, what involved a few mobiles, a laptop and a watch, when I happened to look at the watch, what was on me wrist. It said five to six. That didn't give me a lot a time for negotiating. I had to run then, and when I got to the station — one what didn't have its ticket barriers up yet — I could see the train coming. It was a cool night. Down on the platform, She Who was shivering in her fleecy top, looking round and smacking a rolled-up magazine against her palm like it was me own hairy bottom.

I raced up just as the train pulled into the platform. 'Sorry, darl,' I go. I kissed her on the cheek, what was cold.

'Hmph.'

We found a seat in the downstairs part a the carriage. She plopped down all sulky. Her hair, what is pretty, fell in front of her face.

'C'mon, babydoll. Give your daddy a kiss.' I went to tickle her under her chin but she jerked her head away. I caught a whiff a her perfume what was full a flowers like me nan's garden. 'You smell sweet, babydoll.'

'Where'd you get that watch?'

Shit. I wasn't sposed to keep that.

'Like it? It's yours.'

'It's a man's watch.' She looked closer at it and frowned. 'It looks very expensive.' She was looking at me all suspicious. Sometimes, I swear, she be like me own personal lady cop.

'It was on special.' In factuality, it was on this bloke's side table, in full view of an open window, what was pretty special from me own point a view, but I wasn't gonna go into unnecessary detail.

It was then that the pair a coppers boarded the train.

Two

At first I stressed, cuz I thought the coppers knew about me seeing the man about a dog what wasn't really a dog, and the watch what wasn't really me own watch in factuality, but I saw they was just checking tickets, so I relaxed again. After September Eleven, the New South Wales Government put more coppers on the Sydney trains. Makes sense, eh? Like Osama bin Laden was gonna make his next appearance on the express to Bankstown, and New South Wales's finest could catch him and be heroes like the firemen in New York. But if Osama bin Laden was in the hood, he wasn't going anywhere near the trains. So the coppers spent most a their time checking people's tickets and telling them not to put their feet up on the seat.

'Did you buy a ticket, Zeki?'

'You worry too much, darl.'

'I don't think so. I think I worry the right amount. Maybe I don't worry enough.' I could see she was in a puff. 'Well?'

'Well what?' I put on me best, most innocent face, what wasn't really.

'Zeki, how many times —'

'Relax, babe.' To illustrate how this was done, I flipped over the seat in front so it was facing us and put up me feet. 'This is the life, eh?'

'Zeki,' Marlena said, 'you do have a ticket, don't you?' She wasn't letting it go. 'Zeki?!' I already owed She Who a hundred bucks for paying me last fine, what might a been the reason she was getting so tense on me. She worked this job emptying bedpans and washing floors in the children's ward at the hospital. Even though she loved kids, the job was pretty terrible and she earned fuck-all — pardon me French. Still, she managed to save. At least when I wasn't around.

'Everything's under control, darl.' I winked. In factuality, I knew I had to improve on the situation, what was looking as hairy as me auntie Elma's upper lip. The coppers were moving through the carriage in our direction. 'Tickets, tickets.'

Marlena pulled her own ticket outta her bag. She looked at me with big eyes and a tight mouth.

I gave her me most charming smile. 'Chill, darl.'

'I'm so chilled I'm shivering.'

'It's only a ticket. Anyway — anything happens, you don't know me.'

'*Zeki*.' She and Mum, they got the same way a saying me name like it really means something else, like 'Stop it' or 'How could you?'.

'Shh. Trust me, baby.'

She Who took a breath and opened her magazine. I could tell she was only pretending to read.

The coppers was checking all the people's tickets. When they got to us, I looked up like I be pleasantly surprised. 'G'day,' I go. 'Howzit goin'?'

One a the coppers had a face like a country boy, what be made a freckles and sunlight. He said 'G'day' back. The other, what was older, didn't say nuffin. He had a face like an arrest warrant. He smelled a belt leather. He was staring at me feet.

'Mate,' goes Detective Sergeant Freckles, 'you know you're not supposed to put your feet up on the seat.'

'Oh, mate, I know, I know,' I go. 'But I got ankylosing spondylitis, gotta keep me ankles up, you know? Doctor's orders.'

He looked at me like he wasn't sure if I be bullshitting him.

Marlena made a noise that sounded like the bark a them small dogs with big ears what are more like rats than dogs. See, her uncle got ankylosing spondylitis. It's such a funny word that after he told us about it, I went round repeating it for days in all kinds a funny voices, though not in front a him. Not after the first time, anyway. 'Pardon me,' she goes, coughing into her fist and frowning. She looked down at the magazine, what had a spread on Brad Pitt and that Friends chick.

'My brother has ankylosing spondylitis,' goes the other copper. 'It's a disorder of the spine. Nothing to do with ankles.'

'Maaan!' I go, like I was fully surprised. 'I'd better get me a new doctor, eh, mate?' I put me feet back down on the floor, giving each one a shake and checking them out like I couldn't believe they was okay down there. 'The things them quacks will tell ya.'

I could see Freckles was trying not to smile. His partner wasn't laughing. 'You wouldn't be carrying a train ticket now, would you?'

'Aw, look, mate, I'm not gonna lie to you. It's like this — I forgot.'

'Do you forget often?' This from Freckles, me mate.

'Yeah, actually.' I figured I might as well be honest. 'Bit of a bad habit.'

'Ever been in trouble with the law?' Bad Cop asked.

'Mate. I've been Inside four times. But I'm clean now.' What was almost true.

Bad Cop nodded and asked to see me ID. I gave him me driver's licence. He walked over to the door of the carriage to call it in. Freckles apologised. 'Sorry, just protocol.'

'I know, mate,' I go. 'Just doin' yer job.'

'So,' Freckles goes, 'what were ya in for?'

'B 'n' E. Hot goods. That kinda thing.'

'Hot goods?' The copper laughed. 'Stoves and microwaves and stuff like that, mate?'

I grinned. 'You got it, mate.' I was thinking this was going all right when the other bloke returned.

'Right-ee-oh, Mr Togan. Gonna have to ask you to come back to the station with us.'

'Mate, sir, me folks are expectorating me. Big family dinner. Rellies gonna be there, me nan, you know what it's like. Give me a fine for not having a ticket, fair enough. But I didn't do nuffin. I'm telling ya, I'm clean as a whistle. Cleaner probably. People spit into whistles.'

Marlena wasn't pretending to read no more.

'She with you?'

'Never saw her before in me life,' I go, giving her the once-over. 'Though I wouldn't mind an introduction.' I winked at Freckles and whispered, 'Quite a foxy lady, what d'ya reckon?' Freckles frowned. Both coppers quizzed She Who Don't Deserve This with them eyes. She stared down at her magazine what had a pitcher a Tom Cruise and that Spanish chick with the same name, except in Latino, while her cheeks turned as pink as that pickle what they got in Leb shops.

The train was approaching a station. 'Coming?' Bad Cop asked, what wasn't really a question.

Just as we got to the end a the carriage, I turned and called out to Marlena, 'Tell me folks I ran into some friends, darl. I'll be a little late.'

When we got to the cop shop, these two blokes what was wearing suits and ties was there waiting for me. One was chewing gum. He popped it when I walked in. The blokes nodded to the coppers, what nodded back. Now I was really beginning to panic. I thought maybe they did know about the man and the dog what wasn't a dog in factuality after all. I eased the sleeve a me shirt down over the watch what wasn't really me watch.

'Zeki Togan?'

'That be me,' I said, holding out me hand for shaking, what the blokes didn't do. So I turned it into a move from me hip-hop repertoire and kinda pointed at each a them in turn as I asked, 'And who do I got the honour of addressing?'

'We're from the Department of Immigration.'

I almost laughed out loud then. 'Thanks for the service, mate,' I told them, 'but you're a bit late. I immigrated here with me family when I was six months old. That was a long time ago. And now, speaking a late, if you'll be excusing me, I gotta go to exactly that very same family, what be firing up the barbie —' I looked at me watch, remembering too late it wasn't exactly me own watch, 'right about now.' I turned to go. The guy what was chewing gum grabbed me wrist and, before I had time to react, slapped on a pair a cuffs.

'What're ya doin'?!' I reckoned they'd worked out it wasn't me own watch after all, but you always gotta act innocent, specially when you ain't.

'We're taking you into Immigration Detention.'

I almost laughed again. 'You got the wrong guy.' I thought I knew the one they were probably looking for. One a me rellies from the Old Country was in Australia on a tourist visa what finished two years ago. He was washing dishes at me uncle Baris's kebab shop for cash wages — not that I was gonna dob him in or nuffin. I may be a crim, but I got me honour.

'No, I think we've got the right one.' The first bloke popped his gum again and signalled to the second one. 'Wanna read Mr Togan his bedtime story?'

The second Immigration bloke held up a piece of paper and began to read. 'According to Section 501 of the *Migration Act 1958* . . .' I looked over at Freckles, what was looking down at some paperwork like it suddenly be very interesting, like it just grew a pitcher a girls with bikinis on. Then I looked at Bad Cop, what looked straight back and seemed to be enjoying himself. The wind banged a tree branch on the window but no one seemed to notice but me. Two lady coppers walked past the door of the office we was in. One said something what I couldn't hear and the other laughed. They were babes. I've always had a soft spot for a woman in uniform, what I seen a lot of in me time. Somewhere in the station they was making coffee. It smelled good. I wondered if they had any doughnuts. Coppers always had doughnuts, even on TV. I wouldn't a minded a doughnut. I like to eat when I'm stressed and I was feeling mighty stressed, what is a natural reaction to being cuffed, specially when you done nuffin to deserve it, what in my case was for once. The Immigration guy was still reading from that piece a paper. '. . . powers to deport non-citizens who . . .' It was all Greek to me, what, being Turkish by originality, I didn't understand a word of.

But something he was saying snagged in me ear. 'Non-citizen?' I said. 'But I's a . . .' Then I stopped. I was gonna say that I was a citizen. Then I remembered that, in factuality, I wasn't. See, when me family immigrated, we was given permanent residence. When I was nineteen, Mum and Dad decided we should all take out citizenship. You shoulda seen the queue at Immigration. It was a hot day, and hotter inside than out. I couldn't be arsed waiting in there with all them other wogs just for a piece a paper, specially on a day like that. It'd be hours before it got to be our turn. So I told me folks I was going to the toilet and nipped off to the pub to put away a few coldies. I ran into some mates. One thing led to another, and by the time I remembered about getting back to Immigration, it was eleven o'clock that night. I told me folks I'd go back the next day but never got around to it. Boy, did me dad give me a walloping over that.

They were all staring at me. 'Did you have something to say?' The Immigration bloke what been reading that paper drummed his fingers on the desk. I realised me gob was hanging open. I shut it.

And so, as it turned out, I wasn't late for dinner that night. I never got there at all. I got to Villawood Immigration Detention Centre instead.

Three

In factuality, Villawood isn't that far from me folks' place, but once we turned off Woodville Road onto Christina, and then turned up Birmingham, what is opposite Leightonfield Station what I never even knew a train to stop at, it began to feel like we was going to some kind a secret place what didn't have no connection to the suburbs what surrounded it. Birmingham, what is a road with factories on, was completely empty at that hour. Not a person in sight. Birmingham hooks to the right, and that's when you see the first gate, what has guards on, and when you drive through that you see razor wire around a big compound, what I later found out was called Stages Two and Three. The road forked, and we went to the right. We drove past some old Nissen huts, and some trees, and a minute or two later we was pulling up at what looked like a little fortress in the middle of nowhere — they told me it was Stage One, the maximum security part a Villawood.

Stage One held more than ninety men, mostly in three dorm rooms, what weren't big but what held forty men each. I never seen anything like it even in prison. An officer took me into one a the rooms and pointed to a mattress on the floor, what had the kind a sheets on what be grey even when they be clean. Right away, I got farts, smokes, sweat and dirty socks in me nose.

I looked around. Some Vietnamese and Chinese were sitting in groups on their cots, playing cards. A big Maori dude was lying on his back, staring at the ceiling and punching his fist into his hand, over and over. A little Eastern European bloke sat in the corner muttering to himself. A Fijian dude what was covered in tatts came up and asked for a ciggie. His name was Mingus. Me and Mingus went outside, into a tiny concrete courtyard with a punching bag and a couple of old picnic tables. The walls was topped with coils a razor wire. A Chinese bloke sat flicking old tea bags up at the razor wire, what was hung like a Christmas tree with them. Mingus told me some a the guys had been there seven, eight months. They were mostly criminals what Australia wanted to deport but their own countries wouldn't take back. He told me a lot a them were hard-core. The more he told me, the more confused I got about what I was doing there.

One a the blues walked over and handed me a Detainee Information Booklet what set out all the detention centre rules about head counts and lockdowns and Codes a Conduct and the importance a taking a shower every day and all this other bullshit, what I chucked in the bin for a joke.

I asked Mingus where I could get some chow. It was already after eight. Me stomach, what had been looking forward to Mum's home cooking, was getting pretty cranky.

'Dinner's over, bro,' he told me. 'They serve it from four-thirty to five-thirty round here. You miss it, that's it.' He musta clocked the look on me peach cuz when he finished his smoke, he said, 'Wait here.'

'Ain't got nowhere else to go,' I said.

He came back with a packet of instant noodles.

'You're a legend, mate.' I gave him another ciggie.

In factuality, the noodles weren't even enough to fill a man's tooth, much less his stomach. But it was better than nuffin. Anyway, it was only for one night. As soon as I finished, I went to the public phone to call She Who. I wanted to tell her where I was, and that I needed a lawyer urgent — an immigration one, not a criminal one, what was for once. They needed to bail me outta there quick-smart.

She wasn't home yet and her mobile was switched off — still at me folks, I was guessing. They took me own mobile off me when I got there, and they didn't allow incomings on the public phone after eight at night. I didn't wanna call me folks and get them all worked up. Couldn't face the drama. So I left a message on Marlena's home phone with the Stage One number telling her to call me in the morning.

I could tell it was gonna be a long way to morning, specially since I gave away the rest a me smokes and spare change to the Chinese and Vietnamese for protection — I knew how things worked even before the Fijian dude spilled it out. Even the Islanders what looked big and were covered with tatts was respectful a the Orientals, what was well organised and what knew kung fu from the time they was born.

I didn't wanna hang around that dorm any longer than I needed to. Taking a walk to check out me surrounds, I came upon this nice-looking bloke what was sitting on a chair in the corridor reading a book. He looked to be around me own age, in his late twenties. Later I found out he was younger than he looked, what comes from having a tough life. He was wearing clothes what was neat and clean but not flash. Cuz he didn't look like a crim, he peeked me curiosity.

'Yo, bruvva,' I said.

'*Salaam aleikum*,' he goes, getting to his feet and touching his right hand to his heart. 'I am Azad.'

'Zeki.' I went to give him the bruvvas' handshake.

He laughed when his hand got tangled up and I had to show him what to do with his thumbs. He asked me where I came from. I told him Auburn. He didn't know it. I told him it be in a different part a Sydney's western suburbs.

'I'm sorry,' he said. 'I mean your country.'

I was about to say Australia. 'Oh — the *Old* Country, mate? Guess.'

No one ever picks it. I look like I could be anything. Me skin's so olive it coulda dropped off a tree in any a them Mediterranean countries. Me nose points to the Middle East and me eyes got a slant of Oriental.

'Turkish,' he said.

I was surprised. He was one smart dude. 'Bingo,' I said.

'Sorry?'

'Don't worry about it. Where are you from?'

'I am a Kurd.'

'Like what be made a yoghurt, mate?'

'Sorry?' He rolled his Rs like they was tyres.

Azad didn't get me sense a humour in them early days. 'Just a joke, mate. Me mum puts curds what be made a yoghurt into *tarhana*, what is the best breakfast, I swear.'

He smiled politely and glanced down at the book in his hand.

'Watcha reading, mate?' I asked.

He showed me the cover. '*A Fortunate Life.* It is supposed to be Australian classic. A visitor in Port Hedland gave it to me. I like to read to improve my English. Do you know it?'

'Not personally,' I said. 'Me and books aren't what you call real acquainted.' I felt in me pockets for me ciggies and remembered I gave them all away.

He took a pack from his pocket and held it out.

'Ta.'

'Take the pack,' he said. 'I am trying to give up, *Ensh'Allah*.'

'Oh, mate,' I said, lighting up. 'If you don't mind me saying so, you don't got what they calls da meaner of a crim.'

'Pardon?'

'You don't look like no criminal.'

'I'm not.' His dark eyes flashed in a way what made me think I shouldn't a said that. His back went real straight. 'I'm an asylum seeker.'

I thought about this for a minute. 'Like a boat person, mate? What be on the news?'

He nodded.

'Huh. I never met an illegal before,' I go. 'I mean of the immigration variety.' What wasn't strictly true, of course, but I'd already forgot about me uncle Baris and his hiring practices.

Them dark eyes flashed again. 'I am not illegal.' Azad explained me all about the Refugee Convention, what wasn't a convention like what they got at convention centres, but some kind of international law. Apparently, it said it wasn't illegal to seek asylum even if you did it illegal, or something like that. Anyway, I insured him that I wasn't too hung up on issues a legality.

'So why didn't they give you a visa?' I asked him.

He explained that his case officer rejected his application for asylum after his first interview. He appealed to the RRT what stands for Refugee Review Tribunal and what in factuality is just one person what determinates your refugee status. But the RRT gave him a dodgy translator what spoke a different kind of Arabic from Azad and no Kurdish. Azad's English wasn't good then like it was when I met him. The RRT rejected him again, but Azad's lawyer said that was cuz a the Dodgy Brothers translator, so he's taking the case to the Federal Court. The court hearing wasn't gonna happen for another five months, and even if he won, he'd have to go through the whole process all over again, what made me head spin just trying to understand it. 'And I am already in detention two years and one day,' he said.

I was horrified. 'You been in this place two years and one day?' I never done more than thirteen months at a stretch meself and I was a pro.

'Not all the time here. I was in Port Hedland detention centre, in Western Australia, until a few weeks ago. After September Eleven, I thought, "That's it." This government hated boat people anyway. Now they were saying we might be terrorists. I thought, they will never understand that I am a dissident and a refugee. They will never give me visa. They will try to send me back to Iraq. And then the Americans will bomb Iraq again, because Bush blames Saddam for what happened in New York. I am sick of bombs. I am sick of death.' Azad told me more Kurdish people died in one town from being gassed by Saddam than what died in both them towers put together. Cuz it wasn't all over the televisions a the world like September Eleven, and cuz it didn't happen to Americans, no one hardly noticed. 'I had enough.' He decided to escape from detention. 'They caught me before I even had the chance to take one breath of free air.'

'Bad luck, mate.'

'Maybe not. I am a refugee. Better this way, even if it is slow. I don't want to live like a criminal, running from police all the time. I will fight for my right to walk with my head held high. I am not less than other people. My father, who was killed by Saddam, taught me this.' He shook his head. 'You know what my name, "Azad", means in Kurdish? "Freedom". Funny, isn't it?'

Zeki means 'smart' — I told him some people found that pretty funny too. 'So what happened when they caught you?'

'They put me in prison for a few weeks, then transferred me here.' He told me he'd heard most asylums in Villawood were in Stages Two and Three. Only the ones they considered 'high-risk' were in Stage One. He shook his head like he couldn't believe it. 'A high-risk poet.'

'You a poet, mate?'

'Yes. We Kurdish people are famous for our poetry.'

'Respect.' I went the knuckles but he didn't know to match them. He backed off like I was gonna punch him or something. 'No, I mean it. I ain't dissing you.'

He sighed and looked at his watch. 'Almost nine-thirty. The news is on SBS. Some Algerian asylum seekers have TV in their room. It was a gift from visitors. What are you doing? Want to watch the news with us?'

'Lemme check me diary,' I said. He looked at me like he didn't understand. 'Just kidding,' I go. 'Lead the way.'

The Algerians' room held just four guys, what was a luxury under the circumstances. But then they told me they been there eight months, what was no luxury in factuality. Azad introduced me to them and some other asylums, Palestinians and Bangladeshis. We didn't get to say much before the news came on. It showed the Prime Minister making some speech.

'Bore-ring,' I said.

'Sssshhh,' they hushed me. They was concentrated like laundry powder on what he be saying.

'I am furious at the behaviour of those people!' The Prime Minister's fist was punching the air and his long, flat lips flapped like something I didn't wanna be thinking about when I be looking at the mouth a the Prime Minister. I was just glad he didn't have no beard. 'I don't want people in this country who would throw their own children overboard!' He went on about how Australia needed to protect its boarders what already lived there or something like that. I didn't know what he was squawking about.

'*Akhoo sharmoota,*' one a the Algerians said, what even I knew was an Arabic curse word meaning you got a sister what was on the game. All a them was getting working up and stressated about the news but I had enough on me mind with me own problems without worrying about the Prime Minister and him overboards. I excused meself and went back to me bunk, where I tossed like a Greek salad till the morning.

Four

'What's happening? Where are you, Zeki? What's going on? Why did they take you there?' She Who always asks more questions than there be answers for. I'm used to it. I cradled the phone between me shoulder and me head so I could light up a cigarette, what I'd bought back from one a the Chinese with me last dollar, what I found in me pocket.

When I told her they'd cancelled me permanent residence what I had all me life and wanted to deport me to the Old Country, she gasped and gasped again. It sounded like she be pumping up a bicycle tyre. 'They're gonna deport you? For not buying a train ticket?' Another gasp. If she put any more air into that tyre it was gonna explode. 'I *told* you —'

'Nah, nah. Told you not to worry about the ticket, darl. That's just how they caught me. When they put me name into the system, they found out Immigration had me number. Woulda happened sooner or later, or so they said. I don't understand it real good, but they got me on something called five-oh-one a the *Migration Act*. Under five-oh-one, they can deport you if you ain't a citizen and you've spent more than twelve months at a stretch in the nick.'

There was a brief pausation, but it didn't feel too silent to me. I can hear everything what goes on in Marlena's brain, I swear. She'd put down her air pump and was punching numbers into her mental calculator.

'Thirteen,' she said. 'You just served a sentence of thirteen months.' Like she was telling me something I didn't know.

'Yep. Thirteen. What isn't turning out to be me lucky number.'

A little over a year ago, see, I was knocking off some a the houses along them back lanes in Surry Hills. Them lanes used to be for when even people in the inner city had dunnies out back and someone had to come and collect the shit from them. Anyway, them lanes were narrow and dark. From a professional standpoint — I'm talking me old profession here — that was all good.

Hopping the fence, I broke into the first place easy, just sailed through them windows. I was having a sticky in the desk drawers when I found a stash a mull and a pipe. I don't mind telling you I enjoy a spot a dope from time to time. So I had a smoke. I was bagging the DVD player when it hit, and it was fucken full-on, pardon me French. Next thing you know I had the munchies, but they had nuffin much in the fridge, only hippy shit like lettuce and mango beans and them squares a tofu what don't even taste like food. So I stuck the rest a the mull and the pipe in me pocket, picked up the bag with the DVD and jumped the next fence, except it wasn't much of a jump cuz I was more stoned than I knew. I fell into a bush what they got growing there. I got all scratched up and me clothes was torn, but I thought it was wicked funny and laughed me head off.

I got inside the second house easy and, mate, you shoulda seen what was in that fridge. Real fancy yuppy food, all types a posh cheeses and olives what was stuffed with fetta and almonds. I stuffed meself like one a them olives, had another smoke and decided to shower and change me clothes. The guy had Armano suits and everything. The pants legs were on the long side, and the waist was tight, but I was one styling dude. I sprayed meself with his cologne, what also be Armano. I'm not sure what happened next. I must've lied down for some shuteye. When I opened me eyes, there were all these coppers and the poofter what owned the place gathered round the bed laughing at me. They shouldn't a done that. Robbers got feelings too.

Anyway, that's when I got done for thirteen months. It shouldn't a been such a big deal, such a long sentence. I mean, I didn't take much a value. But I was sorta on parole at the time.

But back to me phone call. Marlena snuffled, then she gasped again, and then she began to wail. I knew I just had to stand there and cop it.

Maaan, I hate it when women cry. It's the worst thing, I swear. If they tell us what we done wrong, we can at least argue that we didn't do it, or make a joke or try to explain.

But when them tears start to fall, they make you feel so guilty. Every one a them salty drops is an accusation. They're accusing you a cheating, they're accusing you a lying, they're accusing you a letting them down again. Even if it all be true, it ain't fair. There ain't nuffin you can say back to tears.

Five

Ten days after I got to Villawood, they brung in a whole Vietnamese gang fresh outta Long Bay. There wasn't enough beds in Stage One to go round, so the blues told Azad and me to pack our stuff cuz they was moving us to Stage Three. I was just happy to get outta that dorm. When you put forty men in a room, they do a lotta shit you don't really wanna know about. We'd heard that in Stage Three there was four per room max.

It was about eleven ay-em when they put us in the back of a white van with our gear. When we drove out the gate a the compound we looked at each other and grinned. Even though we knew we wasn't going far, and we guessed that, wherever we was going, there'd be razor wire there too, it felt that good to be outside of the walls, and the fence, and riding in a car too, even if it be locked from the outside. At the top a the road we could see that big yard I saw when they brung me in that first night.

The morning they took us over was bright and sunny. The sky was clear and blue. Inside the yard there was some grass, and even some gum trees — what we didn't have none of in Stage One — and a whole lotta white plastic tables and chairs. If it weren't for the parallel cyclone fences and the coils a razor wire running long the top and bottom a them, it woulda looked like an okay sorta place to have a barbie. We drove round the outside a the yard, past a brick office building, what was also inside the fences, and up to a big gate.

A young, blonde female guard walked over from the office. She was twirling a clutch a keys in her hand. 'Nice tits on it, eh?' I said to Azad, what frowned in a way what made me think he understood but was pretending not to. Azad's a real gentleman, in addition to being Kurdish and a poet and smart. Don't get me wrong — I can be a gentleman too when I need to. But at that particulate moment I was feeling pretty excited at being moved and it also felt like I hadn't seen any females in years.

That wasn't exactly true, cuz I'd only been Inside for ten days. She Who visited me of course. But visits in Stage One was only for short times and the visiting room was the crowded little kitchen where we took our meals. There was never enough chairs, but the blues waited till people were almost fighting for space before they opened the door to the tiny concrete yard outside. And the whole time, there was at least twenty or thirty pairs a hungry male eyes on your woman, what was not a good feeling, specially for her. The other females what I saw were other blokes' women. What you're not sposed to stare at, even if everyone does. And of course, there was Mum, what isn't the same thing, and the Villawood psych Nadia, what is an old lady whose main job was insuring that no one topped themselves. The one female blue they got in Stage One was a big Samoan what was virtuosically a bloke. So that blue was looking pretty good to me, even in them baggy blue trousers and plain white blouse what all the guards wore. As I said, I like a woman in uniform. She was making some joke with the officer what was driving the van. Then she peeked inside at us. Her eyes snagged on Azad for a moment. Then, like she just remembered what she was sposed to be doing, she went to open the gate. The van drove into the space between the two fences, what was wider here than in other places round the compound. She locked the first gate behind us, and walked over to open the second. We drove through that and the blues waited for her to lock the second gate as well before they drove us into a garage what belonged to the Property Office.

'She never took her eyes off you once, mate,' I said to Azad while we waited for them to unlock the van and let us out. 'You're in like Flynn.'

'What means "in like Flynn"?'

I told him. He put his head in his hands.

Stage Three was all men like Stage One but not as hard-core, and there was more variety, what I like. There was Chinamen and Vietnamese and Islanders here too, but also Lebs, them Indians what don't cut them hair, and Moroccans, and Pakis, and Bedoons what are from Kuwait and what are kinda like Bedouins except stateless, and others including a

Scottish bloke what spoke funny. There were heaps more asylums and visa overstayers than crims too, what made it a more relaxed hood. Next to Stage Three was Stage Two, what you could see through a fence and what had better facilities and women and families in, and what we shared the big Visiting Yard with. All up, there were about four hundred people in the two stages.

They put us in with this Moroccan dude, an overstayer named Ali. Ali, what had dreadlocks and an Australian girlfriend, told us that if we behaved and were there a long time, they'd eventually put us in Stage Two.

'Stage Three is good enough for me, mate,' I said. The room wasn't nuffin to write home about, but at least the toilet wasn't in the same space what we slept in. 'I got no intentions a staying long.'

Ali shrugged.

I'd been Inside almost two weeks already, what was two weeks too long, and it still didn't make no sense that I be locked up like some foreigner, though I spose that's what I was, technologically speaking, even though I had permanent residence what I thought meant what it said about being permanent. As for this five-oh-one bullshit, I couldn't get me head round that one at all. The point was, I did the crime then I did the time. There had to be some mistake. I was looking forwards to talking to the lawyer what She Who found for me and what was coming to see me the next morning.

Six

There was no mistake. The five-oh-one business mighta been bullshit, but it was serious bullshit. Me lawyer, Mr Gubba, explained all this to me the next morning. We was sitting in a small room in a demountable what was next to the Visiting Yard. He wore a posh suit. He had dyed blond hair what was blow-dried and a tan what had to be from one a them solipsariums. He charged by the minute and spoke slower than anyone I ever met.

Gubba told me that he was gonna appeal me deportation orders to the AAT, what stood for Administrative Appeals Tribunal. The AAT had the power to overturn the decision by the Department of Immigration and Multicultural Affairs, what was called DIMA. He told me the AAT was like the RRT for asylums and the MRT for visa overstayers what stood for Migration Review Tribunal.

Them alphabets was just one part a the Villawood language, what be English made up a all the accents and dialogues what people speak in them own countries plus what the officials be on about. I was getting pretty fluid at it.

Gubba told me that they used to apply five-oh-one only to people what committed fully serious crimes. They started using it for small fries like me in the mid-nineties. He said that he was gonna raise this in the appeal. He was also gonna argue that if they was that worried about me, they shouldn't a let me outta prison. But I wasn't sure it was such a good idea to say that.

'So when's this appeal gonna happen, mate?' I asked Gubba.

His shoulders went up and down. 'Maybe a month.'

'A month! Every day in this place is like a year, I swear. Look at me — it's only been two weeks and I'm dying in here, mate! Look at me!'

He looked at me. 'Nice watch,' he said after a minute. 'I used to have one just like it.'

I didn't wanna ask what happened to it. 'Here, take it,' I said, unfastening the band. 'Just get me outta here.'

He gave me a smile what was on his mouth but not in his eyes. 'Keep it. I don't have any magic formula for getting you out, watch or no watch. However, there is something called a Bridging Visa.' He explained that that's a visa what they can give you so you can get outta detention while they process your case. A Bridging Visa required a bond, but the amount was different from case to case. Gubba said it might be a couple a thou, but he couldn't say for sure.

We filled out the forms for the appeal and the Bridging Visa.

'As for my fee . . .'

'Speak to me missus,' I said. 'She'll fix you up.' She'd be fixing me up too when she realised how much he cost, and that she was gonna have to raise a couple a thou for the bond too, but I didn't wanna think about that. 'And what she can't do, just put on me tab.'

After me meeting with Gubba, me head was full a numbers like five-oh-one and alphabets like AAT and visas what was also bridges, what was also toll roads, and they was all fighting for space in there. I went back to the room. Ali took one look at me, closed the door and pulled a joint outta the pocket of his jeans. 'Oh, mate,' I said.

I remembered this thing that happened when I was in Silverwater. 'I was sitting with Mum in Visits, feeling sorry for meself while she rattled on about how I oughta get on the straight and narrow. Why couldn't I be like me brother Attila, what got his own shop, beautiful wife, great kids, the whole package, yadayadayada. I was feeling so accused and prosecuted.'

Ali nodded and passed the spliff.

'Suddenly, this tiny black parcel came flying over the fence. Me mum didn't notice nuffin. She was pouring out some tea and gathering strength for a second charge. Me, I was keeping an eagle on it. It had to belong to someone, but it looked like I was in Lady Luck, cuz no one came to collect it. I couldn't go and get it in front a me mum, and I hadda keep an eye out for the blues, but eventually I stood and stretched and bent over, pretending to tie me shoes while I scooped it up and stuffed it down me sock. Then, when Mum wasn't looking, I cheeked it.'

Ali tilted his head to one side. All him dreadlocks was hanging in the air. 'Cheeked it?' he asked.

'You know, stuck down the back a me trackies into the place where the sun never shines.'

He grinned in a way what made me think there be a misunderstanding.

'I don't mean all the way inside, I'm no poofter, wasn't doing it for kicks. Just putting it where I could get a grip on it.'

'Right.' Ali giggled.

'So. After me mum left, I headed to the gate, holding it in, walking like I'd just eaten a prune curry. They strip-searched us after Visits in prison. The screws made you take your pants down and everything, but from the look on me face and the way I was pinching me bum cheeks together, they told me to get to the crapper before I soiled something. I went to me crib, relaxed and down it dropped. I unwrapped it and — *mate*. Just what the doctor ordered.

'I was mulling up when this guy Hadeon, a big-time dealer, came into me cell. You gotta pitcher Hadeon. He's a Ukrainian with a face what looks like it was chopped outta clay with an axe. We called him the Hatchet. He had a criminal record longer than me arms, what you can see aren't that long in factuality on a count a me being so short. But he'd been done for rape and assault and dealing heroin and evil shit like that, so you get the idea. This dude once argued with Hadeon over something stupid. The day after the argument, we was in the prison workshop when they called time for smoko. The dude what argued with Hadeon didn't budge. We're like, "Hey, dude, smoko, wakey wakey, hands off snakey", but still no reaction. He sat staring straight ahead with a half-finished Qantas headset in his hands. It took a minute before we saw the screwdriver handle sticking outta the back of his head and the pool a blood on the floor. Everyone knew it had to be Hadeon but they wasn't able to pin it on him. He was good mates with a blue, a bad muvvafucker just like himself, what people said helped him get rid a the evidence.'

'That's heavy shit,' Ali said, making a face and shaking him dreddies.

'Anyways, there I was, happy as Larry, rolling a fat spliff from the weed in the parcel, when it suddenly occurred to me that I had something what probably belonged to Hadeon. He was staring at me with them beady eyes what were cold and grey like dirty ice. I knew I had to act real cool, even though in factuality, I was shitting meself. "Where'd you get that?" Hadeon asked. He made his eyes even slittier, like he could see what was going on better that way.

'"Mate," I go. "You reckon you're the only one who gets drops?" I made meself look real put down-upon. He looked hard at me, but I didn't crack.

'Finally he goes, "All right, all right." Then I sold him some of his own dope.'

Ali gave me a high-five. 'Man, you're bad.'

I shrugged, like I be modest. 'You gotta make the most a your opportunities — what be one a me Rules a Survival.'

I was gonna explain more about me Rules a Survival when a phone call came through for Ali. I wandered out to find Azad. I found him at the fence between Stages Three and Two, talking to this skinny, sad-looking kid in a baseball cap on the other side. Azad was more excited than I ever seen him. 'Hamid and I were together in Port Hedland,' he explained to me. He introduced us, and turned back to Hamid. 'I hoped you'd be Out by now, brother.'

'Me too.' Hamid spoke real soft. He was nineteen going on ninety, I swear. They kept talking, and every so often Hamid looked up at Azad, but most a the time he kept his head down and you couldn't hardly see his face under the cap.

'Hamid and I used to study English together eight hours a day when we first got to Australia,' Azad told me. 'Sometimes even nine or ten hours.'

'No wonder youse both speak it so good,' I said, what wasn't just being polite. 'Like natives, mate. Me, I never studied nuffin more than ten, fifteen minutes max in me whole life. I get bored too easy.'

Hamid kinda smiled. 'We had so much hope then,' he said. 'Hope and dreams.'

'Yes. You were always talking about wanting to be a doctor. And the first Afghan surfer. After you learned to swim.'

'I say that?'

Azad laughed. 'Yes.' He looked like he suddenly remembered something. 'You still growing your hair?' he asked Hamid, telling me at the same time that back in Port Hedland, Hamid swore he wouldn't cut his hair until he got free.

Hamid looked up and he took off his cap. Azad and me, we didn't even look at the hair much, what was long, cuz in the middle of his forehead was a lump the size of an egg.

'Who . . . ?' Azad's question seemed to get stuck in his throat like that piece a kebab the time me uncle Baris had to perform the Heimlich manoeuvre on me in his shop, what is not a gay sex act even though it kinda looks like one.

'No one.' Hamid put his cap back on and stared at the ground. 'Me.'

Seven

That evening, Azad filled out a Detainee Request Form to be moved to Stage Two so he could look after Hamid. 'He needs me,' Azad said. He told me that back in Afghanistan, Hamid's parents were teachers what ran a secret school for girls. That got them into big trouble cuz educating girls was a crime. Go figure. They put his mum in prison and no one knew what happened to his dad. After his folks disappeared, people told him that the Taliban, what was the bad guys what disappeared them, was coming for him next. He was only seventeen. So his rellies put all their money together to pay a people smuggler to get him somewhere safe. He didn't have no idea about Australia before he came. It was just cheaper than Europe.

The next day, as soon as Visits started, we went out to wait for Hamid. When the two a them seen each other without a fence sticking between them, they hugged and kissed each other's cheeks, what is what men from the Middle East do and what doesn't mean they be poofters.

'What happened with your Federal Court?' Azad asked.

Hamid just shook his head. They both went quiet for a while. I guessed Azad be thinking about his own case too.

'So . . .' I was searching me brains for how the whole business worked. 'You got rejected by the RRT?'

Hamid nodded. 'Yes. The Member, she did not believe I am Afghani. She said I was Pakistani pretending to be Afghani.' He told us how the Member asked him about some rivers in Afghanistan what he didn't know about. She said she'd sent tapes of his voice to some Swedish outfit. 'They sent back a report saying my voice had Pakistani inflections.'

'I spose they'd know all about that in Sweden, eh, mate?' I said.

Hamid didn't smile. 'The Member thought so. That's why she rejected me.' His voice was as flat as me tyres that time Marlena let all the air outta them after she caught me with that checkout chick, what I swear was an accident.

I suddenly thought a something. No way could I name all the rivers in Australia. And Marlena tells me that sometimes I sound like one a them rappers what be from the ghettos in LA or the Bronx, and not an Aussie what be from the suburbs a Sydney. I hoped they wasn't gonna ask me shit like that when I had me AAT or send me influctuations to Sweden.

'What's wrong, Zek?' Azad asked. I looked up. They was both staring at me.

'Nuffin,' I said, wiping the sweat, what was from stressation, off a me forehead. I offered them some a the bickies what Marlena brung the other day, but they didn't want any. So I ate six, what is two each.

'Are you going to Full Federal?' Azad asked, what be the next step after Federal.

Hamid shook his head. He told us that DIMA gave him a letter saying they were making arrangements to deport him. 'But the day after they gave me the letter, the Americans started bombing my country. Even DIMA couldn't send me back to a war zone. And they couldn't deport me to Pakistan, because I don't have Pakistani papers. So they transferred me here to Villawood.'

Hamid told us that really stressed him out, cuz the few friends he had in the world excepting Azad were all in Port Hedland. He cried on the plane over, and the officers what was escorting him made fun a him and called him a girl. He had no idea Azad was gonna turn up in Villawood too. Last he knew, Azad was caught trying to escape. He reckoned Azad be in jail or maybe even deported back to his own country.

'You know,' said Azad, 'I called Port Hedland to speak to you the first day they brought me to Villawood. Some officer there told me they had no one by that name. I thought you got your visa. I thought you were free. *W'Allah*.'

They both smiled for about half a second.

'I am so glad to see you, brother,' Hamid said to Azad.

Two days later, they still hadn't done nuffin about Azad's request to move to Stage Two. I told him they probably filed the request in the Circular File, what is a slang for bin what I then had to teach him.

The Yanks continued to bomb the shit outta Hamid's country. He watched the news every night in the rec room and listened all day to the radio, what a visitor gave him, for news about the war. One day the Yanks dropped one a them daisy-cutter bombs onto Hamid's cousins' village and accidentally smoked half the population. There was a short report about it one night on the news. Hamid went crazy then. He began hitting his head against the wall again. Medical put him on Vals. It didn't make much difference. He just hit the wall slower.

Azad put in a new Detainee Request Form every day. Now that he had a mission, what was to help Hamid, he had more energy and light what was in his eyes.

Two more weeks a Groundhog Days went by like the movie, except with no Bill Murray in. I couldn't believe how fast weeks could pass when the hours be passing so slow. Marlena brung me some more clothes and a small TV and video and a poster a Shakira for me wall. She visited three or four times a week, depending on her shifts, and Mum once a week, on Sundays. I got them to put Azad and Hamid's names down on their forms too, cuz the blues wasn't sposed to let you out unless you had a visitor.

It was already November. It was getting hotter. Summer was coming. Ramadan too.

They brung in an asylum from Kashmir, a tall, skinny bloke in his thirties by the name a Bhajan. One day, we was sitting together in Visits, under the shelter. By way a conversationals, I told him that I didn't know nuffin bout Kashmir except me mum loves the jumpers what they make there.

He looked at me like he be trying to figure out if I be taking the piss. What I wasn't, cuz me mum really does love them jumpers. Next to us, a tradesman was doing something to the Coke machine. His stubbies were hanging low and you could see his crack. There was this chick, a visitor, what was getting something from the snack machine next to it. She was wearing them hipsters. She bent down to collect her crisps from the slot and you could see the topper part a her crack as well, what was better to look at and what had a G-string hanging out. Bhajan and me both looked, and then he turned to me. 'That's funny, Zeki,' he said, nodding and shaking his head in that way what Indians and Pakis do too. 'Because I don't know anything about Australia except that all Australians like to show off half their buttocks.' Bhajan had a pretty weird sense a humour.

A day or two after that, they brung in a whole lot a Thais what was caught working illegal in the restaurants and what needed rooms in Stage Three. So Azad finally got his request, and they took me and Bhajan over to Stage Two as well.

Bhajan and me got put in a building what was called Shoalhaven, like the river but with no water in, at least on the day we moved in, cuz the pipes was all broke. A young African asylum called Thomas was me neighbour on one side. Me neighbour on the other side was this older bloke from the

Philippines, a born-again Christian what stuck his nose in everyone's business. Bhajan's room was down the hall.

They put Azad together with Hamid, what was now trying to get the Red Cross onto finding his rellies. The Red Cross said they'd look, but they had a lotta people they was looking for over there, so it might take a while. Hamid stopped sleeping. They started giving him sleeping pills on top a the Vals, but it didn't make much difference.

I asked him why he didn't just call his rellies himself to see if they were okay. 'They don't have phones, Zeki,' he said, like I shoulda known that.

Eight

One evening, Thomas, Azad, Hamid and me was sitting outside playing cards. It was early, cuz the loudspeaker was still calling people to the phone, what it didn't do after eight. 'Bangladesh, you have a telephone call. Bangladesh, you have a telephone call.' They was sposed to call your name and country together. Some a the blues couldn't pronounce people's names, so they just called them by country, what got specially confusing when they called China to the phone cuz even in there, there was one billion of them, I swear. Sometimes the blues put on funny voices to pronounce the names, what people didn't think was that funny. Thomas told us about this teenage boy from Syria what used to be there and what was named Humam. 'They never got that right,' Thomas said. 'They would go, "Human from Syria, you have a telephone call." He hated it. If they were going to call him Human, he said, they should treat him like one.'

'Twenty-one,' Azad said, cleaning up the pile a stones what we used for gambling.

'Hamid Jafaar, Afghanistan, you have a phone call. Hamid Jafaar from Afghanistan, you have a phone call.'

Hamid jumped up and ran to the phone. We all watched him go, hoping it was news from his family what be good. When he returned a few minutes later, he told us it was only Sue. Sue was a retired teacher what visited asylums and helped them with their cases. She was a big lady, what was comforting just to look at, with a sofa bed for a backside and bolster cushions for arms. If her edges was soft, her brain was sharp. She knew how things worked, and she didn't take no shit from the authorities. The asylums all reckoned that if anyone could fight the government and get them free, Sue could. She'd just wanted to say that she was coming the next day and would call Hamid and Azad and Thomas to Visits. She'd asked if they needed anything.

'What'd you tell her?' I asked, hoping the answer be KFC or doughnuts.

'Freedom,' Hamid said.

'Fair enough.' What it wasn't, really.

The loudspeaker crackled. 'Bhajan from Kashmir, phone call. Bhajan from Kashmir, you have a phone call.' Bhajan waved to us on his way to the phone. We waved back.

'You know what gets to me?' Hamid said, shuffling the deck and dealing out another round. 'If they really believe I am from Pakistan, why do they always say "Afghanistan" after my name?'

'You know what gets to me?' Thomas asked. 'That you are still looking for answers to questions like that.' He tapped his cards. Thomas had long fingers the colour a me favourite type a chocolate, what be dark. Azad once said Thomas's hands were artistic, what I don't know about, except Thomas drew excellent pitchers and used his hands to draw them, so I spose they were. 'Hit me.'

I hit him then, for a joke. Just lightly of course. But as soon as me hand touched his upper arm, I felt something what made me hairs stand on end, what is a lotta hairs. It was like the bones wasn't exactly where bones oughtta be. 'What's with your shoulder, mate? Fucken scared the shit outta me.'

'Don't hit me then.' No one said nuffin for a minute. Hamid dealt him another card. 'Again,' Thomas said. Then, 'Twenty-one.'

Later that night, Thomas and me, we was sitting outside Shoalhaven having a smoke. There was some people talking softly on the phones, and every so often you could hear some shouting in Chinese what be from a video they was playing in the rec room. A Burmese guy was sitting in the playground strumming a guitar, and one a the kids was crying, but otherwise, it was pretty quiet. The lights of the compound at night were kinda soft and yellow, what made it seem less ugly but more like hell. Thomas touched his shoulder and made a face, like it hurt.

I gave him a question mark with me eyes.

He blew some smoke into the air. 'You want to know, don't you?'

I shrugged.

'Nothing better to do, anyway,' he said.

I almost wished he hadn't told me. See, Thomas came from one a them countries where they got all them tribes what was always killing each other. You know, like the Tutus and Whatsits. He was from a middle-class family what had a trading business. They all spoke English and French and a bunch a them African languages too. When he was eighteen, he and his sister, what was tall and a babe and seventeen, was sposed to go to Paris, France, where they got an uncle. Thomas was gonna study art at the Sore Bone, what not be a medical school even though it sounds like one, and his sister was gonna be a supermodel on them Paris birdwalks. They had their tickets and everything. Then the massacre happened. When he came to he was lying under the bodies of his sister and parents and covered in blood what was his too. The Red Cross took him to a hospital cuz he was pretty messed up, even if he wasn't exactly dead. Later they took him to a refugee camp on the border what was a lotta tents and not a lotta food. He registered with the UN, what said he was a refugee and put him in the queue for resettlement, what was long. Three years later he was still there. He was only twenty-one and getting migraines from the stress and the sadness and the machete chop to his head. He couldn't walk good on a count a the way they broke his leg, and his shoulder healed kinda weird. He was in pain all the time. He lost all hope and tried to hang himself.

'Full on,' I said. His story was fully stressing me out. 'So how'd you get here?'

He took a long drag on his ciggie, and stubbed it out on the ground. 'The aid worker who cut me down from the noose helped me find my uncle in Paris. My uncle sent me some money and I paid a people smuggler to get me to France. The smuggler took me to the airport and gave me a false passport and ticket. He wished me good luck. Then he disappeared. When I looked at the papers, I almost had a heart attack. The ticket was for Sydney.

'You know, Zek, I didn't want to come to Australia. I didn't even know where it was. I wasn't sure if the smuggler cheated me or just made a mistake. When I tried the mobile number he gave me, a recording said it wasn't in service. By the time I arrived at Sydney airport I had a migraine. I told them I was a refugee. They took me into a room to ask me questions but because of my migraine I could barely talk. Next thing I knew I was here, in Villawood, being called a "queue jumper". And this is where I've been ever since. Two years later. Damn this place. Damn it to hell.'

He looked around.

'I wonder. Can you damn hell to hell?'

Nine

That fucken loudspeaker never shut its metal mouth, I swear. It called people to Muster. It called people to the phone. It called people to Medical. It called people to Visits. It called people to the DIMA office. Gubba had told me I'd be hearing about me Bridging Visa any day. So, although I hated the sound a the loudspeaker as much as everyone else, I had me ears out like they was satellite dishes — what they kinda look like, in factuality.

It finally happened when I was having a yarn with Anna, the blue what was blonde, what Azad and I met the day we got transferred to Stage Three.

'Zeki Togan from Turkey, come to DIMA. Zeki Togan from Turkey, come to DIMA.'

'Yes! Yes!' I punched the air. 'It's me lucky day.'

'Go on, then,' Anna said, giving me a friendly shove. She coulda told me then what apparently everyone in the world knew except me — whenever Immigration had good news for you, what wasn't often, they gave it to you in a letter. They didn't call you to the office.

Stupid, happy me, I moon-walked all the way to the office. The door was open.

Me case officer was Turkish. She waved me in.

'G'day, Mrs Kunt.' I pronounced her name like 'koont', what is the correct way, what most Australians don't do.

'Hello, Zeki.' Other detainees what had her for a case officer said she was really nice, but she never so much as cracked a smile around me. I got the feeling she thought I be disgracing the community. I wasn't gonna let that bother me. Not that day.

'Whatcha got for me today, Mrs Kunt?' She handed me an envelope.

I started to rip it open. 'And the winner is . . .' I looked up. Still no smile. I couldn't help it if she had immunity to me charms. I whistled as I shook out the letter.

It took a minute for it to sink in. Then it did just that, like a large stone with me heart tied to it and thrown into the middle a Sydney Harbour. The whistling died in me mouth.

The good news was I could get me a Bridging Visa. The bad news was that they was requiring a bond a twenty-five grand. 'Twenty-five grand! How am I sposed to raise that?' I shouted. 'That Russian dude Boris what got a Bridging Visa two days ago only had to pay three thousand. And the Malaysian girl, Amira, hers was one and a half. This is fucken bullshit! Pardon me French.'

Mrs Kunt didn't even blink. She put her elbows on the desk and folded one hand over the other, making a little platform for her head to sit on. She stared at me with her big brown eyes and raised one eyebrow. I could smell her perfume, what had spice in.

'You're Turkish,' she said, like she be telling me something new. 'Maybe it's just *kismet*. You know *kismet*? Destiny?'

'Mate, I come from Kismet Bay. What is a real place.' I stood up and stormed out.

Kismet?! Kiss my arse, more like. I was still muttering and kicking the ground when the loudspeaker called me again, this time to the phone.

I wiped the mouthpiece on me trackydacks. People round there was always so pissed off they be spitting. The phones weren't too clean. 'Yo.'

'Zeki?'

'Hey, darl,' I said.

'What's wrong?'

'Nuffin.'

'Zeki, don't bullshit me. I can hear it in your voice. Something's happened.'

When I told her, She Who Has Every Right busted her dams. I held the receiver away from me ear. Like I told you, tears do me under. They are me underdoing. I was already feeling pissed off and sorry enough for meself as it was. I didn't need this. I was hanging for a smoke when I saw Thomas come walking down the path. I waved at him and he waved back.

'Ciggie?' I was doing the word without the sound.

'Zeki? Are you there?' Marlena's spooky — I swear she knows what I be doing even when she can't see me.

'I'm right here, darl.' I rolled me eyes at Thomas. He smiled without showing teeth and held out a pack a smokes. I took one and lit it. He had one himself, leaning against the wall and crossing them wonky beanpole legs a his while he listened in on the rest a me conversationals. I didn't blame him. There wasn't any entertainment in there except other people's business.

'Zeki, if you're not out by Christmas, I'm gonna have to tell my parents.'

Marlena's parents never approved a me. They think I be bad news. But since I got outta the nick in September, She Who had been telling them all about how I be going straight, working a proper job and all. She still hadn't mentioned the little problem a me being in Villawood. They'd invited me for Christmas dinner, what be a big thing in her family and what meant they was accepting me at last.

'Darl, just tell 'em I gotta work.'

'On Christmas Day?'

'That was always a good day for working in me old profession. People being out at their rellies 'n' all.'

'Zeki!'

'Only kidding, darl. We'll think a something. We still got a month and a half. I should have me decision by then, what'll put me back in the Free World. They'll never even have to know about this little episode. You worry too much. She'll be right.'

When I finally got off the phone I wiped me brow, like I been put through the mall, what is the feeling you get when you been forced to shop all day instead of going to the pub.

I looked at Thomas and shook me head. 'Women!'

'At least you have one,' he said, shrugging him weird bony shoulders.

'Fat lotta good that does me, mate,' I bellyached. 'I been Inside a whole month now, what is putting a strainer on the relationship. I got a Bridging Visa but can't afford the bond for it and me AAT hearing isn't even coming up till just before Christmas. I gotta get out by Christmas or I'm stuffed. Anyway, by then I'll have been in this hellhole more than two whole months.'

Thomas's mouth twisted up. Then he turned around real quick and limped off like he had an appointment he just remembered. It occurred to me that he'd been Inside almost two years. Me and me big one.

Ten

Like I told you, I never knew much about asylums before I came here, though I heard about them on the news like everyone else. I didn't think much about them situation neither. I had enough a me own troubles. Besides, lotsa people what be immigrants — like me own family — they figured the asylums was giving everyone else a bad name what came here legally. Everything you heard about the asylums in the media was bad. When I first got in here, Mum was afraid they'd be even worse than the crims I was mixing with in Silverwater. I had to insure her the ones I was meeting was better than some a the people I knew what was living on the Outside. What is true, specially the people I tended to know, on a count a me old profession.

What I learned about the asylums was that they was only here cuz they was running from heavy shit, like ethical cleansing and Saddam and torture, what be real torture like with electrical shocks and sensible deprivation and broken bottles up the Khyber, and not torture like what I say She Who be putting me through all the time.

Take this dude Babak what had a room not far from mine in Shoalhaven. Back in Iran, Babak owned thirty-six thousand chickens and wore silk shirts made in France. Babak got real pissed off each time the government here said the asylums only came for a better life, what was a lotta times. Each time one a them ministers got on the TV and said that, Babak spat on the ground and told us all again about his thirty-six thousand chickens and his silk shirts from France. He'd still be in Iran, what he says got better food and better mountains and better everything than Australia, except for his cousin what was a dissonant what criticised the government and then hid on Babak's farm. The security forces raided the place and shot the cousin and a whole lotta chickens and Babak's young son too. Babak was lucky he wasn't home or he'd be dead as well, though he says he'd rather be. His wife, what was pregnant, and his five-year-old daughter was on that boat what sunk on the way here from Innonesia last month and they drowned to death.

I was learning lots about the world, and what I was learning made me even more fucken determined — pardon me French — to stay in Australia where I belonged. As I said, I immigrated with me family when I was six months old. Only time I ever travelled back to the Old Country in me twenty-nine years was when I was five. The first thing they did over there was cut half me boy off. It wasn't even that big in the first place. I couldn't wait to get back home before they took a knife to anything else.

See? I said 'back home'. Even then I thought of Australia as home. I reckon spending most a me life in Oz makes me fair dinkum, even if I never got me papers. So what if I got a bit of a past, what was the basis of this five-oh-one problem? We was taught in school how the nation was built by convicts. Well, that's just another name for crims. I reckon being a crim makes me more Aussie than people what was born here but what never broke the law even once in their life.

Eleven

Angel came into our lives in the beginning of December. I don't got words for how beautiful Angel was, except that it was like light was always coming off her. She came from Cambodia and her skin was kinda gold in colour. Azad said her eyes were 'like liquid sadness', what just proves he's a poet. She was only seventeen, though she told DIMIA she was older cuz she didn't wanna get into more trouble for being a minor.

Oh, that's right. DIMA had become DIMIA by then. Late in November the government added Indigenous to Immigration and Multicultural Affairs. The detainees joked that was so the government could have just one department to deal with everyone what was not coloured white.

Anyway, the day they brung Angel in, me and Azad and Hamid, we'd just been to Muster. According to the human rights groups what care about asylums, the blues were sposed to call it 'roll call' cuz we was human beings not sheep, but they never did, even though they got the chance five times a day.

The three of us was heading back to our rooms. It was Ramadan, so we was fasting from dawn to sunset every day. I know I'm not a very good Muslim, but Ramadan is the one time a year when I try to be. One month for God, the rest for me. I reckon that isn't too bad a deal. The days were getting hotter. Azad and me had just stopped to let Hamid catch up. He was having one a his bad days. He was trailing head down and floppy-pawed like one a them puppies what always got beat up instead a loved.

Even though he perked up some after he and Azad got to hang out again, Hamid suffered the depression pretty bad. He could never sleep at night even with the pills they got him on, and he was tired all day. And observing Ramadan in detention wasn't great. They made arrangements for us to be able to have *sohour* before dawn and *iftar* after sunset, and they let the community from Outside bring in special foods, like dates and juice for breaking the fast. Mum brought in lots a good Turkish food too. But it wasn't the same. Everyone talked about how, in their countries, everything kinda stopped for Ramadan. It's a special time, and each night, after *iftar*, everyone goes visiting, sometimes till it was time for *sohour* and morning prayers. There were good TV shows and a great atmosphere. I told them it was kinda like that in Auburn too.

One thing that made it harder Inside was that lotsa shit was always going down what no one should be seeing during Ramadan when your thoughts gotta be pure.

Like what had happened the day before. We was sitting in the Yard with some visitors what came for the first time. They was Christians. They'd brought all this food and juice cuz they didn't know about us fasting. We was sitting at this table, smelling the food what we couldn't eat till later and some of it not even then cuz it wasn't *halal*. They was asking questions about people's cases, and about the situation in Detention. We answered even though we knew they weren't gonna be able to help. We was polite, cuz we knew they meant well. All around us, people what wasn't Muslim were eating and drinking juice and water, smoking cigarettes and laughing, and some a the women visitors were wearing short skirts and tops what showed off their tits what was hard not to look at. Thomas, what was a Catholic, was in another part of the yard with a white-haired Father from the church what helped asylums. They had their chairs pulled up close and was deep in conversation, what is what we was struggling for at our table. Suddenly one a the lady visitors looked up and cried out, 'Shivers!'

We looked where she was looking. Someone had dragged one of the longer tables over by the fence. There was a bed sheet draped over it like a tablecloth. The sheet hung down to the ground. The table had some food on but no people, and it was shaking like the coins on a bellydancer's hips. A table with a cloth on was the Villawood equivalent of a shaggin' wagon.

'*La ilaha illallah*,' Azad said under his breath — There is no God but Allah — and he quickly looked away from the sight. Him and Hamid and Bhajan excused themselves and went back inside soon after that. I felt sorry for the visitors, what felt bad, even though they hadn't done nuffin wrong. So I sat talking with them for a while till they left, what they did soon after they learned that I was a five-oh-one and not an asylum.

The worst thing about Ramadan on the Inside was that everyone missed their families, what was worser still for people like Hamid what didn't even know if he still had one and Azad, what saw his dad taken away and his mum and sisters killed when they was trying to get across the border to Iran.

Anyway, there we was the next day, walking back from Muster. Azad and me stopped to let Hamid catch up. That's when we noticed her, this skinny chick sitting in a corner, all twisted up on herself, long black hair hanging over her face like a curtain. She was shaking all over. 'Are you all right?' Azad called out. She didn't seem to hear the question. Azad angled his head to say we should go over.

'Hello?' Hamid kneeled down by her side. 'Are you okay?'

She looked up then and her hair fell back and their eyes met, and I swear it was like one a them romantic movies what Marlena likes what goes into slo-mo at just the point where I wanna hit the fast-forward. Or maybe it just seemed like that later. Anyway, Angel raised her hand to brush the rest of her hair away from her face. That's when I noticed the bruises on her arms. It was like someone had scraped some a that gold off her skin so you could see she was just made a flesh and blood like the rest of us. She musta caught me staring, cuz she tugged her sleeves down and wrapped her arms around her chest. I was pretty sure I seen something else on her arms too what she might be wanting to cover up.

She looked up at Hamid again and made her lips into something like a smile. Then she reached out to touch his face, like she wanted to comfort him instead. He jumped like she'd given him a shock. Suddenly she pulled her hand back, clamped it over her mouth, spun around and started dry heaving like she was trying to turn herself inside out. This was getting way too heavy for me. I tried to catch Azad's eye, but he was staring at her and biting his lip.

Finally, she stopped heaving, but she looked pale and was shaking again. She looked over with half-closed eyes to see Hamid still kneeling there.

'Come,' Hamid said, real gentle. 'We're going to take you to Medical. You need a doctor.' She nodded. Turns out she was on her way there when she got too sick to continue. He handed her a clean tissue from his pocket. She dabbed at her face with it. Hamid helped her up and put her arm around his shoulder. Her head flopped down against his neck. Azad put her other arm around his shoulder and they slowly took her to Medical.

I felt a tug on me sleeve. I looked down. Abeer, a little Palestinian girl, looked up at me. She motioned for me to squat down. She cupped her little hands around me ear. 'What's wrong with the new girl, Zeki?' she whispered. 'And is she Hamid's girlfriend?'

'You're asking a lot a questions today, mate.'

'Grown-ups always say that when they don't want to tell you the answers.' She stuck out her tongue at me. 'Come on, Zeki, come see my new pet.'

I figured the others had the situation under control. I followed Abeer to the building where she and her family had their rooms. They'd been in detention for two and a half years. She brung out a gecko, what she held in her hands.

'What's the little fella's name?' I asked.

'Visa.'

'Cute.'

Later, I caught up with Azad and Hamid in Hamid's room. They told me Angel was back in Lima Dorm. Lima was the female-only dorm, what was next to Shoalhaven and what got locked down. All single females got put in Lima. You could see them in the kitchen and the rec room and in Visits, but after five o'clock if you wasn't in Visits and you wanted to talk to a Lima girl, you hadda do it through the fence. The officers said it was to protect them. But the detainees said it was so no babies got made and born in detention, cuz babies born in detention gave Immigration even bigger headaches than even the asylums did. But the detainees said it wouldn't a been such a problem if they didn't keep people here for long enough to make babies and then have them in the first place.

'What'd they say at Medical?' I asked.

Azad rolled his eyes. 'The usual. They gave her a Panadol and said she should to drink lots of water.'

'Donkey doctors,' Hamid said, and he sounded angry. But it was true. The Medical in Villawood was bullshit. I never seen anything so dodgy even in prison. A few weeks ago Hamdi, this old Lebanese bloke, broke his arm. They told him to rest and gave him a Panadol, no joke. They didn't like taking people to hospital cuz they hadda pay for it. They only took Hamdi to hospital after his arm got infected and swollen and he was screaming with the pain. Another time, this Nigerian woman, Vanessa, had a miscarriage. The whole baby didn't come out, what I don't like thinking about. They didn't let her go to hospital neither until she got toxic with it and nearly died. The point was, Medical wasn't looking after much besides its own arse, what was tight. It made Hamid, what wanted to be a doctor himself, crazy to see it. He said that if he got to be a doctor, he'd come back to Detention and treat the detainees proper.

'So what's her story?'

Hamid bit his lips. Azad frowned like I shouldn't a been asking. I kinda guessed anyway. See, they was always bringing in girls from brothels what worked illegal. And I'd been keeping bad company long enough to recognise cold turkey, what was not a sandwich meat.

I could see they wasn't in a talkable mood. 'Catch youse later, eh?'

'Eh,' said Azad.

'Eh,' said Hamid.

I was feeling kinda unsettled and in need a some detraction. I looked at me watch. It was a long way to *iftar*. I went to see what Thomas was up to. He was with Abeer's little brother, Bashir, teaching him how to draw. They was into it. I watched for a while but then I got bored. I was missing She Who pretty bad. I joined the queue at the payphones. It took forty minutes to get to the front a the queue, what was annoying but at least it killed time, what was good.

Finally I got to the front. I wiped the mouthpiece on me trackies and dialled. It only rang twice when she picked up.

'Hey, babydoll. Any chance of a visit?'

'I dunno about today, Zeki. I have to work at four.' Visits began at one-thirty but people had to start queueing by twelve-thirty if they wanted to be in by two, and even then they might not get in till two-thirty or later. They made people line up outside the fence in the sun, what was hot. They took so much time processing the visiting forms, She Who reckoned they was learning to read and write at the same time. We was just talking about this when she said something what took me heart by the balls.

'Um, Zek. You know Peter?'

'Peter Pink-nuts? Peter the poofter from church what your parents think you should go with?' I knew I shouldn't be talking like that when I be fasting, but I couldn't help meself.

'It's Peter Pinknett. He's not a poofter.'

'Now you're defending him?'

There was a long sigh. 'I'm not *defending* him. I'm just saying he's not a poofter. Anyway, I think you should say "gay". You know My Le hates it when you call gay people "poofters".' My Le was Marlena's best friend. She was a beauty therapist what worked with poofters.

'What, is this a conference call with My Le now? Look, darl, you know I got nuffin against poofters. So long as they not be moving in on me own best girl.'

'Can we start this conversation again?'

'Ten minutes!' someone shouted from a back a the queue.

'Yeah, ten minutes!' someone else joined in.

'Shut up,' I said.

'Did you just tell me to shut up?' Marlena asked.

'No, no, darl, I was talking to some dickheads in the queue.' I gave them the finger over me shoulder.

'Time!' Dickhead Number One shouted.

'Finish up!' Dickhead Number Two added.

I ignored them. She Who blew out some air. 'I'm starting again. You know Peter?'

'Yeah, and what about the pink-nutted poofter?'

Another silence. 'He asked me to the movies. And my parents think I should go. I don't want to, Zeki, I really don't, but I just . . .'

For years now, Marlena's folks been pressurising her to ditch me for good. What they didn't think I be. They always had these stooges what they thought be better for her than me. But she never even thought a giving in before.

'I still haven't told them you're Inside. But if you're not out by Christmas . . .'

'Babydoll, you know I'm gonna win at the AAT. I'm gonna be outta here by Christmas, no wucken furries. Gubba was that confidential about it . . . Fuck. You're not really thinking a going to the movies with Pink-nuts, are you, darl?'

'Zeki, you're not supposed to swear during Ramadan.'

Maaan. Sometimes she's like me own personal lady cop *and* the religious police, all rolled into one. 'You're right. I shouldn't. C'mon, darl, you're not really thinking a doing it, are you?'

She took a few quiet breaths what I could barely hear, me heart was banging that loud in me chest. 'No, not really.'

'Time! Time! Off the phone!' Every dickhead in the queue was shouting by now.

Twelve

Not long after Angel arrived, Hamid went off the pills. He wanted to look after her and said he couldn't do it if he was doped up. They both put in Detainee Request Forms what asked for permission to see each other more than what was normally allowed. Nadia, the psych, told the management that allowing them to meet in the daytime would be a good idea for their mental health. So they let her come into Stage Two between nine ay-em and twelve-thirty pee-em and again between one and five. They wasn't allowed to go inside Hamid's room, or they'd stop her coming. Hamid started sleeping at night again cuz, he said, he had something to wake up for.

Every morning, he'd get up at eight and meet Angel at the gate. She'd have some breakfast, what he didn't on a count a fasting, and then they'd go to the computer room to play games or to the rec room for billiards. They'd walk around. He'd wait for her to eat her meals, and she'd wait for him when he went to prayers. In the beginning, they did a lotta sitting around the playground in the compound, while she went through the withdrawals. She was cleaning up. It was tough. But she was doing it.

One day she appeared with her hair all washed and shiny and her pretty lips smiling, and that's when we all noticed how beautiful she really was. She had heaps more self-steam than when she first came. We were all feeling happy for Hamid, what was looking pretty good himself. He stood taller, holding his back straight like me dad's always telling me to do, and even his eyes were brighter. In factuality, he was a handsome little bugger, what I never noticed before. Me auntie Elma is always banging on — when Uncle Baris isn't listening, anyway — about how Afghani men be the best looking. I always thought that was cuz they was the only ones what had more facial hair than her. Looking at Hamid though, I could kinda see her point. Not that I'm a — *gay* — or nuffin.

Hamid introduced Sue to Angel. Sue was already trying to figure out what to do for Hamid. She'd asked a barrister to look at taking his case to the full Federal or High Court. The appeal period had already passed, so it wasn't looking too hopeful. Now Hamid made her promise to find a lawyer for Angel as well. 'More important than helping me,' he told her.

Ramadan finished, and visitors from the community brought in food for the three-day feast of *Eid*. Me mum cooked up heaps a good stuff for me and me mates.

Finally, it was the day before me AAT hearing. She Who

came to visit. She gave me her ring to hold for good luck, what I slipped onto the gold chain on me neck.

'What else you got for me, darl?'

She started to show me what was in the plastic bags she'd brung in — videos and ciggies and stuff. 'Nah, nah,' I said, motioning for her to come sit on me lap. 'I'm talking about some a your sweet lovin'.'

'Tsk — everyone can see, Zeki.'

'Pretend they can't.'

'*Zeki.*'

In the end she sat down on me knee and gave a quick peck with tongue in. 'You can collect the rest when you're out.'

Back in me room, me and me boy had a conversational with Mrs Palmer and her Five Daughters to relieve the tension, and then I checked out the goods. *Scarface*, *Mr Bean*, *Total Recall* and a couple a Jackie Chans. Phone cards and cigarettes and apple-flavoured tobacco for the hookah pipe what was owned by a Bedoon called Khalid. Instant pasta, instant noodles, instant soup. Instant everything for people what had time to burn. We woulda been better off with inconvenience food. What else . . . chocolate, juice, jelly bears and Tiny Teddies, what was for me. Marlena's got a thing for bears. She calls me her Big Bear cuz I'm so hairy, got a furry back and everything.

'Zek.' Little Chinese guy stuck his head in the door. 'You girlfriend come today?'

I nodded and beaconed him inside. 'Yeah, mate. Shop's open.'

'Noodles how much?' He also wanted two packs a smokes and one international phone card. A coupla Pakis came by for phone cards as well. The teenage brothers Farshid and Reza, what are asylums from Iran, paid for individual ciggies what they smoked in my room, so their mum wouldn't find out. Chaim, an Israeli visa overstayer what was claiming refugee status on a count a being a dissonant what supported the Palestinians, bought the apple-flavoured tobacco. He liked hanging with the Arabs what smoked the hookah, and they liked him cuz he supported the Palestinians and told good jokes. It didn't hurt that he always bought the tobacco for the pipe, neither. Another Chinese bloke came in and rented the Jackie Chans. Even after counting out what I had to pay back to She Who Managed Supply, I made me a neat profit. It went straight into me sock, the one I hid in the video slot a me VCR. There was over one grand in there. I thought to meself, I'll come outta here laughing.

I stared out the window at the sky. A faint glow on the horizon, beyond the razor wire, reminded me that it was all still happening out there. The clubs, the pubs, the bars, the action. Life. Life and me, we'd been separated by a great big parallel fence with coils a razor wire top and bottom for more than two months. We was getting back together soon. I was stoked. And for the sake a She Who Has Suffered Enough, I wasn't gonna fuck it up this time — pardon me French.

The next day, two guards came to escort me to the AAT. They put me in cuffs and then in the van, and we went to someplace in Parramatta. It wasn't much of an outing, but I could taste that Free World air like it be chocolate. Gubba, me lawyer, was looking more blond and tanned and blow-dried than ever. He was one smooth dude. He told the Member, what be an Indian lady, that I had no home but Australia, and that I'd gone straight, though I swear he glanced at me watch for a second when he said that. After, he told me he thought the hearing went well. He figured I'd be outta there in a week, ten days max. Just in time for Christmas.

Thirteen

Fucken Tribunal had to take their fucken holidays at Christmas before they made their fucken decision, didn't they? Pardon me fucken French.

I didn't even get to complain about it proper to Gubba cuz he was going on his hols as well. He phoned to tell me on the twenty-third a December. 'Sorry, Zeki. It's not the ideal outcome.'

'Mate, ya gotta get me outta here —'

'Sorry, Zeki, can't chat. Have to catch a plane. I'm off for two weeks myself. Noosa. I'll speak to you when I get back.'

'Slip, slop, slap,' I said.

Fourteen

On Christmas morning, She Who called to say she was coming to visit later that arvo, after the lunch with her folks, and that we had to talk. This is not a sentence what a man wants to hear coming from the mouth a his beloved at the best a times. And this sure wasn't the best a times.

Eleven ay-em Muster came round. I dragged meself over to the office. I noticed on the way over that some a the blues was wearing Santa hats. I swear they was doing it mostly for themselves. I never knew any prisoner what be cheered up by the sight of a screw in a dumb red hat. In the office there was a blue with a Santa hat on what I didn't recognise from the back. When he turned round me heart skipped a beat.

Remember what I said about the evil crim in Silverwater, Hadeon, the one what was mates with a screw what be just as evil as him? The screw's name was Clarence, and that was him.

I swear, Clarence's mum musta pushed him out at the top a the Ugly Tree — and he hit every branch on the way down. Ugly with a capital E, I swear. Me and the other greens — what be the name for prisoners, what wore green uniforms, not people what hug trees — we used to call him Meat and Two Veg. He had a head like a side a beef, a nose like a potato and hair the colour a carrots what he cut like he thought he was a US Marine. His lips were thin. He had a scar on his cheek where someone once went him with a knife. Someone told me it was from a girlfriend what caught him porking her thirteen-year-old daughter in her bed. His eyes was the creepiest thing about him cuz they was big and pretty like girls' eyes, with thick lashes. And now, them eyes what I never wanted to see again, they was staring straight at me.

'If it ain't Zeki Togan,' he goes, in a voice greasier than a Kings Cross pizza at three in the morning. 'How nice to see you again.' He showed his teeth, what were neat and white, but I wouldn't exactly call it a smile what he gave me.

'Likewise, I'm sure,' I said. 'What're you doing here?'

'Working for the Shit House now. Got assigned here.' The Shit House was what they called Whacking Co, the private prison management company what ran this place on the half a the government and what had the initials WC. 'I thought it was just gonna be reffoville. I didn't think I'd be seeing loser crims like your good self. I guess I was wrong.'

'You wanna see losers, mate, just look in the mirror a few times a day,' I advised, holding me fingers against me forehead in the shape of an 'L', what spells out 'loser' even though it only be one letter.

'Sign language for "I'm a dickhead", is it? Anyway, a change is as good as a holiday, eh?'

I didn't say nuffin.

He smirked, like he just thought a something. 'I'm assuming that if you're in here, you're going back to the Old Country.'

'After you, mate,' I went.

'This *is* my Old Country.'

'You Aboriginal, mate?'

He snorted. 'Yeah, well, *they* never did much with the place, did they?'

I knew I was gonna get meself into trouble if I kept talking to the muvvafucker. 'You tick me name off?' I said, looking pointingly at the list.

'All done. Happy Christmas, loser.' He put his third finger on his forehead, what spells something else what is rude.

I walked outta the office in a worser mood than before.

Angel passed me on her way in. 'Hey, Zek,' she goes. Her voice was soft and gold and fluttery like the budgie what we used to keep before it got eaten by the neighbour's cat. 'Happy Christmas.'

'You too, Angel.'

She gave me one a them bright smiles. I smiled back and watched as she turned and went into the office, her long black hair swinging along the line a her hips.

I could just make out Clarence's oily tones as I walked away. 'Well, well, well. What do we have here?'

When I got back from Muster, I found Thomas sitting on a plastic chair outside our building, hunched over his drawing pad. He'd put in a Detainee Request Form to go to Christmas Mass at a real church, on the Outside. They'd just laughed. Now, he was drawing Christmas wreaths what were made a razor wire and a Jesus what was hanging from the fence instead a the Cross what he usually hangs from. Across the bottom a the pitcher a Jesus, Thomas wrote the words, 'Inasmuch as ye have done it unto one of the least of these my brethren, ye have done it unto me'.

I read that out loud a few times and scratched me head. 'What's that when it's at home, mate?'

Thomas told me it was words from the Christian Bible. It was about how you're sposed to look after people even if they be a stranger or locked up or both.

I gave him the knuckles. 'Respect,' I said.

'And they call this a Christian country,' he said, like he didn't believe it much. 'Oh no, here comes Nadia.' He pretended to be too absorbed in his drawings to see her. It didn't work cuz Nadia, the Villawood psych, was a big lady what you could see pretty easy.

'Hellooo, Zeki,' she sang out. 'Hellooo, Thomas. Happy Christmas.'

'Happy Christmas, Nadia,' I said for both of us, cuz Thomas wasn't never gonna get round to it.

'How are we today?' She smiled and opened her mouth like she was getting ready to catch the answer with it.

Thomas looked up. 'We are fantastic, Nadia,' Thomas said. 'We are terrific. Today is the day when baby Jesus was born.

He was a refugee. He was born in a manger. We are refugees. We were born in mangers too. But here, in Villawood, we have food and shelter and medical care. We never even knew what chairs were before coming here. Now we sit in them all the time. We never had it so good in our whole lives.'

Nadia's smile, what had slipped down her chin, struggled back up to her cheeks. 'There's no need for sarcasm,' she said. 'It's not very helpful.' She said the words 'very helpful' like they be a song what had three notes up and one down.

'Nice to see you, Nadia.' Thomas bent over his drawing pad.

'We'll talk later, Thomas,' she said and toodled off to find someone else to depress.

After Nadia left, Azad walked over. 'What's happening?' He looked at Thomas's drawings and gave him the thumbs up. He was putting on a brave face but you could tell he was feeling down too. You didn't have to be a Christian to be depressed about being Inside on Christmas, what everyone knew was a big holiday in Australia when everyone got with them families and had barbies and went to the beach. So everyone was feeling down that day. Moods on the Inside was like colds or flus. They got passed from person to person just the same, except with moods you saw the sickness in people's eyes and the way they held themselves, what was not exactly in the direction of up.

It didn't help that bushfires was making the sky look like the dome a hell. The temperature had been up in the mid-to high-thirties for days. You could smell the burning gum trees, and the wind made it feel like you was baking in one a them fancy ovens like what She Who wants us to get one day. What with that and the general mood and Clarence's reappearance in me life and the fact that She Who wanted to talk, I knew it wasn't gonna be an easy day.

But me, I got a philosophy a life, what I had to remind meself about sometimes. And that is — when times are tough and you can do bugger-all about it, the First Rule a Survival is to kick back. So I took meself out into the Visiting Yard to do just that.

Fifteen

I was shaking a Coke outta the machine when I looked up and saw this lady coming out the vault door from the office where they process the visitors. She was with Sue. Now, I reckoned she was a bit of all right. Classy style, nice eyes, dark wavy hair. Probably about forty. I love older women. I never had one in factuality, but the idea always appealed.

The moment the guard let them through the gate to the Yard, Babak — he of the thirty-six thousand chickens — raced up. He tugged Sue off to one side like she be a barge, what he moored at his table. On the table was a stack a papers tall enough to kill a man. They'd barely sat down when he was shoving them in her direction.

This left Sue's friend on her lonesome. She was looking nervously at the fences and the razor wire, then round the Yard.

I soiréed over to her. 'G'day,' I said, 'how ya goin?'

'Hello. Happy Christmas,' she said. 'I'm Sue's cousin? April?'

'April. That's a pretty name. What is only suitable.' I held out me hand. 'Zeki.'

Her eyes ran down me forearm. Them eyes was as blue as the sapphires I once found in this lady's jewellery box. It was them sapphires what led to me first stint in the nick. April looked at both me arms. I clenched me fists so me muscles showed. I wasn't that fit — in fact, I was getting a gut — but me arms were ripped. Didn't mind showing off me arms at all.

I noticed she be growing beads a sweat on her upper lip.

'Hot as buggery, innit?' I went, then added, 'Pardon me French', so she'd know I was a gentleman what don't usually swear in front a ladies.

She touched her own wrist and the snap-on band they put on visitors. She looked at me arms again. She hadn't been admiring me muscles after all. She was trying to work out if I had a wristband. 'You sound so . . . Australian.'

'A happy li'l Vegemite, that's me.'

Thomas appeared just then, shaking her hand and looking at her like she was vanilla ice cream. 'You must be April. I saw you come in with Sue. I'm Thomas.'

'Ah, so you're Thomas! Great. Nice to meet you. Happy Christmas.' She held out a bag with some candy canes and gingerbread men. 'You too . . . Zeki, was it?'

'Still is. Thank you.' I chose a gingerbread man and bit its head off. I always do that first cuz I don't like it looking at me all accusing while I eat the rest of it. I got enough in the life to feel guilty about without worrying about the feelings a gingerbread man.

'Happy Christmas to you too,' Thomas said. He didn't take nuffin from the bag. 'Sue told me you were coming today. She said maybe you can help me.'

'Oh, did she? . . . Uh, look, I . . . I'd like to help. But . . . This is my first visit. I'm still in a bit of shock.'

A gulping sound from somewhere below our knees made us all look down. This little Iraqi girl, Noor, snot all over her face and one pigtail undone, was crying for her mum. Abeer, me little Palestinian mate, ran over. 'Come,' she said, pulling Noor over to her own mum, Najah, what put Noor in her lap and held her till she stopped crying.

April's eyes went very round. 'Is that her mum?'

'No. Her mum is in Woomera,' Thomas said. Woomera was another detention centre what be thousands a kilometres away, in the desert. 'They brought her here two days ago by herself.'

'But separating a little girl from . . . that's . . . outrageous,' April said. 'It's too cruel.'

Thomas shrugged. 'We're used to it,' he goes, what wasn't exactly true.

April glanced over at Sue. She was already lost in the forest a Babak's paperwork. Babak saw April looking and tapped Sue on the shoulder. Sue looked over like she just woke up and didn't know what bed she be in. 'Sorry, April!' she called out. 'You all right there?' Pointing at Babak's papers, she said, 'It's a bit of an emergency. I just have to . . . '

'No worries,' April said. 'Do what you need to do. I'm with these two gentlemen.' Then she blushed, like she'd said we'd all just hooked up, like we was at some club.

'Good-o,' said Sue, giving her the thumbs up, and went back to it.

April wore one a them smiles people wear at a party where they don't know no one and they don't reckon they're gonna have a great time, but they know they ain't getting a lift home till midnight so they better make the best of it.

'Let's go sit over there,' Thomas suggested. His tone made it clear to me that no part a the word 'let's' be spelled with the letter Zeki. Sometimes the asylums was like that with them visitors.

You know, for one crazy moment I wished I was one a them. The asylums. They was in this country — what — two, three years, not a day of it outside the razor wire and they knew every classy lady and cute chick from the Blue Mountains to the North Shore, I swear. Some of them had women writing to them from Perth and Adelaide and country towns all over Australia. Me, I lived in Sydney me whole life and who did I know? She Who Busts Me Balls. Oh maaan. I was feeling fully apprehensible about her visit.

April, what didn't know any a the subtextuals, turned and gave me a join-us type wave. I didn't wanna seem too eager. It's never good to let the ladies think you're keen. I looked round like I was considering me options. I nodded to some other Turks, and winked at that cute new Chinese girl what overstayed her visa — Ching or Chong or something like that. You know, one a them names that sounds like what happens when you drop a tray a cutlery down the steps. Ping pong ting tong. I waved to Bhajan, what was with some lady what visited him every week.

Finally, I strolled up to where April and Thomas was sitting, me Nikes kicking up little clouds a dust. I was glad I was wearing a clean T-shirt, me gold chains and me best trackies — the nylon blue-and-orange ones with the white stripes and the zips what start at the ankle and go up to the knee. They was unzipped to show off the Nikes. I'd put some product in me hair, what takes after Mum's not Dad's, thanks God, and it was standing up in spikes. I reckon in that gear I could almost pass for the good-looking one in *Pizza*.

For all that, me arrival didn't make much of an impact. April's eyes were glued to Thomas's face. I pulled up a chair. He was telling her his story. When he got to the point where he tried to hang himself in the refugee camp, April's eyes was leaking like taps what had worn-out washers.

Thomas's story was too full-on for me, even if I heard it before. I needed to focus on something else or I was gonna stress out. April's chest heaved. That was one excellent set. I focused.

'I can't believe they didn't give you a visa,' April said.

Thomas leaned forward and locked his eyes onto April's. 'Sue told me about your husband.'

'She . . . Gee. What did she say?' April frowned and glanced over in Sue's direction.

'She said your husband is the Minister's doctor. And that they are friends too. April, I have a letter in with the Minister for a four-one-seven. Sue helped me write it.'

'A . . . sorry?'

'A four-one-seven. It's when the Minister himself decides to give you a visa. Which he rarely does. But a connection could make a difference. Sue said your husband could be that connection.'

Talk about putting on the pressurisers.

'Surely once the Minister hears your story, he'll give you a visa anyway.'

'April.' Thomas shook his head. 'If this Minister was locked in detention by some accident, he wouldn't give *himself* a visa to get out.'

'Ha.' April laughed. Thomas wasn't smiling. 'Oh, look,' she said, 'I'm sorry. But . . .'

Thomas put his head in his hands. 'Forget it. I wish I'd never stepped foot in this stupid country.'

'Oh, God, don't say that.' She reached out to touch him on the shoulder. She must've touched what I touched that time cuz her hand came straight off like she been electrocutioned. He raised his head and looked at her with red eyes.

'Maybe I can . . .' April blew her nose on a serviette with a honk. 'Pardon me.' I handed her another serviette. 'Thanks. Uh, when is the Minister supposed to make a decision?'

'Who knows. Maybe tomorrow. Maybe one year from tomorrow. Maybe when hell freezes over.' Thomas squinted up at the sky, what was full a burning.

'Maybe.' April spoke in a small furry voice like a kitten, what was deep too, like the kitten be at the bottom a the ocean. 'Maybe you should look at this as your journey. We say when things happen to you, bad things or good, it's your journey . . .'

Thomas looked at her with his eyes still narrow. 'A journey,' he repeated, flat as a tyre with nails in.

'I just meant there are ways of looking at things . . . like trying to accentuate the positive . . .'

'April, this is your first visit. I don't want to be rude. But I've been Inside two years now. For nothing. That's on top of three years lost in the refugee camp. My home was burned to the ground. My family is dead. I want to study — I'm not allowed. I want to walk for more than a hundred metres without running into a fence — I'm not allowed. I'm only twenty-three. I should be enjoying the best years of my life — I'm not allowed. There's nothing positive about any of that.' Thomas finished speaking and moved his baseball cap round so the beak, what usually covered the machete scar at the back of his neck, was covering his eyes. Then he lowered his head and crossed his skinny arms over his chest.

I could see April's spirit reeling outta her like fishing line what got tuna on.

No one said nuffin for a while. We watched as a group a ladies came in with Christmas pressies for the kids. One a them put a pair a gauzy pink angel wings on Abeer. Abeer mumbled 'Thank you' and then just stood there like she didn't have wings at all. Noor got a sparkly crown but she didn't look like she be feeling like a princess. April's eyes went all watery again.

I could see she be feeling bad. Thinking to detract her, I asked, 'What do you do in the life, April? Are you a doctor like your husband?'

'Me? Oh. I have a little bookshop? Sometimes I edit books, too?' April was always asking questions what weren't questions in factuality.

'What sort of books?' Thomas asked, lifting the beak of his cap a millimetre or two.

'Spiritual development, self-help, that sort of thing?'

'Self-help?' he goes.

'Oh,' she goes, 'it's like I was talking about before. It's about finding the right path.' Thomas looked at her like he still didn't get it. 'I suppose the classic self-help book is the sort that tells you how to make friends and influence people.'

'People in Australia must be very stupid if they need a book to tell them how to make friends.' Thomas the diplomat.

She looked like she didn't know what to say to that. 'Well, there's more to it . . .' She rattled on for a while, using lots a big words like self-axleisation and vigilisation.

'You believe in all that?' he asked after a while.

'I . . . I suppose. I mean, it's pretty good advice, even if some of it's kind of obvious.' She fingered a crystal what was hanging from her neck on a silver chain and then let it go. It fell into her tits. I tried vigilising meself as that crystal.

'Why did you come here, April?' Thomas wasn't mincing his words that day, that was for sure.

April sighed. 'I've been having . . . a hard time? Sue said it'd be good for me to get out of myself, to meet some people with real problems.' She bit her bottom lip, like she knew she just said something dodgy.

Thomas was onto it like a pelican on a water rat, what I actually saw one time in the harbour. 'So . . . *we're* supposed to help *you*.'

April took his words like a slap. 'I didn't mean . . .' Her voice wobbled and her eyes went shiny again.

I figured I better infuse the situation. 'That's interesting what you been saying bout all them books.'

They both turned and stared as if trying to remember who I was. 'I'm not much of an innalectual meself,' I continued. 'I was never much chop at reading. The teachers said I was dyspeptic. But I write hip-hop songs sometimes. I reckon I could write a book.'

April blinked. 'Maybe you should then,' she said.

'Maybe I should read one first, eh?'

That's when I noticed her dimples. 'That wouldn't be a bad idea.'

Thomas mumbled something and jiggled his leg like he wanted to shake it clear off.

'Where's this bookshop a yours?' I asked.

'Leichhardt?'

She said the word like she didn't think I'd know it. 'I know Leichhardt,' I said. 'Norton Street. Spag bol. Eye-tie pastries. The best coffee after Turkish.' I punctuated the last statement with one a them cool hip-hop moves where you punch down the air, second and little fingers expended, thumb out, elbow up.

'How . . . ?' She looked puzzled.

'I watch a lotta hip-hop videos. Not bad, eh?' I thought she was talking about me moves.

'No, I mean ... I don't get what you're doing in an Immigration Detention Centre.'

I felt the shame come flooding in. I was saved though cuz just at that moment Azad, Hamid and Angel walked up. April looked at Azad like he be a dessert she didn't even know she'd ordered.

Sixteen

'Yo,' I greeted them after they'd done the intros with April.

After everyone sat down again there was what Mum calls an Auckland Silence. Me mum went to New Zealand once and said it's pretty quiet over there.

'Was there big queue to get in?' Azad asked.

'I couldn't believe it,' April said. 'It took two hours!'

'I'm sorry,' goes Azad.

Thomas stood up. 'The wait to get out is even longer.' He walked over to a table what had other Africans on.

April's eyes went like blue buttons. 'Is he . . . ?'

'He'll be right,' I insured her.

She turned to Azad. 'I didn't mean to complain about the queue. We were just hoping to get inside earlier.'

Hamid smiled. 'We're here twenty-four-seven. Welcome anytime.' Everyone laughed. Hamid was in a great mood count a the Management deciding the day before that it be okay if Angel moved to Stage Two. They didn't know her real age, what made her a minor what oughtta stay in Lima.

April poured out juice for them and, like she just remembered it, reached into the bag what held the gingerbread men and other stuff like candy canes and Tim Tams and pistachios and spread them over the table. 'Please,' she goes, opening her hands over the food.

We all said 'Thank you' but only I dug in. Another gingerbread man lost his head.

'Where are you from?' April asked Angel.

'Kampuchea,' Angel said. 'You know it? Cambodia?'

'Oh my God. We went there last year. On holiday? There and Vietnam. It was a two-week gourmet tour. The food! It was so yum. And Angkor Wat is fabulous. *So* amazing. It's a very spiritual place. But here I am telling you about it!'

'I never been to Angkor Wat,' Angel said in that funny ding-dong way Orientals have a talking, like they was tapping them syllabuses out one at a time. It was cute on the girls.

'Really? How come?'

'I . . . I was working,' she said.

We all sat there real tense, hoping she wasn't gonna ask Angel about her job. I reckoned I'd better break the ice cube.

'I'm Turkish,' I volunteered. 'In originality.'

'Oh, I was wondering. Huh.'

'And I'm from Afghanistan,' Hamid said.

As she turned to Hamid, her eyebrows shot up and her mouth made like a cat's bum. 'Gee, that's . . .' She didn't know if she should say that it be good or interesting or just plain terrible that he came from there. 'Incredible.'

'And I'm Kurdish,' Azad said. 'From Syria . . . how do you say it — *via* Iraq.'

'"Via", that's a great word! Huh. Your English is so good. And the rest of your family . . . are they in Iraq?'

Azad nodded.

In me head I was jumping up and down and waving stop signs and red lights at April, but she didn't see them. There were times when you don't ask questions. In prison, you don't ask what people got done for. A mate a mine what's been to Darwin said that you don't ask people why they moved to the Northern Territory neither. It was like that at Villawood, but not cuz people did something wrong like what made them go to prison or the NT, but cuz it be too fucked up to talk about, pardon me French.

'Maybe someday they'll be able to join you here,' she said, chirpy like the budgie before the cat got it.

'I don't think so,' Azad said quietly. 'They were all killed.'

April's hand flew to her mouth.

'It's okay. Not your fault.'

We were back in New Zealand.

'How do you,' April started again, 'how do you survive here, in this awful place?'

'For me, faith,' said Azad. 'God is great. And poetry.'

I reckoned Thomas survived on him wits and Hamid and Angel on love. As for me, She Who Knows Me Inside Out and Sideways and Even Upside Down always says I survive on me optimism. She calls me the Infernal Optimist cuz she says I could look on the bright side of hell if I had to.

'Wow,' said April to Azad. 'That's beautiful. Poetry and faith.'

'Did you celebrate Christmas today?' Hamid asked.

'Actually, I'm Jewish?' April said like she was asking us if it be all right. Later she told me she was nervous that all Muslims might be like Osama bin Laden what blamed the Jewish for everything.

'You are the People of the Book,' Azad said. 'We are cousins. We all believe in one God.'

She was like a puppy what licked his face all over with relief. I remembered someone once told me Jews are like us other wogs what can never keep our expressions in check like Anglos do with their stiffed upper lips. 'True. Though you might say I'm a typical post-Holocaust Jew. Sometimes I don't know what I believe exactly.'

'But you believe in God,' Azad said, what wasn't really a question.

'I suppose,' she said, what wasn't really an answer.

Azad stared at April and she stared back and Hamid stared at his feet, what were in plastic sandals what were too big for them.

Angel stared at me. She was the only one what noticed that I was choking on me gingerbread man. 'You all right, Zeki?' she asked. Without waiting for an answer, she gave me a whack between the shoulder blades. I coughed and a little leg with frosted boots on came shooting outta me mouth and landed in the middle of the table.

'Sorry,' I said, scooping up the leg and popping it back in me gob. I washed it down with juice. 'Whew.'

Angel giggled. She put her hand over her mouth. She started to shake, and then she began laughing like she was gonna split her sides with it. Everyone started to laugh then, even me, though I was careful to swallow first. It was sweet seeing Angel laughing like that. Her brown eyes went like quarter-moons with them points on her cheeks.

'Zeki always makes us laugh,' Azad told April.

Thomas chose that moment to return. He sat down, mumbled something, and reached for a candy cane. He'd calmed down. April looked at him, relief all over her face. 'We have these in my country too, for Christmas,' he told us, holding up a candy cane.

'Really?' April said, very enthusiastic, like that be extremely interesting. He nodded. No one could think of anything to say after that. April looked at me like she just remembered I was there. 'So, Zeki, what's your story?'

Seventeen

'Everyone makes one mistake in the life, right?' I reached for a Tim Tam. As I told you, I eat when I'm stressed.

She nodded and leaned forward. Her tits swole up over her shirt's scoop-neck in a slow, milky wave. I caught a whiff a her sweat. It smelled nice, like honey yoghurt. 'Yeah?'

I struggled with this next bit. See, there are two types a women. Those who love an outlaw and those who don't. I was hoping she be the first type, but I didn't like me chances. 'I suppose you could say it was a self-help kind a mistake.'

'Sorry? A self-help mistake?'

'Yeah. I helped meself to things I shouldn'ta.' She still wasn't with me. I spilled it out. 'Break 'n' enter.'

Her eyes and mouth made three perfect Os and she straightened up. Despite the heat, the air round her chilled by about ten degrees. If this kept up, I was gonna have to go in for a jacket. 'But how . . . why are you here in Villawood?'

I told her about the day I was supposed to get me citizenship with me family. 'I meant to go back, but never got round to it. I hate queues.'

'You should jump them. Like us.' Azad grinned.

April turned to Azad. 'But . . . I thought you didn't jump any queues,' she said. 'There were no queues to jump where you came from. That's what Sue said.'

Thomas gave her a look like *duh*.

April blushed. Her eyes grew watery again. I looked from her to Azad, what had gone completely blank, like an uncharged mobile. He was cracking pistachios with his teeth. The ground around his chair was littered with shells.

April returned her attention to me. 'You know,' she goes, kinda smiling but kinda not, 'we were broken into once and they took all our CDs. Hope that wasn't you.'

'I *never* pinched no one's CDs, I swear.'

'Really? Is that true?'

'Not exactly,' I admitted. 'See, there was this dude what had Snoop Dogg's *Doggystyle*, the one with "Pump Pump" and "Serial Killa" what you can't get in the shops no more. So I left some things I'd normally a taken, like the DVD player. You gotta give people a fair go, I reckon. Anyway, I'm here on a count a five-oh-one.'

'Five-oh-one?'

'It's a kind a libel law. Any non-citizen what spends more than twelve months in prison is libel for deportation on the basis a character.'

April took this in. 'Well,' she said after a pause, a smile tugging up her lips. 'You certainly are a character.' Her body relaxed some. The mercury rose.

'Spose I shoulda waited in that queue. Now . . . oh shit.'

Marlena was coming down from the gate. And the look on her face was one of total accusation.

'Excusing me. I got a visitor. Nice meeting you, April. Uh, you mind?' I took another Tim Tam for the road. I met She Who halfway between the gate and the table. Straight off, she gave me one a them looks what said I be in trouble. Oh maaan. What'd I do to deserve this? I knew if I asked she'd have an answer, so I only thought the question to meself.

She was wearing her nice trousers and silver sandals with heels on. Seeing as there was no more tables or chairs available, we was gonna have to sit on the ground. 'Want me to go in and get a blanket for us to sit on?'

She shook her head. 'I want us to talk.'

We found a patch a grass what wasn't dead yet, and what had some shade, and sat down.

Some Koreans sitting in a circle a chairs behind us busted into a song about Jesus.

'Christ,' I joked, 'not a minute's peace in here.' We turned to look. The Koreans all looked to be around twelve, even the old ones, with them smooth skin and boxy faces. The chicks was wearing blouses what were buttoned up to the collar spite a the heat. A few metres behind them, a pair a Tongan sheilas was getting it on, or close to it, on a reed mat laid out by the fence. One a them moaned. The Koreans turned to see what was happening. They gasped like the sight made their brains need a lot more oxygen than what they had.

Clarence stormed over, shouting 'Cool off! Cool off!' at the Tongans, what they didn't do for long.

'Hard-core lesbian action,' I whispered, winking.

'Zeki.'

I took another tack. 'Nice toenails,' I said. What they were in factuality, being painted red with green decals for Christmas on.

She gave me a little smile. 'I did 'em myself.'

'You're the best.' I meant it.

'Zeki.'

'Babydoll.' I held out me arms what was for her to fall into.

She didn't fall. 'I told my parents you're here. They think I should dump you. They said this five-oh-one thing is the last straw.'

'I didn't do nuffin! Did ya tell 'em that? It's not like I'm in prison.'

She looked up and stared pointingly at the fence and the razor wire and the guards, and then at her wrist band and then back at me. 'No, not at all,' she said, rolling her eyes, what are the prettiest.

'This place is bullshit, darl. It's total bullshit. You know I don't belong here. I'm as Aussie Aussie Aussie oi oi oi as the next bloke. I drink VB. I follow the footy. I don't know nuffin but this country. Anyway, I'm virtuosically outta here.'

'Well, that's what Gubba says.' She shook her head. Her hair fell in front a her face and she pushed it back behind her ears what had the gold earrings in what I gave her two

Christmases ago. She loved them earrings. She never knew I didn't exactly buy them from the shop. 'I don't trust Gubba, Zeki.'

'What d'ya mean?'

'I dunno,' she said. 'Something about him. The other day I was in there for fifteen minutes. He charged seventy-five dollars. More important than the money, though — what if he's wrong, Zek? What're we gonna do if that Tribunal thing decides against you, if they decide to deport you?'

'Darl, listen to me. No one's gonna deport me. And babe, just fix him up, will ya? You know them lawyers. They shake your hand, pat you on the back and still manage to come up with a third hand for lifting your wallet.'

'*My* wallet,' she goes, like she be correcting me.

'That's what I said,' I joked. '*Your* wallet.'

She gave me a bailful look, what is a look what says you gonna have to pay to get outta the situation it be putting you in.

'I'll make it up to you later, I promise. Speaking a which . . .'

I glanced round to make sure there was no blues in the vicinity. I dug into me pocket for what I owed her for the vids and smokes and stuff what I sold to the other detainees, and pressed a wad a bills into her hand. She was a natural-born businesswoman, I swear. But she always laughed when I said she should go into business. It was true, though — she was ace at managing supply. When I told her that, she replied that she had to be, cuz I always came up with plenty a demands. Anyway, she did a quick count and stuffed the cash into the waist of her trousers what was, in factuality, round her hips and not her waist. Being a little plump, her tummy spilled out over the waistband a the trousers like the top of a muffin. She was one beautiful woman.

I leaned in and whispered. 'Did you smuggle in the mobile?'

'Zeki, you know I hate it when you ask me to do this sort of thing. It really stresses me out. It's *contraband*.' She said the word like it meant something bad. She brushed some dirt off her trousers like she was angry with the cloth they was made of. Then she sighed and pulled a big Christmas pudding outta one a the bags. 'It's in here. In the pud.'

'That's me girl! And the charger?'

'That too.'

'You little bewdy.' I wanted to get me business affairs in order before I got out, and to do that I needed to make a few phone calls in the privacy a me own room. I went to give her a kiss but she wasn't real happy with me. She turned her cheek. I got worried. 'You're not really gonna dump me, are you?'

She gave me a look what said I was on probation, what is something I have been on a lot in me life. 'The woman in front of me in the queue,' she goes in that accusing tone, 'she had a roast chicken and the guard swung it through the metal detector. If they'd have done that to the pudding I'd have been caught for sure.' She sounded like she was gonna bust into tears.

'But they didn't, and you wasn't,' I pointed out, reasonably enough, I reckoned. 'And how about the other stuff?' I moved me fingers like I was rolling a joint.

She shook her head. 'No. Not gonna either.'

'I swear, darl, it's no sweat. How many times do I have to tell you? Wrap it up in cling wrap, stuff it down your bra and spray them sweet titties with perfume. The screws won't find it in a million.'

'It's a federal offence, Zeki. You might like it Inside, but I don't.'

That pissed me off. 'I like it Inside? *I like it Inside?*'

'Keep your voice down,' she whispered.

'What is this — church or something?' She gave me a look then. I knew I'd stepped over the line. She's a good girl, in factuality, and when I thought about that, I really didn't know what she was doing with me. Still, a few ounces a maryjane down her bra wouldn't a killed her. The Moroccan bloke Ali's chick did it all the time. After he got released, the supply dried up. He said he'd be back to visit, said he'd come every week, but he hadn't showed his face yet. I understood. When you're Out, you're Out. You don't wanna know nuffin about the Inside. When you're on the Inside, all you wanna know is Out. You think about it all the time. You think about it till your head hurts.

That's the great thing about dope. Dope keeps you from thinking too much, what be an occupational hazard on the Inside. When you're locked up, your brain races like dogs after one a them mechanical rabbits, but it's like someone's got rid a the off switch on the rabbit. Dope gives them dogs in your head a rest.

This was something Miss 'The Law is the Law' never seemed to understand.

The Infernal Optimist

'Okay,' I said, 'forget the ounces. Just one joint? For me personal usage.'

'You know, Zeki,' she goes in that tone what sounded like Miss O'Meary from Year Ten what learned us English, 'sometimes I think my parents have a point.'

By the time I sweet-talked She Who Must Be A-Pleased into giving me a smile, it was seven o'clock. I insured her there was nuffin to worry about except putting a slab in the fridge and polishing up me dancing shoes.

The blues was clapping their hands at stragglers and the loudspeaker was blaring. 'Visits are over. All visitors must leave the Visiting Yard. Throw your rubbish in the bin.' Mate, that whole place was rubbish, but there wasn't a bin big enough for it.

Clarence, what was on gate duty, hustled Marlena outta the Yard. He sneered as he swung the gate shut between us. She shuffled up the slope to the vault door with that funny, cute gait a hers, more a waddle than a walk. Me sweet muffin wobbled on her heels as she waited for a second guard to come and open the vault door from the inside. She turned her head and gave me one a them looks. That was the moment I hated the most. I felt shamed a being Inside and didn't want her to go. I never knew whether to stand and watch till she was all the way through or turn and go like a man, pretending to be cool. I scrounged around inside one a the plastic bags what she gave me and pulled out a stick a liquorice. It was twisted up like me heart.

'What are ya, a big girl?' Clarence said. 'Or ya gonna say there was somefing in yer eye?'

'If you don't shut up, you'll have somefing in *your* eye, mate,' I replied, quick as snakes. 'Me fist.'

'Ooh,' he goes, making a face and batting them spooky girl eyes at me, 'I'm scared.'

'You better be, muvvafucker.'

'C'mon, Togan, you're holding things up,' Anna yelled at me from the other gate, the one to the compound. She pronounced me surname like it rhymed with 'bogan'. I was used to it.

'I mean it, arsehole,' I said to Clarence. Then I turned on me heels and strolled to where Anna was waiting, not hurrying, taking me sweet time.

'Watcha got there?' Anna goes, pointing at the bags with her chin.

If it were one a the other screws, I'd say, 'None a your fucken business,' even though technologically it was, but Anna was all right, so I didn't give her no shit. I opened the bags. She looked inside. 'Some of that chocolate for me?'

'Take it.' I held out a big fruit and nut bar.

'Just kidding,' she said, pushing me hand away.

'Anyway,' I go, 'you know where to find it.' I winked. 'Shop's open all night long.'

'Cheeky monkey.' She grinned. 'Happy Christmas anyway.'

Back in me room I opened the box a Tiny Teddies and poured out a handful. I picked out Happy, Sleepy, Grumpy, Cheeky, Silly and Hungry. Anna called me Cheeky but I felt more Grumpy and Hungry. I popped the whole Teddy family into me gob.

Even the best food tastes like cardboard when you're on the Inside.

Eighteen

April came to visit again the next day, what was Boxing Day. Everyone was impressed with that. Almost everyone. 'Where's Thomas?' she asked. It was clear she hadn't seen him stomping off when she appeared at the vault door.

'He here one minute ago,' Angel told her. 'Join us. He be back soon.'

'Gee, this place is awful, isn't it?' April said, settling into one a the plastic seats. 'All this razor wire! And the prison guards. And Sue told me that when they give you jobs, like cleaning, they pay you a dollar an hour, and in phone cards? I can't believe it, the whole thing is so depressing.' She went on like that until everyone was staring at them feet. Talking about how terrible Detention was wasn't a great conversational gamble. The odds a getting a favourable response wasn't too good. Lotsa new visitors did it. Maybe they needed to. But we didn't need to hear it. We was living it. April made a face. 'But I guess you know all that, don't you?'

'Mm,' Hamid agreed.

April looked around. 'Oh, there he is.' Thomas was talking to some visitors on the other side of the yard. She looked over at him nervously. 'See, what I haven't been able to say . . . to tell him . . . is that Josh, my husband, left me?' Everyone looked up again with horrorfied expressions on them faces. 'It happened after September Eleven. He said that seeing so many people die so suddenly made him think he should die without regrets? The thing he was going to regret the most, apparently' — April rolled her eyes — 'was not getting it on with his nurse. That really hurt me. Last week . . . well, he started calling again. The nurse dumped him and he wants me to take him back. I thought he had some nerve, and told him so.'

'You should forgive him,' Azad said.

'Do you think?' April looked at Azad and bit her lip. 'I told him no way.'

'That is not good,' Azad said, like he be an authority.

'Huh,' she said. 'I'd already smudged the bedroom with sage and mugwort to get rid of all the negative energy? And I was beginning to feel okay about it. Then, after visiting here yesterday, I lay awake all night thinking. I decided . . . well, I decided that I'd talk to Josh — for Thomas's sake. I think that was part of Sue's plan from the start. But I need to find out more about Thomas's case first.' She looked over at Thomas again and made a brave face. 'I'd better go talk to him. Would you excuse me? I'll be back.' She strode off in Thomas's direction.

Hamid shook his head. 'What she do to the bedroom?'

They all looked at me. I shrugged. I never heard a no one smearing them bedrooms before. 'Fucked if I know.'

We all sank into our own thoughts like we was Sanna the bikini girl and our thoughts was the quicksand in that old movie *When Dinosaurs Ruled the Earth*. It's one a me favourites on a count a having both dinosaurs and bikinis in, what doesn't happen enough in movies. Hamid rubbed the palm a one hand up his other arm to the elbow a few times. Then he switched hands and did it to the other arm. Azad took out his lighter and flicked it on and off. Angel twirled a strand a hair round her finger. I was jiggling me feet, just like Farshid and Reza were doing over at the next table. I reckon if anyone worked out a way to harness the nervous energy in that place, it coulda powered all a Sydney.

Finally Thomas and April came walking back together. As they sat down, April reached into one a her bags. 'I almost forgot!' she said. She pulled out pressies for all of us — an art book for Thomas, a medical dictionary for Hamid and a man-bracelet for Azad what was silver. I got a posh journal what was all blank pages for me to write me book in. She said the art book and the medical dictionary was from her own bookshelves at home and the bracelet and journal from her shop. She apologised that she couldn't do proper shopping cuz a the holidays but we was all amazed by the gifts, what be fully thoughtful. She still seemed kinda nervous, like she was stepping on poached eggs, but the conversation went easier after Thomas came back.

Some musos came into the Yard with their instruments and set up under the shelter. They had a darabuka what is one a them Arabic drums, a Yamaha keyboard what they plugged into the socket for the Coke machine, a guitar and a violin. Nuffin like this never happened before. We went over to listen along with most everyone else in the Yard.

We made a big circle round the musos. First they sang some folk songs and Irish ballads. Then they invited us to sing and play too, but at first no one did on a count a shyness. Then one a the Iraqis stood up to sing an Egyptian love song and a Palestinian took over on the darabuka and Reza, what got a nice voice even though it cracks sometimes on a count a his reaching pubalescence, sang a Persian love song. Azad sang a Kurdish one. Bhajan sang us one a him poems. Then this Albanian chick what was getting out soon with her family sang 'Bombastic Love' and 'I am a Slave 4 U', what was awesome. After that the musos played some dancing music and Farshid asked the Albanian chick to dance. They was just getting into it when one a the Iraqis cut his grass. Farshid didn't look too happy, but then a uni chick what was visiting got him to dance with her, what cheered him up. I asked April to dance and was showing her some flash moves when she got shy and wanted to sit down again. Some a the kids danced too. Abeer tied a scarf round her little hips and did the belly dancing, while the ladies what cover with the veil sat to one side watching and clapping and doing that Uluru thing with them voices.

When there was a break, I stood up. 'For those a you what don't know me, I's the Zekster, and what I's gonna perform for youse all is a one-hundred-fiddy per cent original number.' Some a me mates whistled and hooted. I made these phat sounds with me mouth like I be scratching vinyl and doing some drum beats and performed me best B-boy moves as I rapped:

It's another day in Detention
That be life in suspension
For the Zekster
What grow fat like a cat what grow mould what grow old
The Zekster say, yo, look at yourself
You be sitting on the shelf
Gonna get on the pension
Fore you're outta Detention
Bro it make me hypertense
Yo, just looking at that fence
Being in be too intense
In Detention. In suspension.
Can't go without a mention
A the refugees
What the government owe apologies
For keeping 'em years in Detention.
Years in suspension.
We all need release from da tension!

Everyone laughed and whistled and applauded. I was one talented homey, if I have to say so meself.

The party was just going off when the loudspeaker crackled. 'Will visitors please make their way to the gate. Will visitors please make their way to the gate.' They never put a question mark in them influctuations cuz they don't mean it as a question. Visits was over. Clarence and the other blues walked round the Yard clapping them hands, but not like they was applauding.

'Aw, c'mon, mate, giss a break,' I go to this Maori bloke, Tip, what was a reasonable bloke for a blue. 'Let us go to seven-thirty or eight for once. Live on the wild side.'

'Sorry, bro, wush I could. But rules are rules.' Tip says 'wush' instead a 'wish' on a count a being from New Zealand where everyone speaks funny. 'Besides, our shuft ends at eight and we gotta tidy up the paperwork before we can get off.'

Our shuft never fucken ended — pardon me French.

After the visitors disappeared through the vault door, we cleaned up the Yard and divvied up the leftovers from the food what they brung. By quarter past, the place was quiet as a mouse, what wasn't really that quiet on a count a the loudspeaker calling folks to the phone and Medical and some a the detainees arguing outside the laundry over the dryers, what was never enough. The end a Visits, specially on a day like that, was like when you're coming down after an E, what sometimes makes you feel almost sadder after than you was happy before.

Nineteen

'Yeah, Zeki. Come in.' Azad was sitting on his bed.

'Watcha doin, mate?' I asked.

'What's there to do?' He looked around his room, what only got some books and clothes and a prayer rug and some stuffed animals on the bed what visitors brung him like he was a little kid. He collected feathers too. They were lined up on the shelf by his books — feathers from cockies and maggies and currawongs and even one or two from a kookaburra. He'd been spending more time by himself since Hamid and Angel got together. There was something in his hand.

'What's that?'

'Seashell.' He showed me. Someone gave it to him for Christmas.

'Oh, mate, I miss the beach,' I go. 'This country got the best beaches.'

'I wouldn't know,' he goes.

I held out me pack a smokes. He shook his head and sighed again.

'Shit. Sorry, mate.' I stuffed it back in me pocket. 'Forgot you was giving up.'

'*Ensh'Allah*.'

There was a knock on the door. I looked at me watch. Eight o'clock. It was Anna. 'Room service,' she goes, what is a joke for when they come to your room for Muster instead a making you go to them. We showed her our IDs like she didn't know who we be, and she ticked our names off the list. 'Have a good one,' she said and left.

'She was giving you lusty eyes, mate, I swear.'

'What means "lusty eyes"?'

I showed him.

'Stop it.'

I gave him more lusty eyes. He threw plush toys at me till I stopped.

There was another knock. It was Bilal, an Iraqi dude what lost the plot. Bilal had his coffee mug in his hand. '*Salaam aleikum*, Bilal,' Azad greeted him.

'*W'aleikum salaam*.'

Azad reached onto the shelf for his jar a Nescafé and spooned out some brown crystals into the mug. Bilal nodded and left. Every night he got coffee from Azad, hot water from Thomas, four spoonfuls a sugar from this Liberian bloke, creamer from a Russian and a spoon to stir it with from an Iranian. Then he went to a Chinaman's room to drink it. The sugar used to come from this Palestinian dude. When the Palestinian got released on a Temporary Protection Visa, Bilal went around talking to himself for hours, not wanting to drink his coffee without sugar but not wanting to take it from anyone else, either. The next evening they brung in the Liberian what was an asylum what came by plane. Bilal decided that the Liberian would be his sugar man. But the Liberian didn't have any sugar. He didn't have nuffin. He didn't know what was going on. They'd taken him from the airport straight into Villawood. He was crying and scared cuz he didn't know Australia locked up refugees and he didn't have a clue what this Iraqi headcase was doing standing in his doorway with a mug a coffee. That was two months earlier. He just left the sugar on the shelf by the door now.

'You know Abeer's dad, Mohammed?' Azad said a few minutes later. 'He told me they knew Bilal two years ago, when they were all together in Woomera. He said he was perfectly normal then, like you and me.' He shook his head. 'That's what scares me the most about detention, you know,' Azad said. 'Losing my mind.'

'Mate, I know what you mean,' I go. 'Of course, me mum says that if I lost my mind, no one would notice it be missing.'

'Your mum says that?' That made him smile for a second. 'Ha.' The smile faded. 'Sometimes I wonder if I lost my mind a long time ago, when my family was killed. It's like I don't feel much anymore, like I am cold inside. Maybe I'm crazy as Bilal but can't see it. I think I'm okay. But how do I know? *W'Allah*, how do I know?'

I shrugged. If he didn't know, I sure as hell didn't.

'You know the Chinese guy, Fang, the one in Falun Gong?' Azad asked.

'The one what looks like he's trying to push things what are made of air along shelves what are also made of air?'

'That's him,' Azad said. 'Fang told me an old Chinese story. This old man dreamed he was a butterfly. When he woke up he wasn't sure if he was an old man dreaming he was a butterfly or a butterfly dreaming he was an old man dreaming he was a butterfly.'

'Whoa,' I said. 'That's fully spinning me out.' I thought about it. 'Was he a butterfly then?'

Azad laughed. 'Maybe.'

'I reckon April's got a bit a butterfly in her.'

'April? In a way. Like she is flying around looking for a flower to land on.'

That's one a the things I liked about Azad. He could always take the conversationals to a deeper level, like one a them diving bells on the television what goes looking for ocean fish with lights on. Me, I was just talking crap about how pretty she was.

'Fang told me another story,' Azad said. 'When Mao was the ruler of China, he decided to kill all the birds that were eating the farmers' grain. So he got everyone in China to stand outside their houses and on their roofs and to bang their pots and pans together at the same time. All over China, birds were too scared to land. They flew and flew until they got so tired of flying they just dropped out of the sky and hit the ground dead. You know, that's what it feels like sometimes, being a refugee, being without a home, a safe place to land. Like one of those birds.'

'Mate, you should write a poem about it.'

'I started to.'

'What happened?'

'I don't know. I haven't been able to write lately. Writing poetry is like stretching your wings and — what is the word? — *soaring*. You can't do that in a cage. I don't read as much as I used to, either. I keep telling myself I'll write and read again when I'm free . . . I don't like to let the other asylum seekers see it, Zeki, but I'm tired. I'm so tired.'

'You wanna go to sleep?' I asked. 'I'll leave if you do.'

'No, don't. It's not that kind of tired.'

'How's your case going?' I asked.

'Do you really want to hear?'

I told him I was all ears, what is true cuz they're so big I used to get called Dumbo when I was young. It is also true cuz I be a good listener. She Who says this is one a me best treats.

Oh maaan. I was thinking how I was gonna give her one a me best treats soon enough. I was gonna give it to her all night long. I was thinking about this and in my imagining Marlena turned into April and then they was both in there and I was in the middle like *köfte* in yoghurt. Cuz a this I missed some a Azad's explanation, what had too many legal details in and was flying over me head anyways, making me feel like one a them suburbs in the flight path what hears the roar a the planes but can't see what the people are doing inside them.

'I don't know.' Azad said them three words like they was real heavy, like they was barbells what he was dropping on the floor, *thump, thump, thump.*

I musta missed something.

'What was the most time you ever spent in prison, Zeki?'

'Thirteen months.'

'For what?'

'Break-and-enter, and violating the conditions a me parole.'

'Think about this. I committed no crime. But I've been in twenty-seven months so far. I could be in another twenty-seven. Sometimes I think I will never get my freedom, and I swear, Zeki, the second I *know* that, really know it to be true . . .' He made like he was cutting his wrists. 'I did it before, in Port Hedland, after my RRT. If I do it again, I won't fail.'

I didn't know what to say when the asylums started talking like that. It made me real uncomfortable. I reckoned a change a subject was in order.

Like I just thought a something, I said, 'Seen that new English chick, mate? Overstayed her visa by five years, apparently, working illegal and everything before they caught her.'

'You don't have to worry about her. She'll get out. She has the right skin colour for this country.'

'That's not me point, mate.' I was trying to cheer him up. 'They say she's a model. Not just any old model. *Long-jer-ay!*' I made bowls with me hands and held them in front a me chest. Last backpacker they picked up, nympho Canadian babe, did half the single male population a Villawood before they deported her a few days later. If she'd a been Inside just one more day I'm sure I'd a had a chance too. Azad didn't say nuffin, like he didn't care one way or another. I tried again.

'She's one hot mama.' Still no reaction. I made two fists, pumped me elbows backwards and me hips forward. Then I repeated the gesture for emphasis.

He shook his head. 'Not interested, Zeki.'

'Mate, if you're not interested in this one, I'm gonna have to take your pulse. You might be dead.'

'Don't bother,' he goes. 'I checked already. I've been dead a long time now.'

Me phone vibrated in me pocket. It was She Who. 'Cuddly-wuddly-poo?' she goes. 'Big Bear?' I told Azad I had a call, told Marlena to hang on, stuck the phone back in me pocket, and went back to me room to take the call.

Twenty

When I said I was sorry I couldn't take the call right away, Marlena said she didn't mind. She loved that thanks to the mobile we could talk anytime. She even liked the sounds what got into the phone through me trackies just then, *swishswooshswishswoosh* from the nylon and *fookfookfookfook* being the sound a me runners. She said she could hear what was going down around me too but not totally clear, like when you come outta the water with some a the ocean in your ears. I loved it when She Who was in that sort a mood. When she just be loving me and not criticising everything I do. It got me going. So I told her all about the treat I was gonna give her, though I left out the bit about April being in it too. I told her how I was gonna take the little man in her boat for a long row in the river. That little man, he was gonna go through whirlpools and rapids and them long, slow, wet bits what rivers have. She said I was too naughty, but I knew she liked it cuz she was breathing funny and calling me encouragable. She wasn't wrong there.

After we got off the phone, I headed straight out to find that backpacker chick. She was already talking to Chaim, the Israeli. There's only the quick and the dead round here. Survival Rule Three: Be quick.

I wished I could get on the Internet. We had a 'computer room' up near the soccer field. In it were six computers older than me *dede*'s bones and not much use except for playing games on. There was no Internet access. When I was Outside and She Who Watches Over Me Every Waking Moment finally made some Zs, I'd get into them chat rooms. You meet some hot chicks that way. I chose the name AussieStud, except me spelling's not that hot and so the first time I logged on I was AssieStud. That turned out okay, cuz I got loads a responses from ladies with a preference for back-door action. But me typing was dead slow. By the time I finished replying, the chicks had pissed off outta the room. On me last stint in the nick I took a typing course, but fat lotta good that did me there.

It's funny. The asylums what was transferred to Villawood from immigration detention centres in Woomera and Port Hedland all called Villawood 'half the visa' when they first arrived cuz it was that much better than those places. I wouldn't know. I'd never been locked up anywhere but prison before. Personally, I prefer prison. You know why you're there and when you're getting out, what is the most important thing. Plus, there's courses and work and stuff to fill up the day. On me last stint in the nick I almost got to be a fully qualified air-conditioner repairman by the time they let me out. Time before that I learned auto mechanics.

By comparison, the courses they got in Villawood were bullshit. Like yoga, what was a lady what told us to breathe with our stomachs instead of our noses, what was dumb cuz you can't. Then she showed us how to do the doggy style what wasn't the doggy style what I like. The only good part was when we got to lie down at the end with a blanket over us, but then she told me off for going to sleep. Apparently me snoring made it hard for the others to mediterrate.

I was feeling antsy. So I took a walk, what didn't mean much in that small place. Same old faces, same old buildings and me runners wearing a rut in the same old rut they was wearing in the day before. Some new people came, like Chaim what got here two weeks ago, and some went, like the Moroccan bloke, Ali, and some people came and never went anywhere again but crazy, like Bilal. But even with them comings and them goings, in the end it was same old, same old.

I wandered past the playground and the telephones and laundry, and turned left up the path past the women's centre and the building what had families in, and the Rec Room what had billiards and TV what the Chinese was always watching them movies on, and then on to the bullshit computer centre and soccer field. It was late and some people was out having conversationals. But there was nuffin happening. Night-time, what I used to love and what be when all the fun be happening on the Outside, is the worst time on the Inside, I swear. It be time what needs filling. But everything was quiet under them yellow lights. I headed back towards Shoalhaven down the other side a the soccer field, past another dorm where someone was playing African music, and then by Medical and the kitchen. I came up to the place what we called David Jones after the department store, what even the asylums knew from TV, but in factuality was a storeroom full a second-hand clothes what was donated.

Angel was sitting outside David Jones with Hamid. They was facing each other. She'd kicked off her thongs and rested her bare feet on top a his, what was bare too and balancing on the topper part a his sandals. She was wearing a strappy top and a denim mini. She'd pinned her hair up but some strands had fallen free around her neck, what looked pretty. She was holding one a them styrofoam cups from the mess. They was talking quietly. I noticed Angel had a flower in her hair, what was unusual cuz there weren't no flowers growing Inside. I wouldn't a been surprised if you told me it just grew outta her, I swear. I didn't wanna disturb them, so I stopped to consider me options.

There was a crunch a boots. Clarence came round the corner from the other direction. When he saw Angel and Hamid, his fugly mug turned even fuglier, what I wouldn't think possible. 'Oi — who gave youse two permission to be out by yourselves?'

'We don't need permission,' Hamid said, his jaw going all tense.

'Oooh,' Clarence goes, like he be mocking Hamid. Then he turned his attention to Angel and waggled a thick finger in her direction. 'Hey, Angel, don't I know you from way back?' except he said the last words funny, like 'svay pak'. She didn't say nuffin but her hands started tearing the cup into pieces like she was mad at it. Hamid stood up like he was gonna fight Clarence but Clarence moved away before Hamid could get his sandals back on.

I didn't know all the details. But by then I knew Angel was sold by her own mum when she was nine. They was very poor. Her dad had pissed off somewhere. Her mum was sick and needed money for medicine. So her mum handed Angel over to a man what seemed nice and what said she'd be working in his factory in the city. He gave her a doll to play with. But he didn't take her to no factory. He took her to a place what is like a red-light district in the bush and what specialises in young girls and what was called Svay Pak. It made me sick just thinking about it. I had a nine-year-old niece, me brother Attila's daughter, and I'd a fucken killed anyone what touched her, I swear. Or what tried to touch me little mate Abeer, the Palestinian girl what was also a detainee and was eight. There is some things what is just wrong, what even crims know.

When she first went to Svay Pak, Angel was always screaming and crying and scratching at people's eyeballs. They gave her smack to calm her down. She had a full-on habit by the time she was thirteen. The bosses sold her the smack and took the money outta her earnings, what was already fuck-all, pardon me French. When she got to be sixteen, them johns over there was thinking she be too old. The bosses had a plan. They knew that in Australia, sixteen was still young for being on the game. So one a the men, he got a fake passport what said she be his own daughter. She went along with it cuz she heard this was a big country and thought she might be able to escape. They put her in a house with locked doors and barred windows and stooges to guard it. Angel tried to escape but got caught and they beat her and did shit to her what I don't wanna think about neither.

A customer what seen her bruises tipped off the cops. They raided the place and nabbed the men. Some a the girls escaped. Angel hid behind the wardrobe in her room. When the coppers found her, they threw her in Villawood. We met her right after that.

She was scared to go back to her country cuz she still owed the men a lotta money and their mates there would be waiting for her. Sue was helping her make a claim for protection. But apparently the men told the police she had wanted to come to Australia — what was true in a way, but what made her case complicated. Her lying about her age made it complicated too, cuz the story got some holes in it as a result. The good thing was that she had no papers and DIMIA couldn't work out what country she really came from. Even though she said she be from Cambodia, the Cambodian embassy didn't known nuffin about her. Some a the Vietnamese said she might be from Vietnam, cuz apparently she spoke Vietnamese real good, and then DIMIA thought she might be from Thailand, though the Thais said she spoke Thai with an accent. She could speak a little Chinese, and French too, and she knew English even before she came to Australia. Svay Pak was an international kind a place.

She still had the doll, what was missing one arm. When she played with it she seemed like a little girl. It made me eyes burn.

Twenty-One

The day after Boxing Day was a Thursday. There wasn't many visitors cuz people was going back to work or off on their hols. Anna was on the gate again. She let me through to Visits even though I didn't have no visitors. She was good like that.

Farshid and Reza were squatting down by the edge a the yard and staring into the no-man's-land between the inner and outer fences. I went to see what they was looking at. Abeer ran over as well. Turns out a currawong had walked into the middle a the coil a razor wire. He was looking all round and up into the sky like he was deciding whether to fly. We could all see that if he opened his wings they'd be shredded like lettuce in a felafel shop, except black and white instead a green. Abeer's eyes went big.

'Stupid fucken bird,' goes Farshid what was sixteen and pissed off with life. 'It can fly anyvere it vants and it comes here and gets stuck in the razor vire. It deserves vat it gets.'

Farshid and Reza are Iranians what say 'vee' where words got double-yous but what otherwise speak English like they was born here. Reza shot his brother a look. Reza was thirteen. He wasn't as tough as Farshid, though they both been in Detention with their mum almost three years already. I got an idea. I reached into me pockets for some toasted sunflower seeds what I been snacking on and chucked them through the fence onto the ground outside the coil. The currawong tipped his head to one side, picked up his feet and, keeping his wings tight to his chest, stepped outta the coil and pecked up the seeds.

Reza grinned and I could tell Farshid was happy too, even though he was pretending to be cool about it.

Abeer reached into her pocket and pulled out her gecko, Visa.

'I bet that currawong would love Visa.' I made a grab for it what wasn't really a grab, what was just for teasing.

Abeer punched me with her free hand. 'He's my pet!'

I pretended to be knocked sideways by the punch.

She stuck out her tongue. I stuck out mine. Then I strolled off like Lord Muck, King a the Birds. There was probably a lesson in there somewhere, but I never been too good at lessons.

The next afternoon there was gonna be a soccer game between Stages Two and Three. Everyone was talking about it at lunch. 'You playing?' Angel asked.

'Yeah,' I said, patting me stomach, what was getting round, 'I's the ball.'

She giggled again. 'I like you, Zeki,' she said. 'You always make me laugh.'

Hamid pretended to look hurt then. 'You like Zeki? I thought you liked me.'

Thomas rolled his eyes. 'Let's go,' he said, slapping his thigh. 'It's going to start soon.'

'*Yela, yela,*' Azad said. 'Let's go.' He and Hamid ran ahead, cuz they was sposed to be playing.

During the game, Farshid punched that Iraqi boy what danced with the Albanian chick. They was on the same team, too. The Iraqi got a black eye what swole right up. The blues threatened to report the incident to the police, but both boys told them to fuck off, in exactly them words and at the same time. The whole thing was stupid cuz the Albanian chick and her family got their visas and left the morning after Boxing Day anyway. They was already in Brisbane, where they got cousins. They wasn't never coming back, not for Farshid, not for the Iraqi.

Them bushfires burned for days. You could smell the ash and eucalypt oil. You could also smell other things what was in the Villawood air, like fear and stressation. But you know what I said about the bad moods what people catched like colds on the Inside? Sometimes it worked the other way round. On the thirtieth a December, in spite a the fact that nuffin was happening on anyone's cases and it was thirty degrees in the shade what there wasn't much of, and the Mess had just put on one a them most ineligible lunches, and lotsa the regular visitors was away on hols, and we was people what was feeling like animals in a cage — in spite of all them things we was all in a pretty good mood. I remember that afternoon in particulate cuz it was the last fully happy memory I got of us all together.

We was sitting around shooting the shit — me, Azad, Thomas, Hamid, Angel and Farshid. 'Where's your brother?' I asked Farshid.

'Dunno. He's gone all veird lately,' Farshid said. Just then Reza wandered up with a tiny bleeding cut above his mouth.

'Ohhh. What happen to you?' Angel asked.

Reza touched his face and blushed.

'You vere shaving!' Farshid figured it out first. Though he was only sixteen, Farshid already had sidies and a semi-respectable goatee.

'Congratulations,' said Azad, giving him the thumbs up.

'And I thought it was just dirt,' Thomas teased. 'I was wondering when you were going to wash your face, man.'

'You should talk,' said Hamid, what was being naughty.

'Black is beautiful. You're just jealous because someone put milk in your coffee.' They did the high-five. 'But let's get back to Reza. Where else you getting hair, man?' Everyone cracked up at this, though Angel opened her eyes wide and threw her hand over her mouth like she be shocked, what we knew she wasn't really.

'Shut up,' Reza said. 'Stop looking at me, everyvun!' We all looked even harder. 'Cut it out! Cut it out! Talk about something else!'

'Yes, we no tease Reza any more.' Angel, what was sitting next to him, leaned over and gave him a hug what made him blush all over again. 'We talk about something else.'

'But it's fun teasing Reza,' Thomas said, what wasn't gonna quit.

Reza gave Thomas the finger. Thomas grabbed his hand. 'Okay, we'll settle this by arm wrestling. If I win, we get to tease you all day.'

'And if I win?'

'We don't.' Thomas shrugged.

Reza won. 'Okay, ve talk about something else now.'

'What about *Moulin Rouge*?' Azad suggested. April had brung *Moulin Rouge* in on video and we'd all watched it together in the rec room. 'I like Nicole Kidman very much. She is beautiful.'

'Of course, mate,' I said. 'She's Aussie.'

'No way.' Thomas laughed like he didn't believe it.

'She's a Sydney girl,' I insured him. 'In factuality, I used to date her, but then I met Marlena and Nicole met Tom so we split.'

Angel giggled. 'Bad luck for Nicole,' she said.

'You sure about that, Zek?' Hamid asked.

'I don't talk about it much. But she always calls when she's in town. What, don'tcha believe me, mate?'

'I think Zeki smoke too much happy weed,' Angel said.

'Wha?' I go, opening me palms and raising them to the sky like God be me witness, what I knew he wasn't really. 'Wha? Why don't you believe me?'

'No way is Nicole Kidman from here,' Thomas goes like he knew it for a factual. He shook his head from side to side real slow. 'Australian girls are not that good-looking.'

'Maaan, how would you know? You ever been to Australia?' Thomas gave me the finger.

'They made the film here too, y'know,' I said.

Farshid leaned back in his chair and crossed his arms. 'So maybe ve agree Nicole Kidman is Australian. But no vay is *Moulin Rouge* Australian movie.'

'Yeah,' said Reza, his voice going up and down like an out-a-control lift. 'Australian movies suck. Visitors bring them all the time but they're boring. There's never any good action and everything's like real life, except stupider.'

'No, mate,' I protested. I was being fully patriotic about it, even though I didn't see a lotta Aussie movies meself for the same reason. I told them the director, Bazza McKenzie, was definitely Australian and the movie was made in Foxtel Studios. They was still not buying it. So I got them all to bet phone cards.

Twenty-Two

'We've got karaoke for you tonight, bro.' Tip, the Maori guard what was me mate, told me. 'The songs are in all dufferent languages. And we've got crusps and soda.'

'Great,' I go. Big fucken whoopee — pardon me French. The good mood a the day before had faded like the curtains in Mum's lounge room when I forgot to look after them that summer I was minding the house. It was New Year's Eve, and all I had to look forward to was getting hammered on fizzy drinks and eating 'crusps' what was probably the cheap ones and not even chicken-flavoured, while a bunch a depressed, locked-up people sang dumb love songs in Hindu and Parsnip.

Being the Infernal Optimist what I is, about a month earlier I'd told She Who to get a special frock for the big night. I called up a mate and got him to get us two tickets to this big party at the Leagues Club sponsored by that radio station what plays all the good stuff, and what was gonna go off. There was gonna be live music, deejays, the works. The tickets wasn't cheap neither, even if me mate worked in security at the radio station and knew where they was stashed. I mean, I had to give him something for his trouble. And I swore to meself it was gonna be the last time I did anything with even a whiff of illegality about it. Going straight for real was me number-one New Year's reservation. I just had to get outta Detention first.

Under the circumstances, I sure wasn't gonna make it to the party. A few days earlier, I told Marlena she'd better ask a friend. She asked My Le, that beauty therapist what likes poofters and what she been mates with since Year Nine. My Le was a smart chick. She worked a good job in a day spa at one a the big hotels. She was a babe, too. I had me own New Year's reservations about My Le, though. Like Marlena's folks, My Le always reckoned She Who could do better than me. Who knew who those two beautiful ladies might meet at a party like that? Any kind a Don Juan could be there, even Peter Pink-nuts. All I knew was that if that Don Juan was me I'd be making moves on Marlena for sure. The whole business was doing me head in.

I needed to get completely blotto, tanked, non-compost, off me fucken face — pardon me French — if I was gonna get through the night without thinking about shit like that. But me chances a that was looking like Zero, what was not a famous swordsman.

But that's the thing about being an Infernal Optimist. Even when I feel like I'm going under, I keep one eye on the horizon in the hope I might see me luck come sailing in.

That afternoon, Mum came to visit. Now, Mum's pretty strict with the law and religion. She wouldn't touch alcohol, much less smuggle it in. She got a policy a zero tolerance. When I wanted to have a beer around her I always poured it into a lemonade bottle first. When Marlena first saw that, she couldn't believe it. 'It doesn't even look like lemonade,' she said, amazed I got away with it.

I shrugged. 'Me mum just figures it's a kinda lemonade she never seen before.'

'Won't she smell it on your breath?' Marlena asked then.

I told her that even if Mum did, she wouldn't recognise it as alcohol. That's the great thing about Mum being so strict. Can't do that sort a shit round me dad though. He's strict *and* he's been round the world and back.

Anyway, that day Mum came with some *boerek* pastries what she makes with honey and walnuts, and the prayer schedule what is printed by our local halal butcher and what gave the exact prayer times for the month a January. She brung me a prayer schedule like that every month I was Inside. Maaan. It always made me feel so accused.

Mum couldn't stay long cuz she had to get back to work at the Community Centre. After she left, I gave the rest a the pastries to Noor, Abeer, Bashir and the other kids, and the prayer schedule to some Algerians what was gonna use it. Prayer is one a the Five Pillars of Islam and one day, I swear, I'm gonna get onto it. But Charity is a Pillar too. I was doing the best I could.

I didn't feel like going back inside. Azad and them were in the Yard, but they had visitors what be proper people, what I could tell only liked to visit with the asylums. You know how in real life some people is held in higher steam and some in lower? It was the same in Visits. To respectable visitors, asylums was the kings, overstayers was the common people and five-oh-ones, we was the bottoms in the heap. Chicks like Angel figured somewhere between the people and the kings, though in them own heads they felt more like us, cuz most a them never been treated good in them whole lives, and when they was treated good, it was usually in exchange for something else.

Looking round for some company I spotted Ivan, this Russian guy what overstayed his visa and what I was mates with. He was leading some visitors to a table. He beaconed me over and introduced his visitors. They was Russians too. While they chatted in their language, I was studying them and thinking they had the weirdest bodies I ever seen. Even the skinny ones had these funny-shaped guts on them. Then, when none a the blues was looking, all them funny guts — what turned out, in factuality, to be plastic bladders full a vodka — came sliding outta their shirts. It was like me whole fleet had steamed into port. I reckon Tip, what was on duty at the gate when Ivan and me was smuggling the bladders a vodka back into the compound, knew something was going on but wasn't gonna say nuffin. Back in the room that night, Ivan and me proceeded to get inked. Azad and Hamid didn't drink so they was at the karaoke with Thomas.

'*Budem zdorovie.*'

'Up yer bum.'

We knocked back another and another and another.

Ivan told me that '*zek*' is old Russian slang for a prisoner in the Gulag, what apparently be lotsa islands with prisons on.

'That'd be right, mate,' I said. 'It's me fate. She Who says I be like flowers what are always reaching to the sun except I'm always stretching to get meself behind bars. She reckons that when I was born they took away the unbiblical cord so I wouldn't have nuffin to hang meself with in the maternity ward.'

He shook his head and refilled our glasses. 'Chirs, big irs,' he said in his Russian accent.

'Boodem anchovy,' I said in me Aussie one.

Maaan, that vodka was good. It'd been a long time between drinks. Before I knew it, I was legless as a Paralympian. I went to pour some more vodka but I missed the glass. Ivan looked horrorfied. 'No wuckers,' I said and licked it off the table. I don't remember too much after that except waking up on Ivan's floor around two pee-em on the first day a the new year, two thousand and two, with one a them dolls what is in other dolls what is in other dolls in pieces round me head, and the loudspeaker calling me to Visits. Ivan was snoring into his pillow, cuddling an empty glass like it be a teddy bear. I hauled meself up to the windowsill and whistled to Abeer's little brother, Bashir, to fetch me sunnies so I could walk back to me room first and freshen up.

Twenty-Three

Me melon was still in a shocking state when I got to Visits. The Yard was swarming with visitors. Hamid and Angel was sitting at a table with Sue. Since they been together and eating regular, they got some a them skinny angles off, what looked specially good round them cheeks. I went to shake hands with Sue. 'Happy New Year.'

'Happy New Year, Zeki.'

'Sue is going to get me Bridging Visa,' Angel told me.

'I'm going to *try* to get you a Bridging Visa,' Sue said kinda gently.

'Respect,' I said, what I really meant. I went the knuckles with Sue what knew how to do them back. She was pretty cool for an old lady what be fifty.

Sue laughed. 'Zeki, you are so Ali G.' She was talking about this black dude what had a TV show. Apparently he wasn't black in factuality, but he did the bruvvas' handshake and the respect knuckles while interviewing people what didn't know he wasn't a black dude in factuality.

'I takes that as a complimentary,' I go, cuz Ali G got all the moves and was a master a style.

Sue smiled. She turned back to Angel. 'Now I absolutely insist that you live with me when you get out,' she said.

'I don't like be trouble to anyone,' Angel said.

'You won't be any trouble at all,' Sue said. 'I have an extra room and I'll be glad for the company.' She patted Angel on the wrist with her big hand.

'Thank you so much, Sue,' Hamid said. 'I feel better to know she will be safe. Then when I get out we will make our own home. We will get married. I will work and go to medical school.' Since getting with Angel, Hamid been full a confidence what he never had before too.

'April's here too, Zeki,' Sue told me, pointing her out.

I got the hint and got up to join April. She was sitting at another table what was piled with food including a roast chicken, what I craved cuz a the grease, what be one a the basic food groups when you be hungover. Some a me mates what is not Muslim swear that bacon's the best but I never touch it on a count a me religion. I know I'm no mullah, but I do got me limits. As I got near the table I raised me sunnies for a sec to check something out. 'Hot chips!' I exclaimed. 'Oh, mate. You're a legend, April.' She gave me a peck on the cheek, what was almost as good as chips.

'Happy New Year,' she said.

'You too, mate.'

She laughed and watched as I tucked in. 'If I didn't know there was no alcohol allowed in here I'd swear you were hungover.'

'Funny that, eh?' I nodded from behind me sunnies and picked up another drumstick.

'Uh, Zeki, could you . . . I don't want to sound, uh . . . if you don't mind, I'd like to save some for Azad and the others.'

'Sorry, mate,' I go. 'I be forgetting meself.' I took two more chips and settled back in me seat, patting me belly, what was stretched out and content.

'So what did you get up to for New Year's?' I asked her. Me heart gave a sudden jolt. New Year's. She Who Could Be Anywhere, With Anyone, still hadn't called me.

'Not much. I went to my sister's place. It was pretty quiet. I didn't feel like . . . partying.'

'Maaan. If I was Out I'd a been partying.'

'I just kept thinking, I can party but *they can't*. It's not just partying. I think, I can walk down the street but *they can't*. I can go out for a coffee but *they can't*. I can go to the movies but *they can't*. I can't stop thinking about it. Everything feels so wrong now. I know this is only my third visit, but I feel completely . . . *destabilised* by this place. Like there are two parallel universes and I am living with a foot in each one. If that makes sense.'

'Better than having both feet in the wrong one,' I go. 'What is what it feels like from the Inside.'

'How true that must be.' April looked at me like she was seeing something what she hadn't seen before, what made me nervous that I hadn't washed me face properly and something was stuck to it, like a piece a drumstick or that Russian doll. I ran me hand over me peach. Nuffin seemed outta place. 'I'm discovering you're actually a very wise person, Zeki. An old soul. I think you've done the loop a few times already.'

'That's for sure,' I said. 'Me head's still spinning.'

'Ha. And you've got a great sense of humour.'

Maaan. I wished She Who Is Always Saying 'Grow Up' and Asking 'Is This a Joke?' could be hearing all this. Maybe She Who met someone at the party. Maybe she was getting it on with him right now.

'You okay, Zek? You seem to be hyperventilating.'

'Hooooo.' I blew out some air. 'I'm all right.' I tried to push the thought a me girl getting it on with somebody else — a somebody else what looked a lot like Peter Pink-nuts — outta me head. The thought wasn't letting me push. It was leaning back and wearing rubber soles.

'You sure?'

'April, what do you do for self-helping when you got bad thoughts what you don't wanna be thinking?'

'Well, you could try some of those visualisation techniques I mentioned the other day. Visualise putting those thoughts behind a locked door. If that's not enough, put them into a wooden box and lock it. You can then put the box behind the locked door, or, if you really want to get rid of it, push it off a steep cliff.'

I vigilised putting Marlena behind the door, and chucking Pink-nuts off the cliff. I was feeling better already. 'That just reminded me a something Azad once told me,' I said. Even just hearing Azad's name made April perk up, I swear. 'It was this story what comes from China about this old man and a butterfly what is dreaming, or maybe the old man is dreaming, or maybe the butterfly catches the old man, or something like that. Maybe there wasn't a butterfly. No, I'm pretty sure there be a butterfly in there somewhere. I don't think I'm telling it right. Maybe you better get him to tell it.'

'I know it.' She smiled. 'It's a famous Taoist parable.'

'A Taoist . . . What's that when it's at home, mate?'

She oppressed a giggle.

What I liked about April was that she just kept hammering away till I got it, and she never showed me no condensation, like she thought I be stupid, neither. She told me about parables, what are stories what are for giving you lessons — what makes all me mum's stories parables — and about met-oh-fours too. A met-oh-four is something what stands in for something else, making it clearer, what this particulate explanation is probably not doing. But April said I do met-oh-fours all the time, that I'm a natural at it, what is one reason I really could write a book, apparently.

'So Azad knew that story,' she said, like she be talking to herself. 'That's amazing. I already felt this connection . . . I mean I feel so . . . close to him. His spirit. I don't know, it's silly. Oh here's Thomas. And Azad.' April jumped up to kiss them hello.

Thomas bent down and offered her a cheek. When she went to kiss Azad, he stiffened a bit. For some a them what come from societies where men and women don't even touch unless they be married, it's kinda weird getting kissed and hugged all the time by the ladies what visit. Hamid told me it freaked him out at first. He was still getting used to seeing women's faces and they was already kissing him. Farshid told me he doesn't mind getting kissed, except he wished it wasn't just by old ladies.

They was all wishing April Happy New Year.

'May it bring you all peace and freedom,' she goes.

'I'll drink to that,' I said, raising me cup a juice.

'Zeki apparently drank to everything last night,' Thomas informed April. I reckon he was annoyed cuz we didn't invite him too. April's look a surprise made us all laugh.

'But . . . isn't alcohol forbidden?'

'Many things that are forbidden go on in the world,' said Azad. 'Why should it be different in here? Anyway, Zeki wasn't hurting anyone but himself. It's problem between him and God.'

'And me head,' I said. 'What is normally attached to me body.'

'That's so true.' I don't think April was talking about me head being normally attached to me body. I don't think she even heard me, in factuality. When Azad spoke, April's hands flew into the air like she was gonna pray in the same way we do, and her voice went all breathy as well as furry and deep, like the kitten at the bottom a the ocean be hyperventilating.

Thomas drummed the table with his fingers. 'Sorry. April, can we go for a walk?'

'But . . .' She looked all worried at Azad, like he was gonna melt if she left him alone in the sun.

'No worries,' Azad said, Rs rolling like they was on the highway. 'We aren't going anywhere.' We all guessed she'd spoken to her husband and that Thomas needed some private time with her. None a the asylums liked to talk about them cases in front a the other detainees. While everyone hoped everyone else could get free, they hoped it most for themselves. So if they discovered some way out, they wanted to be the first outta that particulate gate, specially cuz gates outta here had a way a swinging shut after they be opened. Another was that people didn't want all the details out there in case there be spies reporting back to them countries. Visitors was expected to know this and not talk about asylums' cases to others, even if the others be friends.

In factuality, there wasn't much in the way of secrets in that place. By the time April and Thomas returned to the table, Azad and I had discussed all the possibilities, including that of April getting back together with her husband on a count a working together on Thomas's case. Azad thought that would be a good thing. He believed in the sanity of marriage.

'If they don't get back together, maybe you could marry her,' I said. 'I reckon she'd be into it.'

'*La ilaha illallah*,' Azad said, like I be testing his patience. 'Don't talk rubbish. Anyway, April is old. She is like an auntie.'

I felt sorry for April, what wouldn't wanna be hearing this.

April returned to the table alone. Thomas was heading back into the compound.

'He's gone back to get some files,' she explained. 'I've . . . agreed to meet my husband?' April hadn't yet learned the rules a behaviour concerning the confidentials. 'You know, I wish . . . I wish I could help all of you,' she said, looking at Azad in particulate.

'You help Thomas, that is like helping us all,' said Azad.

Thomas reappeared with two full-up cardboard boxes of paperwork in his arms. Azad and me cleared the table. After Azad chucked the rubbish in the bin and I wiped the table off with a serviette, Thomas plopped the two boxes onto the middle of the table. They landed with a big thud, and the table wobbled like She Who when she be wearing high heels. Some files skidded off the top a the boxes and onto the table, scattering papers from arsehole to breakfast.

'Goodness,' said April, her eyes widening at the sight of all that paperwork. 'Gee.'

Just then, me phone vibrated in me pocket. I sneaked a look at the number what was calling. It was She Who.

'Excusing me,' I said, and hurried to the gate. There, Clarence was arguing with some Chinese bloke, a visitor, what wanted to send some cooked food to his wife, what was Inside.

'No cooked food allowed inside the compound. It's the rules,' Clarence said.

'*Ta bing le.* She sick.'

'Well, she wouldn't wanna be touching that slop, then, would she?'

The Chinese bloke said something else in him language, what sounded angry.

'C'mon, c'mon,' I said, pointing at the gate. Clarence looked at me and then at the other bloke like he was trying to decide which one of us he'd rather be doing over. He didn't choose me, what was for once, though I never seen anyone unlock a padlock, lock it again, and then, while I waited in the middle section, unlock the second one so slow in me life, I swear. I jogged all the way to me room. I pulled me phone outta me pocket and took a deep breath. 'Happy New Year, babydoll.'

A sigh. 'Happy New Year, Zek.'

'So, darl,' I said, me nuts in me teeth, 'how was the party?'

'It was great.'

Great? Without me? 'Yeah?'

'Yeah.'

'Really?'

She sighed. 'I wished you were there.'

'Goes without saying.'

'I'm getting sick of being by myself, Zek. Of having a boyfriend who's always locked up somewhere. You know, I thought when you got out of prison last time that that was it.'

'Me too, darl. Believe me, it's not much fun on this side of the fence, either. So . . . who was there?'

'Lotsa people. Peter.'

'Oh yeah?' *Shit. Fuck. Muvvafucker.* I tried to sound real casual. 'And what was Pink-nuts up to?'

'Oh, *lots.*'

I swallowed. 'Lots? Like what?'

'You'll never believe it. He and My Le hooked up . . .'

'For real!'

I danced round the room as Marlena filled me on all the particulates.

Twenty-Four

April returned two days later. She said it was on a count of all the paperwork she had to sort through for Thomas. 'You know, Zeki, nothing in my life is as important to me now as asylum seekers and their freedom.'

'Huh,' I said. We was sitting by ourselves. Thomas hadn't come out yet. 'Why? If you don't mind me asking.'

'Why?' she repeated. She stole a glance at Azad. He'd already said hello but on this particulate afternoon he was being visited by some uni students what was translating his poetry and gonna publish it in a magazine. Farshid and Bhajan was sitting with them too. They'd spread a blanket on the ground, and brung fizzy drink and chips and cards to play Go Fish. Kids like that didn't like mixing with overstayers, much less five-oh-ones, even though we was people what needed visits too. 'Why? I don't know. It just feels important. Maybe it's a Jewish thing. We always say that if more ordinary Germans and other Europeans knew what was going on with the concentration camps and tried to stop it, or made more of an effort to help the Jews, maybe six million wouldn't have died. I've never been an activist or even political before. But I can't know what's going on here and then not do anything.'

It was kinda weird. A few nights earlier, we was all sitting round talking about something that happened in Visits when Bhajan shook his head. 'Imagine this happening back home, in any of our countries. Some foreigners in trouble, locked up even through no fault of their own. Who would visit them? Imagine women taking them food and clothing, lawyers fighting their cases for free, people coming to see them every day, respectable people too.' No one could. That made me proud to be Australian, even though I wasn't really, and even though it was also Australians what locked everyone up in the first. Maaaan, I wish I'd gotten pasteurised all them years ago with the rest a the family. If I was a citizen, I'd never a been in this mess. I could even be one a them people what visited asylums — except, in all honesty, I probably wouldn't be.

April looked over at Azad again.

'It's good he's with other young people,' she said.

'No young person could be as young as you, April,' I said.

'Zeki.' She shook her head. 'I'm forty-one.'

'No way.'

Azad had his long legs folded up. He was leaning back on his arms, what were lean and brown. One a the girls put her hand on his arm. They laughed at some joke. Another one a the girls, what had a ponytail, pulled off her scrunchie and shook out her long hair. Some strands landed on Azad's shoulder. There was another joke and one a the guys put his baseball cap on Azad's head. Then Azad took it off and put it on another guy's head. Farshid grabbed it and put it on his own head. One a the girls started to sing a pop song then got embarrassed and collapsed in a heap a giggles. They was all just mucking around but they looked like they was having fun. I was shocked when I realised that it was the first time I seen Azad looking like he be young and normal, what he would be if he was outta there.

'No, it's really good he's with young people,' she said again, as if I'd said it wasn't.

I picked up on the subtextuals. 'You know, April, I reckon older women is the best.'

She shook her head. 'Zeki, you're incorrigible.'

'That's what She Who . . .' Shit. Gotta keep me women separate.

'Sorry? She who what?'

'Nuffin. So. You got any kids? Not that you looks more than twenty-one.'

'Ha. I thought older women were best.' She glanced over at Azad again.

'They are, specially when they look twenty-one, like you.'

'Totally incorrigible, you are. I have one daughter, to answer your question. From my first marriage.'

'You was married before?' I was impressed. She was a woman of experience.

'Yes.'

'How old's your daughter?'

'Marley's eighteen.'

'Marley. That's a nice name.' It was just like Marlena without the 'nah', what I wouldn't mind. Sometimes, She Who could be too negative.

April smiled. 'Her father was into reggae.'

'That's cool. She as beautiful as you?'

She smiled again. 'She's quite pretty, but I don't know if she gets that from me. She looks a lot like my mother, actually.'

'Oh, mate. When I get out, you gotta introduce me to your mother.'

'I thought you had a girlfriend.'

'Yeah,' I said. 'That be true, in factuality. But there be twenty-four hours in every day. And Marlena's gotta go to work sometimes.'

April play-punched me. 'Keep your hands off my mother.'

'Okay. But you gotta at least introduce us. And to your daughter, too. She live with you?'

'No. She lives in Nimbin with her dad. She's a bit of a free spirit. And she and Josh don't get along that well.'

'Did you say Nimbin? Her dad one a them hippies? Were you one too?'

She blushed and scrunched up her nose like the memory had a smell.

I squinted, trying to pitcher her in one a them Indian shirts and bell-bottoms with embroidery on. 'Far out.' I reckoned she be more classy the way she was now. I wanted to ask her more questions about her life but Thomas was coming through the gate with another big box a papers. I gave April me mobile number, and told her she could call anytime to speak to any one of us.

I was just wiping down the table with a serviette for the fresh onslaught a papers when there was a flash a white from across the Yard. It was a chair what be flying through the air. The blues began running over to where Farshid was going off like a volcano. 'I'm not a tourist!' he screamed, picking up a second plastic chair and waving it around. 'I just wanna dye my hair!' Then he hurled the chair at an officer.

Nuffin was weird in Villawood, I swear.

The blue put up his arms to block the chair and got hit with it.

'He broke my arm!' the blue shouted like a big wuss. 'He broke my arm!'

Another blue raced over and they both looked at his arm. In factuality the arm wasn't broke, only his pride.

Farshid went for another chair, but before he could get to it, Clarence tackled him and pinned him to the ground. He was pulling Farshid's arms up behind his back.

'Ow!' Farshid cried. Clarence pushed his head into the dirt.

'Let him go! Let him go!' One a the girls what had been sitting with them was screaming at Clarence. She was so worked up she was pogoing, her fists punching the air every time she got airborne.

'Let him go, ya fucken fascist goon! Let him go!' yelled a skinny boy what was wearing one a them shirts with that Latino guy in the beret.

'Fuck off, Ché Guacamole,' Clarence said, sitting down on Farshid's back. 'I'm just giving our little friend here a chance to cool down.'

Farshid struggled and yelled at Clarence to get off him. Clarence raised one hand to his ear and cocked his head. 'Sorry? Can't hear you. Speak up.'

A middle-aged lady stood to one side, wringing her hands like they was a facecloth. 'It's all my fault,' she said to me and April, what had run over too. 'It's all my fault.' Tears poured down her face. I handed her the serviette, forgetting I'd just wiped the table with it. 'Thanks,' she whispered, and put it to her eyes before I could say anything, at which point I figured it was better to say nuffin.

I looked around for Farshid's mum, Nassrin, but someone said she was in Medical. She was pregnant and having a hard time with it, specially since they were still keeping Farshid's dad over in Port Hedland. I was glad she wasn't there. I don't think it woulda helped her blood pressurisation levels what apparently were high.

Everyone was talking at once. It turns out Farshid had asked the lady to bring in some blonding cream so he could put streaks in his hair. The blues at the gate wouldn't let her take it in. They wouldn't tell her why, either. When she got into the Yard, she told Farshid what had happened. He'd gone over to an officer and asked why he couldn't have his hair dye. The officer was one a them real racist dickheads what was always pulling power trips on the asylums. 'Why?' the officer said, what wasn't a question. 'Maybe because I don't like the look of your face. Maybe because you people can't be trusted. That stuff is full of chemicals. If you're not trying to swallow it and commit suicide, you'll be making bombs with it.' That's when

Farshid exploded like he be a bomb himself and started chucking the chairs around.

He hadn't been shouting, 'I'm not a tourist!' He'd been shouting, 'I'm not a terrorist!' I reckoned he better get that one straight if he ever got free and wanted to go on holiday somewhere. 'Get the fuck off me, you piece of shit officer!' he yelled now from under Clarence.

Azad stepped forward. 'Get off him,' he shouted at Clarence. 'Get off.' You could hear the stressation in his voice. He raised his hand like he was going to hit Clarence. Immediately, Clarence pulled back his fist like it was spring-loaded. April's hands flapped in the air like butterfly wings.

'CUT!' The voice a Flora, big Tongan mama what was the Operations Manager, froze Clarence like a pea. 'Go to the office and wait for me there,' she told Clarence. 'Now.' Clarence raised himself up off a Farshid, giving him a kick as he brought his foot over.

'Oh, sorry, Farshid.'

Farshid gave him the finger. Azad helped Farshid to his feet. Farshid brushed off his clothes, what was covered in dirt. His lip was trembling and there was a thin trickle a blood coming outta his nose. He had a small cut above his eyebrow what was bleeding. 'Show's over,' Flora announced. 'Nothing to see.' She shooed everyone away and told Farshid to go into the compound to get cleaned up.

It was lucky in a way that all that happened. Because when Farshid got back to the room, what he shared with his brother, he found Reza trying to hang himself with a noose made a socks.

There was so much shit going down that day that we didn't take all that much notice when they deported Chaim, the Israeli. He was a nice bloke, but it turned out he wasn't a dissonant against his government after all, just a traveller what overstayed his visa cuz he was having too much fun. I reckon he spun the story about being a refugee and dissonant when he woke up that first morning here and saw he be surrounded by Arabs. I think even he began to believe his own story. He was in for one month before they deported him. He said it was like one year.

When he said that I remembered that time when I'd been in for one month and was complaining to Thomas. I had more wisdom by then. I wasn't gonna say nuffin stupid like that when I left.

Twenty-Five

Early the next morning, January fourth, I was in the middle of a fully sick dream what had mag wheels, Marlena *and* Sanna the Bikini Girl in. Suddenly it turned into a nightmare. Marlena, what was sposed to be under Sanna the Bikini Girl, was under the mag wheels, and there was all these people screaming. I sat up in bed like I been electrocutioned. That's when I realised the screaming was for real. I ran outta me room. What I saw blew me away. I didn't know what the fuck was going down — pardon me French. I never seen nuffin like it.

Blues what was in riot gear was smashing into Babak's room through the window. Then they sprayed something through the broken glass. It looked like they was spraying an insect. But if it was an insect, it was screaming and crying in Babak's voice. Farshid and Reza had come running out from their room. They was hitting the blues and trying to pull them away, but they just got knocked to the ground. Everyone was yelling. Me hairs stood on end, even worse than when I touched Thomas's creepy bones that time.

There was blues what I never seen before, in a uniform different from the one the Whacking Co screws wore.

'Azad, what's going on, mate?'

'They're trying to deport Babak.' Azad's hands were in such tight fists that his knuckles had gone all white. He told me that after Babak lost at Federal Court, he'd applied to the Minister directly. The Minister knocked him back. Sue had been trying to get the Minister to look at his case again, but the Minister didn't like looking twice. He didn't even like looking once. Mrs Kunt, what was Babak's case officer too, had asked him to sign the paper for voluntary deportation the day before, but he refused. The blues what wasn't from Whacking Co was from this South African outfit what DIMIA hired to help with forced deportations.

'What's with the spray?' I asked, though I wasn't sure I wanted to know.

'It's . . . I don't know how to say it in English. It stops the blood, bleeding. It's like . . .'

'Anti-coagulant.' Bhajan, what always knew the words for things, had joined us. He said that when they came to get him, Babak barricaded himself in his room and cut himself all over with a razor. The blues didn't want to touch the blood themselves, and they didn't want to call a doctor neither. So they was just spraying him before moving in to take him away. *'Fuck them!'* Bhajan wiped away a tear with the back a his hand. 'We are not animals.'

Looking fully stressated, Tip came up and tried to get us back into our rooms. 'Nothing to see, nothing to see.'

But he was wrong. Cuz next thing we knew, there was a shout from the roof, and there was Hamid.

'You take him, I kill myself!'

Azad jumped like a shock had gone through him. 'Hamid!' he yelled. He turned to me, pulling a piece a paper outta his pocket. 'Zeki, call Sue. This is her number. Tell her what's happening. She can do something.' Then he raced over to where Hamid could see him to try to talk him outta jumping.

I ran back into me room. Sue's line was busy. I didn't know it, but Farshid was already calling her from the public phone. I looked at me watch. It was three-forty-five ay-em. I kept trying, the whole time thinking a poor Hamid up on the roof.

By this time, they'd forced everyone back into their rooms, given Babak an injection, slapped on cuffs and dragged him away. Azad talked Hamid, what was crying and shaking, down from the roof. The blues put Hamid into the Management Unit, what was for isolation and punishment, but Azad was arguing with them to let him go.

Sue tried to get an injunction against the deportation, but it was too late. Babak was halfway to Tehran before the lawyers and magistrates what could do it had their first cuppa. We found out later that the Iranian authorities didn't kill him like he said they would. They did put him in prison and tortured him pretty bad. Azad told me that Amnesty, what be a group what fights for human rights, made Babak what they call a Prisoner a Conscious, what be kinda ironic considering he was knocked out for the whole trip home. Sue took it hard, like it be her fault, what we insured her it wasn't.

The next morning, they deported this other bloke, Jameel, a Pakistani in his early thirties. Jameel and me used to play cards some nights, though like Azad and Hamid he didn't gamble except with stones, cuz he was strict with religion, what was good for me cuz he usually won.

Jameel came from the border with Afghanistan. Opium was a big deal there, but he hated it cuz he could see what it was doing to people. So he informed on some opium growers to the police. Those particulate police turned out to be the cousins a the opium growers. Like Babak, Jameel told DIMIA they'd kill him if he was sent back. DIMIA didn't buy it. They said even if it was true it wasn't enough to make him a refugee. Jameel went quietly. We didn't even know he was gone till we woke up and noticed his room was empty. The other Pakis in detention spoke to his family over there three days later. He was already dead.

Then there was Vesna, what had a husband back in Croatia what beat her up and tried to kill her. They said that wasn't enough to make her a refugee neither so they deported her too. Even the church group what was helping her couldn't track her down after she left. We never knew what happened to her.

It made me skin crawl. Villawood was full a ghosts. And after a string a deportations like that, everyone got even more depressed, thinking they be next.

Thanks God, for all intensive purposes I was outta there. Gubba, what was back from Noosa, told me he expected good news any day. He told me to hang on, just wait for a few more days. He was always telling me we hadda wait for this, hadda wait for that. I told him I don't got the personality of a waiter. I is at least the Mater-D.

For the moment, but, I was nobody, nuffin — a nowhere man like the rest of them.

'I hear you're getting out soon.' Farshid and Reza's mum, Nassrin, was hanging out some laundry. Her face was a bit red on a count a the effort.

'Fingers crossed. Wanna hand?'

'You don't have to.'

'I know I don't have to.' I shooed her aside, thinking how much me mum and Marlena would be impressed if they could see me. I picked up a wet sheet and slung it over the line.

Nassrin leaned back against a post, her hand over her stomach. 'Thanks, Zeki.' She brushed a strand a hair back over her ear. She used to dye her hair light brown and wear make-up every day what the visitors brung her. Lately she was letting things go.

'No worries, mate,' I said. 'How's Reza?'

'I'm sick about him. He vasn't always like this, you know. He vas a happy kid once. It's all my fault . . .'

'Don't say that.'

She looked down at the ground for a minute. 'If, God forbid, he'd managed to kill himself the other day, I vouldn't have a single photograph to remember him by. On the boat over, there was a big storm. The vaves vere that high' — she lifted her hand high over her head — 'and then the boat started to leak. The captain told us we could only keep one bag per family, he told everyvun to throw their extra bags overboard. Ve thought ve were going to die. Of course, ve did what he said. Only after ve vere rescued, and put in detention, I realised that those bags had all our family photos. It's like losing all your memories. And now . . .' She wiped a tear.

The Shit House didn't allow any cameras inside. They said it was to protect the privacy a the asylums, but everyone knew it was so no one could send photos a the shit that went down Inside to the media.

'It's like ve can't even document who ve are,' she said. 'As if stealing our freedom vasn't enough, they have to steal our identity too.' Like Azad, Nassrin could always take the conversationals to a higher level. She used to teach history at uni in Iran but got into trouble all the time. First, she didn't want to wear the veil. Then she thought her students should know about some books what the government didn't think they should know about. Farshid had told me all about it.

'Mate,' I said. I lowered me voice and looked around to see if there was any blues in the vicinity. 'After I get out, I'll come back and smuggle in one a them plastic cameras what don't get caught in the metal detectors.'

She looked like someone turned up her dimmer switch. 'Only if it doesn't get you into trouble.'

'Trouble is me middle name, what I be in all the time.'

'That vould be more than kind, Zeki.'

'It *is* more than kind, mate. It's a promise.'

Promises. I was making a lotta them. I promised Azad and Hamid and Thomas that I'd visit them every week after I got out, Angel too. I promised She Who Deserved Better that I was gonna get a proper job again, and look after her real good. I promised Gubba, what came to see me the other day, that I'd pay him every cent I owed him, even if I had to beg, borrow or steal to do it. I promised Mum, what was at the meeting with Gubba, that was only a trigger a speech, that I wasn't actually gonna steal nuffin no more. And I promised me dad that I'd get me citizenship right away even if I had to stand in a fucken queue, except I didn't use the word 'fucken' — pardon me French — cuz even though he only got one hand on account a being in the Korean War, he could beat the shit outta me and would do it too if he heard me swearing. And I promised meself I'd never eat another meal a chicken and rice as long as I lived.

I dunno where Whacking Co got its chicken, but I swear they was like no chooks I ever ate before. Meat as grey as ciggie ash and what tasted like a poofter's leather shorts after Mardi Gras. Not that I ever ate a poofter's shorts or nuffin. The rice was like flecks a white cardboard what been lying round the tide line at the beach, gritty, salty and tasteless all at the same time.

Azad once told me this story. He was in Port Hedland with this African dude. The African was in Detention for four years before they twigged he was a real refugee and gave him a visa. In that time he'd gone fully nuts, *loco cabana*, but the people what was helping him, they didn't know it yet. He was only Out two days when they asked him to speak at this dinner, one a them fundraisers. He stepped up to the mic and said, 'Chicken and rice.' He paused. He said it again, louder this time: 'Chicken and rice!' Everyone laughed, like he was gonna tell them a joke, like he was gonna turn out to be a Somalian Seinfeld or something. He stared them down. 'Chicken and rice!' he goes, raising his voice more each time. 'CHICKEN and RICE!' No one knew what to do. He just kept shouting 'chicken and rice' until he busted into tears and had to be led down from the stage and back to his seat. Now everyone was feeling real bad, and that's when they served up the dinner. Chicken and rice. He ran screaming from the restaurant.

All I'm saying is I was looking forward to real food. Kebabs, pizza, Maccas. If it was gonna be chicken, it hadda be KFC.

Yeah. A real meal and a good root with me best girl. She Who Is Staunch When I Need a Staunch Woman.

I got a confession to make. Me and Ching — the Chinese chick, you know, Ching Chong Ping Pong — we'd been getting it on lately. Thing is, you gotta do something to keep the equipment in working order. It's like a car — you can't just leave it in the garage for months and months or you might not be able to get it started again when you need it. And Ching was cool. I told her all about Marlena. I didn't want her falling in love with me or nuffin. Don't laugh, it happens. I don't wanna brag, but I've been told I'm a bit of a spud muffin in the sack. Ladies' satisfaction guaranteed. It's true. Funny-looking blokes are always better in the sack than good-looking ones. We aim to please and know we don't always get the chance. And, mate, I can do things with me ears what most blokes can't even do with their fingers.

Maaan. How was it that Marlena could make me feel so Guilty with a capital T when she didn't even know what I been doing? The woman's a witch, I swear.

The loudspeaker, what was right outside me window, hissed into life. 'Zeki Togan, you have a visitor. Zeki Togan, you have a visitor.'

I looked at me watch what I reckoned was already well and truly me own watch by then. It was two o'clock. I wasn't expectorating no one. She Who started her shift at four so it was hardly worth her coming, and Mum wasn't sposed to visit till the weekend. Maybe it was April. I spruced meself up, put a bit a gel in me hair, splashed on some Brut, gave me pits a spray and brushed off the Nikes.

Twenty-Six

Just as I made it through the double gate to the Visiting Yard, it pissed down. Everyone ran for the shelter, dragging bags and baskets and tables and chairs to the one place in the Yard with a roof. I ran too, me Nikes squelching in the mud.

It was hot and steamy under the shelter. The rain came slanting in at the sides. Within seconds, the shelter was packed. It smelled a sweat and wet clothes and stressation and food what be cooked in all different ways according to the different nationalities. Chairs scraped cross the concrete as everyone staked out territory. I was looking round for April when — *fuck me*. Pardon me French, but I swear me heart nearly jumped into me fucken mouth. There was Marlena and Mum — and they'd somehow landed at the same table as Ching.

Marlena plus Mum on a day when I wasn't expectorating them already spelled Trouble, but them plus Ching was like Trouble to the Maximus, like Russell Crowe and them Roman emperors and tigers all together in one small room. When I said I made it clear to Ching about me relationship with Marlena, what I meant was, I tried to tell her. It's just that I fudged one tiny part a the story. I said Marlena was me ex. I was planning on telling Ching the truth, I swear, but you gotta find the right time for these things. Each time I was about to do it, something always came up. Like me boy. She's a minx, old Ching. She gets me boy going, that's for sure. And I'm hopeless after that. When it's over, I swear to meself I'll tell her before it happens again. Then it just happens.

I wanted to turn and run back into the compound but they all spotted me at the same time. I took a deep breath. I greeted Mum and Marlena first. 'It's the dynamic duo.' I kissed them both on the cheek. 'Hey, Ching,' I go, trying to sound real casual. 'This is me mum and Marlena. Me *girlfriend*.' I said the last word real deep and meaningful.

'Oh really? Zeki's girlfriend? Wow. Wow. Nice to meet you.' Ching's big black eyes fucken twinkled with mischief, I swear. She pulled out a pack a smokes and offered them to Mum and Marlena. Mum thinks cigarettes are the work a the devil. She waved her hands around like she was trying to shake them clear off her arms. Ching turned to Marlena then. Marlena never smokes in front a Mum, so she shook her head too. Ching shrugged, popped a cigarette in her own mouth and, one eyebrow cocked in that cheeky way a hers, asked for a light. I wasn't playing that game. I know what she does when you put your hand that close to her face.

'You know I don't smoke,' I lied. She could light her own cigarette.

She did. Then she placed a hand on Marlena's arm, all girly and friendly. 'So, you are Zeki's girlfriend. I hear *so* much about you.' Oh shit.

If Ching said anything I'd be stuffed like a porn star with three dildos.

Mum took out some a her famous pasties. I went a spinach and cheese one and ate it standing up.

'Why don't you find a seat, Zeki?' Marlena suggested, but no way was I leaving her and Mum alone with that fox. I stood me ground and scoped for a chair, but everyone was holding on to the ones they got, even the empty ones, like they was life rafts instead of chairs. Ching flapped her hand at me. 'Go find chair, Zeki, I talk to your mum and Marlena.'

I gave her an imploring look what said 'be good', what wasn't in her vocabulary.

I bolted back out into the rain and spotted a chair what fell over in a puddle over by the playground. It had a dodgy leg and was filthy with mud but I wasn't wasting time looking for another. Back under the shelter I took some serviettes from Mum, wiped the chair dry and sat down. It wasn't like I was wearing me best threads. Soon, but. World, watch out. The *Man* was gonna be back any day now. It suddenly occurred to me how stupid I been. That's why they was there. It was over. Mum and Marlena had come to pick me up and take me home. Fucken *ace*. I wanted to punch the air. *Yes!*

Just at this moment the rain cleared and the sun came out. Life was fucken beautiful, mate.

I was thinking how I was gonna be free and sleeping next to She Who Puts Me Right that very night. You know what it's like when you got someone you can just be yourself around? Like I can fart in front a her and everything. She even farts back. What a woman.

I had to do something about Ching.

Now that the sun was out, other people dragged their chairs back into the Yard. Ching, what was a science student at uni before she overstayed her visa and knows a lot a weird shit, said it was like gas molecules clustering in the cold and then spreading out in the heat. Our table had a good view a the visitors' gate. This Chinese guy came in the gate and next thing you know Ching jumped up, ran over and gave him — wait for it — a big fucken tongue kiss, pardon me French. Me eyeballs was hanging out like boys in the hood. Well excuse me for living! When I looked back, I thought I was busted cuz Marlena and Mum was looking at each other.

'Wha? Wha?' I opened me palms. They couldn't prove nuffin.

Marlena stared down at the table. Mum put on a very special expression a hers that made me think a when she had to tell Dede that the doctor found the cancer in his goolies.

I didn't think I wanted to hear whatever it was they was gonna tell me. I took another pastie and ate it fast.

'Zeki.' Mum had her serious voice on. This was getting worser and worser. Someone died or was in the nick. I could feel it. I was spinning out. 'Marlena? You want to tell him?'

'Zeki.' Marlena bit her lip. 'Gubba called. The Tribunal ruled on your case. You lost. They can deport you.' Tears welled in her big eyes. One fat one plopped right out and landed on her cheek.

'Oh, maaan, don't start crying on me. You know I hate that. Anyway, what're you talking about? They're not gonna deport me. That's stupid talk. Australia's me home.' That really turned on the taps. 'You know I never even been over there except that time when they circumstanced me.'

'Are you listening?' Mum spoke to me in our language while handing Marlena a tissue.

'Yeah. I heard it. Gubba says I lost.' I thought about this for a moment. It didn't feel real. I looked at their faces. Totally crustfallen, like that cake Marlena baked for me birthday what didn't work cuz I slammed the door. All I could think was that I had to say something to make them feel better. 'Fine. Doesn't matter. Whatever. There's always the appeal. She'll be right.'

Marlena dropped her head on Mum's shoulder and started wailing like a siren. How embarrassing was this?

Ching looked over Wing Wong's shoulder. He had her pressed against one a the shelter's columns like she was apricots and he was making paste. Her eyes went wide, and she made a face what said that she hoped the tears wasn't on a count a her.

Women. I'm seriously considering coming back a poofter in me next life. Men have gotta be easier.

'Zeki!' Mum screwed up her mouth at me.

'Yeah, yeah.' I scraped me chair over to Marlena's side, put me arms around her and pulled her towards me. She flopped onto me chest. 'C'mon, babe,' I cooed as I regained me balance. 'It's not that bad.' I patted her back. Clarence was hanging round the shelter like a bad smell. He had a smirk on his ugly dial. I shot him the finger over Marlena's head. 'Babe, we'll talk to Gubba. We'll appeal.'

She Who Was Inconsultable picked up her sorry head and looked at Mum in a way what told me there was more bad news coming.

'Gubba wants ten thousand. He won't touch the appeal until we've paid up — and put another five thousand up front. He said when you lose at the AAT you have to appeal to Federal Court, and that's even more expensive.'

I almost did it. Said *muvvafucker!* in front a Mum. I spluttered for a moment, trying to get me tongue under control. 'The deal was I'd pay him off once I was out and working again.'

'Well, he wants it now. All of it.'

I thought about this a moment. 'You know why sharks don't attack lawyers?' I asked.

They looked at me like someone changed the channels on a program they was watching.

'Professional courtesy.'

Mum managed a laugh. Marlena's lip quivered.

'I'm sorry. I have to go to work, Zek. Your mum's gonna drop me off.'

'Yeah, go, fine.'

'You'll be right?'

'Yeah, yeah, go, go.' I herded them out before Marlena could turn on the waterworks again.

'Bye.' They waved just before disappearing through the vault door.

'Bye.' That's when it hit me. I wasn't getting out. I was fucked. Up the proverbial without a paddle. Done like a dog's dinner. It was fucken bullshit. It was wrong. What were they gonna do, come for me at four in the morning like they came for Babak, or Jameel? I was practically born in this country. I was that angry I could feel the steam coming outta me ears, I swear. I couldn't think. Me palms were sweaty and me mouth was dry. I went over to the Coke machine and chucked some coins into the slot. I hit the button and nuffin came out. I punched the button to get me money back. Zip. Zilch. It was the last straw, what is a met-oh-four for nuffin left to drink through. I swung me leg back and kicked that fucken Coke machine as hard as I fucken could — and you don't gotta pardon me fucken French. I meant it.

Part Two

One

It was like the opposite a that warning they stick on the side mirrors a cars. Objects in the mirror may be further away than they appear. Ten minutes earlier, I coulda touched that world where you go to work, walk down the street, have things to do, people to see. All that now seemed very far away, like it be China or something, except China didn't seem that far away in here, with all them Chinese.

'What're youse looking at?' A man couldn't even break his own toe in peace round there, I swear. The Innonesians at the table by the Coke machine what saw me kick it looked away again. Hauling meself up off the ground, all I could think was that I wanted to get away from all these stooges as fast as I could. That turned out not to be very fast on a count a me toe, what was throbbing. Worse, I had nowhere to go.

Deport *me*? To the Old Country?

Couldn't pitcher it at all. I didn't know no one over there except me rellies. A few years back, they got this idea that I should marry me first cousin what lives there. At the time, Marlena had dumped me on a count a me flandering, what is what she called it and what I not be proud of. Me dad musta told the rellies I was a free man. They sent over a photo a me cousin. She was fifteen years old, and in black from head to toe with only her eyes showing, like a fucken ninja — pardon me Japanese. Me dad thought it was a great idea. I'm like, whoa, *cousin*, hello — Dad, you want your grandkids to look like the British royal family? No way José. She Who Forgived Me in the End came back after three months, what is the longest we ever been apart since we was in Year Ten, except for the times when I was in the nick, and then we was only apart in a technological sense.

No — I wasn't going to the Old Country, no way, no how. If Gubba wouldn't do it, maybe one a them free lawyers what helped the asylums could help me. I reckoned I was a Prisoner a Conscious, cuz I wished I wasn't. If I ever needed a smoke that was the time.

I was pacing the Yard without even realising it. 'Zeki.' I looked over. It was Hamid. He was sitting with Angel and Sue and this other chick, a Burmese girl what didn't speak much English. 'You okay?'

'Yeah, bro. No worries. I just lost me case.' As I said this I made one a them hip-hop moves where you throw your hands in front a your face to point with the second and last fingers at an imaginary place in the middle. It wasn't the right move for what I be saying. Me brain and me fingers wasn't real connected at that moment.

Hamid frowned, like he was trying to work out whether to

believe me hands or me words. 'You lost?'

I nodded.

He frowned deeper. 'What are you going to do?'

'I'll work something out.' I sounded more confidential than I felt.

'Enjoy us.' This from the Burmese chick, what meaned 'join us'.

'Maybe later.' I felt like a fucken blob on the landscape. 'For now, I think I'll just go inside and hang meself.' Sue looked fully alarmed. I spose I shouldn't a said that. Everyone knew about Reza. He had about a million visitors that day what was trying to cheer him up. 'Nah. Don't worry.'

At the gate I pawed me plastic ID down from the board. 'What's wrong, Togan?' Anna asked.

'What's right?' I answered.

'Why are you limping?'

'Don't worry about it.'

'Jeez. Just asking. No need to snap at me.'

Across the Yard, I saw April waiting to be let in through the visitors' gate, but I looked away like I didn't see her. I didn't wanna talk to no one, not Anna, not even April what I like to talk to. While I waited for Anna to find the right key, I stared at the ground and shoved me hands in the pocket a me trackies. I could feel something in there, a square a plastic wrapped around . . . *Yes*. I thought, that's me girl! She musta dropped it in when she hugged me goodbye.

If She Who Always Obeys the Rules could do that, I felt anything was possible. Me mood lifted. Something would work out. I was, after all, the Infernal Optimist.

Two

The smoke made me feel heaps better. Looking in the mirror, I saw me eyes were as red as dogs' balls. I put on me sunnies.

Back in the Yard, I thought, whoa, that's powerful shit. All the kids in the Yard looked like they'd grown moustaches and beards. Abeer had one what was just like her dad Mohammed's. In factuality, she looked exactly like him, but with pigtails on. That was freaking me out cuz I was thinking maybe he got shrunk and put into a frock. I seen something like that once in a horror film. Noor had a moustache just like Saddam. Tip was saluting Bashir, Abeer's brother, what had a goatee, and calling him 'sir'. Even that muvvafucker Clarence was joking around with the kids. This was hurting me head.

Then I saw the woman what was giving out the moustaches. She was a nice lady what brung her own kids into Detention every week to play with the ones what was Inside. She was also giving out scoops what you wave round to make bubbles and the air was filled with bubbles what reflected the sun. I caught some in me mouth what made the kids laugh. Me mouth was full a soap by the time I found me way across the Yard to where April was sitting with Thomas and Azad. April's hair and clothes were wet and steamy from the rain and she was a bit draggled but I like that look, like she just rolled outta bed and into a hot tub with Swedish babes in. 'Hey, April.' I glided over to give her a kiss on the cheek.

'Look,' she goes, pointing at the sky. 'A rainbow! Isn't that lovely?' Still savourising the feel of her cheek on me lips, I nodded in the general direction a the rainbow, what was a big one.

'Nothing's lovely in here.' Thomas the grump. I didn't know that April had just told him her husband had looked at his paperwork. He'd asked how she knew it was genuine, and other questions what got her angry. They had a fight what ended up being about the nurse. He slammed the door when he walked out. She told Thomas all these details what she probably shouldn't a done. She coulda probably got away with saying something like, 'He's thinking on it'.

'Nothing behind the razor wire is lovely,' he said again, like she hadn't heard it the first time.

'Except present ladylike company,' I go. 'You yourself are looking particularly lovely today, April.' Her lips moved briefly in the direction of up.

'You've got a way with words, Zek,' she goes.

I couldn't think of anything to say to that.

'Didn't you tell me that first day we met that you wanted to be a writer, that you wanted to write a book?'

'Yeah, mate.' I couldn't remember saying that in factuality. But it seemed like a good idea. 'I will, mate. When I get outta here I'm gonna be a writer.'

'Then you can steal people's words instead of their things,' Azad said. 'You get into less trouble that way.'

'So true,' April laughed, looking at Azad like he be the wittiest person in the whole world. She turned back to me. 'Have you been writing in the journal I gave you?'

'Every day,' I lied. I was thinking that if I was a writer, then April, what knew heaps about books, could be me editor. We could get jiggy at one a them posh places what writers go to for working on books with them editors, what had a pool and swaying palm trees and them coloured cocktails with umbrellas in. I had to sit with me elbows on me knees to keep me boy from flagging his enthusiasm for the concept through me trackies.

When I tuned back in, Thomas was crapping on about how ugly Australia was compared to his country. I love Australia and it made me upset to hear him talking about it like that. He didn't know it at all. He didn't know how beautiful it be. He'd never been to the Gold Coast or the footie, or even a single Westfield mall. He'd never been outside the razor wire even once.

Thomas listed everything he hated about Australia. They were all things what he experienced in Detention, like bad food and no freedom and stupid officials and donkey doctors and racist guards. Every one a him complaints seemed like they was aimed at April. With each one, she dropped a little lower into her chair, like she was a nail being hammered into a piece a wood. When he finished, she whispered, 'I'm sorry.'

She always be apologising for things what wasn't her fault, what makes her like Azad when I comes to think on it. 'I wish this weren't all you knew of this country.'

'Me too,' said Thomas.

'Do you hate Australia too?' April asked Azad like she was scared he was gonna say yes.

Azad pulled his lighter out of his pocket but then put it back again cuz it was out of fluid. 'I don't know what Australia is,' he said.

'This is Australia,' Thomas goes, stamping his feet in the mud, what splattered up onto me trackies. He smiled with one side of his mouth. 'Sorry, Zek.'

'S'all right, mate.' I shrugged. I was fully mellow from the dope. 'Gotta wash 'em sometime.'

'Actually,' Thomas goes like he was reconsiderating, 'this is *not* Australia. I wanted to take a university course by correspondence while I waited for my decision. They wouldn't let me, even though some visitors said they would pay the full fees for me. The government said you have to be in Australia to study and that from a legal standpoint, I am not here at all.' He pointed to a Malaysian woman pushing a pram on the other side of the Yard. 'See Lili?' he asked. April nodded. 'Her baby was born here in Detention. But the government says her baby wasn't born in Australia. The detention centre doesn't count. Malaysia won't let the baby in because she's stateless. Lili won't go home without her baby and can't get out of Detention because Australia won't give her or the baby a visa either.'

'But, surely, they'll have to . . .'

'They won't,' Thomas said. 'They could be here for the rest of their lives.'

We went to New Zealand for a few minutes.

'I . . . I did a meditation the other day and asked the universe to look after all of you?' April said. 'I want to help, I really do.' Thomas folded his arms across his chest. April opened her mouth like she was gonna say something else, then closed it again. A tear dribbled down her cheek but since everyone else was looking at the ground, I was the only one what noticed.

'I have this dream many nights,' Azad said in a soft voice. 'I'm standing outside a house where there is a party. I hear music and people laughing and talking. I smell food cooking. I walk towards the house and look in the window. There are visitors, and officers, and faces I know from television and movies, and fellow detainees too. You're there, Zeki,' he goes, looking up at me.

I felt proud when he said this, like I done something good for exchange.

'I remember I am supposed to be inside the house too. They are expecting me. So I start to run but my feet stick to the ground, and then I feel someone holding me by the hands and I'm a little kid again and it's my mother and father, and . . .' Azad stared down at his feet like they was a book he be reading. He didn't usually say that much about his personal. 'Anyway, it doesn't matter.' When he looked up again, it was like his blinds was closed.

April reached out and put her hand on his arm.

'I'm fine,' he said, pulling his arm away.

She dropped her hand back into her lap. Then she touched her eyes with both hands.

In me head, it was me what was having me arm touched up. In me head — what was still full a nice mellow feelings on a count a the dope — we was back at that hotel what had the pool and cocktails. I was thinking how I could explain my being with April at the hotel to She Who Always Knows When I Be Telling a Porkie. I'd tell her the truth, what was that I was writing a book and April was me editor and all. Then it hit me. I wasn't getting out. I wasn't going to no posh hotel with April or nowhere else anytime soon. I slapped me hand against me forehead, forgetting I was wearing me chunky ring, and almost knocked meself out. 'Ow!'

'You okay?' goes April. Her voice was squeaky and choked like she was trying not to laugh, but she didn't succeed and then everyone laughed, even Thomas.

Farshid ran by with a soccer ball. All the kids, including visitors, was dividing up into teams according to whether they be moustaches or beards. Some a the older detainees joined in as well, like Bhajan. The visitors was trying to get Reza to play too, but he wasn't in the mood. They asked if we wanted to play. Thomas didn't play nuffin cuz a him gammy leg. April said she wasn't no good at sports. But Azad was keen. When I jumped up to follow him, I stumbled on a count a me toe, what I forgot was broke, and smacked straight into Abeer what was running for the ball. We both fell down on the ground. When I looked over I saw her little face with its big moustache. I started to laugh and laugh and laugh even though me toe was hurting something fierce by now.

Abeer picked herself up, brushed the mud off her frock, straightened her moustache and, pulling her tiny foot back, kicked me as hard as she could. I was being assaulted by a small girl with a moustache. I started laughing again.

'Go, Abeer!' Thomas cheered.

April shook her head. 'You know, if this weren't a detention centre, Zeki, I'd swear you were stoned.'

I really lost it then. I rolled from side to side and hooted and gasped for breath and cried on a count a the pain, all at the same time. It took me a while to realise that there was a lotta noise what wasn't just me or even the kids what be playing soccer. I looked around and through me tears a laughter I saw a whole lot a people outside the fence what wasn't there before. They was waving signs and banners, and banging on drums and shouting, 'Free the refugees! Free the refugees! Lock up the Minister and free the refugees!'

Three

Farshid ran to the fence. Reza jumped up from where he was sitting and raced over as well. 'We want freedom! We want freedom!' they shouted, pumping them fists in the air. All the kids started chanting and lotsa the other detainees joined in, even the ones what wasn't asylums. Azad stood like he was frozen.

Hamid jumped up but Angel clamped her little hand round his wrist and it was like he be chained to the spot. Sue placed one hand on Angel's shoulder and another on the arm a the Burmese chick.

It took less than a second for the blues to sprint into the may-lee, what be Chinese for Big Fucken Mess, pardon me French. They was shouting 'Cert One! Cert One!', their code for emergencies. They was coming at the detainees from this side a the fence and at the protestors from the other. Them white trucks what they patrol the perimeter in sped over too. And then sirens told us New South Wales's finest was on their way. Thomas wrapped his hands round his head in that way what told us he was getting one a him migraines.

April stood up, looking dead nervous cuz she didn't know the life like we do, what is to say she'd never been in trouble or the nick or nuffin. Her hand hovered over Thomas's shoulder like a helicopter what didn't know if it could land, and her eyes darted from him to Azad, what still hadn't moved. It was like she didn't know who to worry about more. Me, I was worrying about meself. If I didn't get meself up off the ground I'd be trampolined by all the people what was rushing around like chooks what have them heads off.

The officer in charge a Shit House intelligence, what it didn't have much of in factuality, ran around recording everything with a video camera. Clarence was charging past April over to where Farshid and Reza was still shouting when April grabbed his sleeve. He turned around like he was gonna deck her. 'Back off, basket weaver!' he barked like the dog he be.

She looked real shocked then. 'Thomas needs a doctor,' she goes, her voice shaking.

'So do I,' answered the muvvafucker. 'Must be sick in the head to wanna work here. Find one, let me know. Now let go of me sleeve before I make ya.' Then the bastard ran over to muscle Farshid and Reza away from the fence.

The Centre Manager came on the PA announcing that Visits was exterminated. He ordered visitors to make their way to the gate and all detainees back into the compound.

Someone shouted for people to set fire to the bins. They said if you burn plastic or rubber, the smoke protects you from tear gas, what they used on asylums in Woomera a few months earlier. I'd wondered why them demonstrators on the TV news was always burning tyres and shit. So that was it. I was getting an education in international affairs and politics what I never had. In the end, no one lit any fires, and there wasn't no tear gas, just shitloads a guards and a handful a coppers what didn't even have riot gear on.

The kids was crying. Abeer's mum, Najah, came running to get Abeer and her brother Bashir, but Abeer stuck her heels into the mud and pushed out her bottom lip and her mum had to drag her away. 'Noor!' She was yelling for her friend the whole time. 'Noor!' She ripped off her moustache and threw it on the ground.

Nassrin was inside the compound but the blues wasn't letting anyone into the Yard what wasn't in it already. So Nassrin just kept screaming for her boys from behind the fence, what got everyone even more worked up.

Then this long-haired hippy chick what was in the protest stepped forward. As she handcuffed herself to the outside fence, she called out, 'We love you!'

At this point, two things happened. Azad looked at her like he be completely memorised, like the sun just came up and she be it, and cried, 'We love you too!'. And April, what was looking all pale and not just cuz she be standing next to Thomas, shouted, 'Marley! What are you doing here?'

'I came down for the protest. What are *you* doing here?' goes the hippy chick. 'I didn't think this would be your sort of scene, Mum.'

'Mum'? Man, if it weren't against me religion, that be one mother-daughter team I'd like to have a match with.

'Besides,' said Marley, 'don't you vote Liberal?'

April turned all the colours a the Mardi Gras. 'Marley!'

Some a the other visitors stared at April like she'd just laid a cable.

A student with dreadlocks what visited Farshid and Reza saw Clarence coming. He yelled 'Pigs!', and went to push him, what wasn't a good idea cuz it only took a second before Clarence got a fist around them hair-sticks. He gave them a yank what made the boy yelp, what is a yell with a P what makes it shorter.

'Go sit on a branch, tree-hugger,' Clarence advised the boy.

An Iranian man what been in Detention for four years and what had lost it like Bilal began screaming, 'You shit fuck officer! Shit fuck rules! Shit fuck place!' Clarence let go a the boy and moved in on the Iranian. That's when I noticed Noor pushed up against the inner fence with a little blonde Aussie girl what was visiting her. They both had them shoulders hunched up like they could hide them heads that way. 'Mummy!' screamed the little blonde girl. Her mum ran over and snatched her away. Azad ran over to scoop up Noor and then ran with her towards the gate to the compound.

As a whole flank a blues moved through the Yard, herding the visitors towards the gate, the coppers argued with some other officers over whether or not to cut the fence where April's daughter had handcuffed herself. The blues told the coppers to work on Marley's handcuffs and leave the fence alone. Apparently when they was on Commonwealth land — what Villawood was — the coppers hadda listen to the blues, unless they was feds, what they wasn't.

After Azad handed Noor to Anna, he came running back again, even though Anna was shouting at him to go inside, that it was a lockdown. He'd just hooked his hands on the inside fence opposite Marley, what was still cuffed to the outside one, when Clarence came up and clapped him on the back of his head.

'That's enough, Romeo. Juliet's got a date with the police. Get inside. Now.'

Azad gave him a look what said he got a lot more passion than what he usually show. That was the last thing I knew, cuz Farshid kicked the soccer ball at Clarence, the muvvafucker ducked and I was sconed. Out like a light.

'C'mon Togan. Lockdown. That means you. Quit mucking around. Togan. *Togan.*'

Anna's voice was the first thing I heard. It came fluttering in on baby angel wings through a thick, dark mist. There was something big and hard and dirty and wet on me face. It was the ground. I picked me aching head up, opened me eyes and spat out some mud. I had an urge to laugh. Then I saw Thomas stumbling by, led by the nurse, his head in his hands, and outside the fence was all them cops.

'I didn't do nuffin, mate,' I said. At least I didn't think I did. I was trying to remember. 'What's going on?' I had a wicked headache. I scrabbled round in the mud for me sunnies.

'You really don't know?' Anna crossed her arms over her chest.

'Don't do that,' I said. 'You're blocking the view, mate. Lemme look at me two best friends.'

'I was gonna ask if you're all right,' she goes, trying to oppress a smile, 'but that comment tells me that nothing's wrong with you.'

'In factuality,' I said, thinking about it, 'me head hurts.' I tried to stand up but I was Dizzy Gillespie. I fell back down on me knees.

'What's going on, Togan? And don't tell me you're proposing.'

Clarence suddenly poked his ugly mug into the frame. 'Moron got beaned by a soccer ball just as all the fun began.'

Fun? One fun thing happens in three months a detention and I missed it?

Four

Later that evening, I got Anna to nuke some macaroni and cheese in the office microwave for me. I stood in the doorway while she filled me in on what I missed while I was eating dirt.

She told me they was keeping Thomas under observation in Medical. Abeer had stopped talking. And in all the confusion, Noor went missing. No one had noticed with all them other things going on. Then one of the Chinamen found her cuddled up in the dryer what is lucky, cuz he was about to chuck his sheets in. Whacking Co didn't want that getting out to the media. Some a them advocates — what is people what do things for the asylums and what the government calls do-gooders, even though they don't think they be doing good — was already making a big fuss about Noor being a small girl what was alone in Detention. In factuality, Nadia been saying that all along too, but now they was thinking a listening to her and moving Noor's mum to Villawood quicker. I said this was good news cuz Noor was getting old eyes like she wasn't a kid no more.

'Where's Farshid and Reza?' I asked, cuz I heard they was in the Management Unit for to punish them. She told me they'd been released but Clarence was giving them the what-for. He said they was troublemakers. He said they was wrong to encourage the protesters. They told him they done nuffin wrong, that Australia was a democracy, so they didn't see why they couldn't speak up for them rights. 'They said they weren't criminals,' Anna goes.

'Tsk. Criminals got rights, too,' I said. I stirred me pasta and took a mouthful. Suddenly I remembered what I'd learned that day about me court decision and me shithead lawyer. It hit me like a punch in the guts. I put me spoon down. 'I got a month to appeal or they'll start deportation proceedings.'

'You'd better get onto it then.'

'Spose.'

I forced the rest a the pasta down and patted me belly. 'It's good trackydaks have them expansible waists, eh?'

'Eh,' said Anna.

'I was planning on getting fit again when I got released, go to the gym, pump up,' I informed her.

'That'd be good,' she goes. 'But you can exercise in here, you know.'

'Here? In the doorway a the office?'

She laughed. 'No, Dumbo,' she goes, like she knew that be me nickname when I was little on a count a me ears. 'In the compound.'

'Nah, mate. No point.'

She shook her head, like she didn't get it. But ask any detainee and they'll tell you the same thing. Azad and Hamid played soccer, and Thomas and me, we had a game a billiards from time to time, and sometimes everyone kicked a ball around, but that was about it. They had volleyball and badminton what no one used, and ping pong what the Chinese was always monopolating. But it was like the razor wire sucked the energy right outta you. It made your arms and legs heavy like they was cased in concrete.

Sometimes I thought the younger guys had it worst cuz it was sposed to be the best time a their lives. But the older men what had families Inside had it tough too. Abeer's dad, Mohammed, was so depressed on a count a not being able to look after his family or do nuffin to help them situation that he spent most a the time lying on his bed. The mums like Najah and Nassrin, they got depressed cuz they couldn't even cook for them kids, what was always upset. At least Najah and Nassrin got a sewing machine in the Women's Centre what they could sew clothes on with cloth what the visitors brung them.

'See,' I explained, 'all the plans we make, to get fit, study, whatever — they're for Out.'

Anna shrugged. 'No time like the present. You know,' she told me, 'my mum was a refugee. From Czechoslovakia.'

'No sh— kidding,' I go. 'You looks Australian to me, mate.'

'Why wouldn't I? I was born here, and my dad's a fifth-generation Australian. Was. He died last year.'

'I'm sorry.'

'Me too. He wasn't that old either. He worked pretty hard his whole life.'

I thought about how even the blues got them problems and them lives, what we normally only thought about insofar as they was a part of our own.

'Sometimes,' Anna went on, 'I look at some of the regular visitors and, quite frankly, I hate them.'

'No way.'

'Maybe that's too strong. It's more like I resent them. They've got enough money and time to swan around here like they own the place, making snide remarks about officers like we're too stupid to know what they're saying, and making things difficult for us. They're always telling us how to do our job — like they know better. And they yell at us about the kids not going to school and about asylum seekers being locked up for years and other things that aren't our fault. It's Immigration that makes those decisions. You know, I wanted to study and travel and have a good life too, but when Dad got sick I had to get a job so I could look after him and Mum. Someone told me there were lots of jobs in security, so I got my certificate and, well, here I am. But they're not better than me.' Her mouth went all tight and unhappy-looking.

'No one's better than you, Anna,' I said, winking. 'You're the best.'

'You're incorrigible.'

'That's what they all say.'

She shook her head and gave me a half-smile. She looked cheered up some. I have that effect on the ladies. I spooned up the last a the cheese sauce and put me bowl down by me feet. I lit up a ciggie. 'So your mum was an asylum? Like Azad and them?'

'No, no, no,' she said like I'd seriously dissed her mum. 'She came here *legally*, as a refugee, after the Russians invaded Czechoslovakia in 1968.'

'They put her in Detention?'

'That's the funny thing. She'd always told me she'd been taken to a place called the Westbridge Migrant Centre but I hadn't put two and two together, you know what I mean?'

'Yeah,' I said. 'That be an expression what mean four.'

Anna looked at me. 'What I didn't realise is that Villawood's just the new name for Westbridge. You know the old Nissen huts between here and Stage One — you can just see them through the fence of the Visiting Yard. They haven't been used for years. That's where my own mum lived for a month or so.'

'Far out. So your mum was behind the razor wire.'

'No,' she goes, drawing out the O like I said something insulting about her mum again. Anna looked down at her desk and straightened a stack a Detainee Request Forms. 'She was actually shocked when I told her what it was like now. She said in her day it was an open hostel. People could come and go. There were classes on Australian history and customs as well as English, and when the refugees got job interviews the government organised a car to pick them up and take them there. They got a dollar a day spending money. She was here in summer and some days they'd get up before dawn and walk or hitch all the way to Bondi, have a swim, buy a Paddle Pop and make their way back by nightfall. That's how she met my dad, when he gave her a lift. They fell in love at first sight.'

'That's romantic.' I was thinking that She Who Loves a Good Romance would like that story. She was always reading romances. And whenever we went to the video shop, we joked that the day Hollywood makes a romantic comedy with kung fu, war and dinosaurs in, we wouldn't have to argue no more about what we was gonna see. I decided that the next time we was choosing a video, I'd surprise her and choose a romantic comedy meself — so long as we could also get one with guns in for later. Then it occurred to me I didn't know when I was ever gonna get to the video shop with She Who again. I put the thought into one of April's little boxes and pushed it off two cliffs.

Just then me phone vibrated in me pocket. Anna's cool, but no way could I let her know I got a mobile. She'd have to take it off a me. 'Anyway, nice talking to you. I better let you get back to it.' With me hand in me pocket, I clicked the button to answer. I'd be in me room in no time.

Five

On the way back to me room, I ran into Angel and Hamid. They wanted to know how Thomas was, and I told them what I knew, what wasn't much. They said April had called on the public phone to find out if everyone was okay. She'd spoken to both of them already and Azad was talking to her now.

After I said goodbye to them I saw Farshid and Reza. They was still arguing with Clarence. The prick looked at his watch and goes, 'In five minutes, I'm leaving here and going to the pub. You losers, on the other hand, are stuck in here.' I couldn't believe I was hearing this. I mean, they was only teenagers. They'd already been locked up for years, and Reza still had the marks on his neck from the noose. Then, like it wasn't already perfectly clear, Clarence added, 'Youse not going nowhere.'

I stepped up. 'Shut yer cakehole and fuck off outta their faces,' I advised him.

'Whoa. It's Big Girl. Got a knock on the melon today, did ya? Gotta be careful, there couldn't be too many brain cells in there to start with.'

I raised me fist, and I swear I'd a gone him, but Farshid grabbed me before I could swing. 'Forget it, Zeki,' he goes, 'He's not verth it.' Farshid spat on the ground like it be Clarence's face.

Clarence looked at his watch again. 'Have a great night, suckers.' He turned and left.

Reza mumbled 'dickhead' under his breath.

Clarence turned his head. 'Oh. And thanks for a great day.'

Me and the boys stood there bagging Clarence and this whole fucken place until something nagged me. I knew I had something to do, just couldn't remember exactly what it was. 'Catch youse later,' I said, giving them the bruvvas' handshake as I went. Reza put two fingers to his lips like he was smoking and made a question mark with his face.

I gave them each a ciggie. 'No charge tonight,' I said when Farshid pulled some coins outta his pocket.

'Thanks, Zek.' They gave me the thumbs up.

'No worries, mateys,' I said, feeling all truistic like I was Mother Teresa her good self.

Just as I got to me block, Ching jumped outta the shadows. 'Boo!'

'I'm not in the mood.' I wasn't, neither.

'Guess what? Guess what?' She was bubbling over like a warm tinnie a VB.

The Christian dude from the Philippines stuck his head out the window.

I wasn't too happy to see Ching but didn't wanna be the night's entertainment either so I pushed open the door and gestated for her to follow what she'd a done anyway.

'My boyfriend is posting bond. I released on Bridging Visa tomorrow!'

'Good for Wing Wong. Good for you,' I said, sitting down. I didn't feel too bad being rude under the circumstances.

'His name is not Wing Wong.' She slapped my arm and giggled.

'Whatever. Ting-a-ling. Bing Bat.' I admit it. I was pissed off she never told me about him. 'Won Ton. Long Dong.'

She was shaking her head like she was annoyed but she couldn't help giggling. 'You naughty, Zeki.' She jumped onto me lap.

'Cut it out,' I said. 'I'm not in the mood.'

She slid up and down me leg and stuck her tongue in me ear. She threw her shirt over her head. She wasn't wearing no bra and her cute tits with them brown nips was looking straight at me. She grabbed one in each hand and made them talk. 'C'mon, Zeki,' said the right. 'One for road,' goes the left. Then she slid onto to her cute knees and started pulling down me trackies with her teeth.

Hey, it wasn't like I had nuffin better to do.

I did get annoyed when she started moaning and shrieking like one of them Chinese opera shows what they broadcast sometimes on Channel 31. She didn't make no effort to keep the levels down neither. Flora banged on the door. 'Togan!' she shouted. 'How many times have I said, *no sex on my shift*!' Great. Now everyone was in on the secret. Oh maaan. Ching did that special trick with her fingernails and the bit behind me goolies and I was off like an exploding Space Shuttle.

I walked her to the door and she bounced off into the mist like Bambi. It had started to rain. Me neighbour poked his head outta the window again and told me the rain was the tears a Jesus. 'He died for your sins, you know.' He put the emphasis on *your*.

'If I wanna feel guilty, I got me mum and me girlfriend,' I informed him. 'I don't need Jesus in on the act as well.' I went back inside. Something was nagging me worse than Marlena. Like I was forgetting something important.

Marlena.

I shoved me hand in me pocket and pulled out me mobile, what said me last call be forty-six minutes long what just ended. Oh maaan. Oh fuck. *Fuck*. I was in big fucken trouble now.

Six

'Hello ba—'

The dial tone bleated in me ear like a sheep with a stuck horn. I tried again.

'Babydoll, I —'

She banged the phone down so hard it almost busted me eardrums. I gritted me teeth, wiped the sweat off a me forehead and tried again.

'Please, darl —'

Azad sat on the chair in me room, eating pistachios. 'Maybe she needs some time.'

'What would you know about it, mate?' I glared at him.

'Nothing. Obviously.' He got up and walked out.

I tore open a pack a biscuits and ate every one. I felt sick. I was sick a Detention. I was sick a the other detainees. Mostly, I was sick a meself.

A few days later, April came to visit. 'Two hours,' she complained. 'It took two hours to get in today.' She crapped on and on about all the new visitors in the queue, how they didn't know anything about anything, not even how to fill out them forms, what was apparently one a the reasons it was taking so long for everyone to get in. She didn't know what most a them was doing there, neither. Some of them was comparing things they'd brought as gifts — CDs, books and magazines, home-baked cakes, curries with rice. 'It's not a picnic,' she said with a little *hmph*, putting juice and nuts and biscuits on the table. There was a lipstick what Angel asked for too, and a pack a cards. She also had a clipping from the newspaper the day after the protest. It had a photo what had Azad and all the kids with their moustaches and beards, seen through coils a razor wire.

'It is not easy for anyone to visit,' Azad said, after he looked at the clipping. 'This place is far from everywhere, we know that.'

'It usually takes me an hour? Depends on traffic.'

'We are very . . . what is the word? Grateful.'

That cheered her up.

'To *everyone* who visits us. You are all good people.' He was saying it like it was a lesson she needed to learn.

Her face dropped a little. I don't reckon April liked sharing the glory. But Azad, what normally looked after everyone's feelings, was doing so less and less. I think it was on a count a the depression, what was growing in him like a mushroom, except not one a them fun ones, and not even one for cooking. A mushroom what got poison in.

'Some people have been visiting for many months.' He wasn't letting it go either.

But Angel got female instincts the way I got criminal ones. She put her hand on April's. 'You very good to us, April,' Angel said. 'You help us a lot.'

April glowed like Homer Simpson after one a them accidents in the nuclear power station, I swear. She gave Angel a big hug. Azad pulled his lighter out and flicked it on and off, even though it didn't have no fluid. April watched him, looking worried.

When Thomas didn't come out, Hamid explained that sometimes people didn't hear their names being called and went back into the compound to look for him. I knew that in factuality, Thomas had heard, cuz a few minutes earlier I'd seen him go to the fence and look into the Yard. But I wasn't gonna say nuffin. Didn't have the energy. It was clear he just didn't want to see April.

'So how are you, Zeki?' April asked. 'You're looking uncharacteristically glum.'

I shrugged. 'I'm okay.'

'Zeki in big trouble with his girlfriend,' Angel informed her.

'Oh no! What happened?'

I made a face. I didn't wanna talk about it.

'He was naughty,' Angel said. 'She found out. Now she not talking to him.'

April stared at me with her eyebrows up. 'You know, Zeki, maybe the Universe is trying to teach you a lesson. Everything in life happens for a reason? What you get is what you ask for?' She started to say something about a book what was also chicken soup, what I didn't get, or care about much, when Azad interrupted. 'What do you mean "you get what you ask for"?' Azad asked. 'Do you think a refugee asks to suffer?' he goes. 'Do you think we asked to come to Australia so that we could rot in Detention? To see ourselves dying a little bit every day? Excuse me.' He jumped to his feet. 'Have a nice day.'

'Wait,' April said. Her eyes had tears in. Women be pure drama, I'm telling you. 'Please wait.'

'Yes?' Azad was talking through him teeth.

'Before you go . . . This is for you.' She handed him a sealed envelope, what looked like it had a card in. She tried to smile. 'I'm sorry.'

Without looking at the envelope, he stuffed it into his pocket. 'Thank you,' he said. Then he walked away.

Angel bit her lip and looked at Hamid.

'Everyone here too stressed,' Hamid said. Then, to prove the point, he dropped his head down like it be too heavy to hold up any more and blew out some air.

Angel looked at him, and me, and April, like she be deciding who needed the most help. 'I know,' she said, cracking the deck, 'let's play cards.'

April gave a little smile. 'I can't believe *you're* trying to cheer *me* up now,' she said. 'Thank you, Angel.'

'Go Fish or Poker?' Angel said, nudging Hamid, what was still staring at his feet.

'Poker,' Hamid said after a while. 'I get used to gambling. It's like life.'

'*Word*,' I said, what be hip-hop for to agree with something, but even more so.

'Pro-ee-ung Tevy from Cambodia, come to DIMIA. Pro-ee-ung Tevy from Cambodia, come to DIMIA.'

Proeung Tevy be Angel's name in her own language. Even I knew the rule by then that they only called you in to give you bad news, but we all gave her the thumbs up what was for hoping it be good news anyway.

'Sue thinks Angel should get her Bridging Visa,' April said after Angel left to go to the office. 'She said that her age and the evidence of her physical and psychological trauma matched the guidelines to a T. You know everything that happened when she was —' I didn't think April was ever gonna get the point about keeping people's confidentials. She looked like she was about to launch into a discussion a the traumatics when Hamid pointed at the cards.

'Your turn, April.'

Angel returned a few minutes later. We read the answer on her face.

'Maybe . . . maybe there's some other way?' April put a hand on Angel's arm. Angel just hung her pretty head.

Seven

The asylums' cause was getting more famous by the minute. It was on the news all the time now. Some Members a Parliament and human rights groups was kicking up a fuss about the children in particulate. What didn't mean the kids was allowed to go to school or that any more asylums was getting visas. But it did mean they was getting lotsa visitors.

Azad and them was talking to this lady what had a notebook and what was writing down everything they said. I wandered over cuz I figured she be a reporter. DIMIA didn't allow reporters into Detention. Some came anyway, pretending to be visitors. I reckoned if this lady reporter really wanted to shock her readers, she should tell them how someone virtuosically Australian like me own good self was locked up like an asylum. But she didn't act too interested in my story, even though I told it with lotsa gestations and wicked impersonations of the coppers on the train and the Immigration guys and even of Gubba with his hair and his tan.

It turned out she wasn't a reporter after all. She was a famous play-writer what was gonna write a play what was gonna change people's opinions about asylums. The next day we met a famous novelist what was gonna write a novel what was gonna change people's opinions about asylums, and a few days after that, a famous director what was gonna make a movie what was gonna do the same thing. I don't know much about plays or books, but I reckon a movie about asylums in Detention would be pretty boring, cuz nuffin much ever happens Inside. So I told the famous director that if he wanted people to go see his movie, it should have car chases and kung fu and Angelina Jolie in.

'Hmmm,' he said, stroking his funny little beard and looking at me outta his square black glasses. 'Interesting.' He said he'd 'workshop the concept', whatever that is when it's at home.

Some a the visitors cried, what put a strainer on us all. Others talked about feeling 'this amazing connection' with the asylums, like they all got cordless phones with no static on. They said things like 'you're not terrorists' and 'you're not bad people' like they was telling the asylums something new. They all promised they was gonna visit all the time, every week at least. We never saw most a them again. Some a the asylums was disappointed at this. I insured them that in the case a the famous ones, it was probably cuz they was busy making them famous books and plays and movies and stuff.

The visitors what came regular, meanwhile, was getting more organised. They was making lists of all the asylums so that everyone was getting called to Visits now, not just the popular ones like Farshid and Reza and Azad. Once, even crazy Bilal got called. He only went out that one time. He said he'd never go back again. He said he felt like a monkey in the zoo or a bear what was in a circus and what had to perform. He figured that a lot a the visitors just wanted to be able to tell their friends they'd been to a detention centre and met the people what was on the news all the time. This made some a the detainees say crazy Bilal wasn't so crazy after all.

Eight

Days passed. Azad was still dark with mushrooms in. He told me he was getting nightmares every night what had snakes and spiders. He was afraid to fall asleep. Even though he was real tired, what you could see in his eyes, he was only getting a couple hours a night, starting around six in the morning and ending when the PA announcements began two hours later. He had a mobile now, too, what one a the visitors smuggled in. Once, around four in the morning, when I couldn't sleep, I went round to see if he was up and felt like a game a cards. I could hear him talking into his mobile. I wondered who he be having conversationals with at that hour, but forgot to ask when I saw him later on.

The fifteenth a January was Reza's fourteenth birthday. The visitors brought lotsa food and juice, and he had three birthday cakes, one what was chocolate with dark chocolate icing on, and one what had lemon icing, and one what had black cherries in, what I liked the best. Reza was in the

Visiting Yard from the start of visits at one-thirty. Around four o'clock he excused himself, saying he'd be back in a minute. Cuz there wasn't no toilets in the Yard, we always had to go back into the compound if we needed to take a piss. Visitors had to go back to the office. But there was Muster at four, and the blues wasn't letting no one go in or out till they finished. Reza had been holding it in for hours, and begged them to let him through. In the end the poor little bugger pissed his pants. That made him feel humeliorated cuz there was young girl visitors his age at the birthday party. Before anyone could stop him, Reza shoved his hand through one a the gaps in the fence and slammed it down on the razor wire. Blood spurted, people screamed, them young girls was crying, and everyone was real upset, specially the little kids like Abeer and Noor, what saw it happen. Nassrin took two steps and passed out. Lucky for her, Farshid caught her before she hit the ground. I helped him get her back into a chair.

Nadia came racing outta the compound. Her eyebrows, what were small like her feet and shaped like them too, was trying to escape into her hair. 'Reza, honey, now what are you doing to yourself?'

'Vat's it look like!' he screamed.

The little feets on her forehead pointed their toes down at her nose. 'This is not rational behaviour.' The words 'rational behaviour' went all the way up the scales and then down again.

'You saying I'm crazy?' he shouted. 'I'm not crazy! I just need my freedom!'

The blues dragged him in to Medical. The doctor told him he was lucky he didn't sever a tendon. That just set him off again. 'Lucky!' he yelled. 'You think I'm lucky!' They gave him a needle, what he didn't want, but what put him out for a few hours. Happy birthday, eh.

On the sixteenth, some a the asylums in Woomera began a hunger strike. On the news, the government called the strikers 'rejectees', 'attention seekers' and worse. It was putting everyone on edge. The air felt heavy, like just before a thunderstorm breaks. You could almost see the sky getting darker and darker with it.

Me own skies wasn't what you'd call bright. I still hadn't come up with a plan for the appeal. Me dad reckoned I should just go to Turkey. This was giving me Anxiety with a capital T, what wasn't helped by the fact that She Who still wasn't speaking to me.

I hadn't given up trying, but. On the nineteenth a January, I was waiting in the queue for the public phones. I remember the date cuz me watch — you know the one — had a calendar on. I'd already used up me mobile credit. I was using a normal phone card, what I got from Hamid, what got it from a church lady what helped the refugees. I didn't like scabbing from the asylums, but they did get a lotta phone cards. Azad was in the queue behind me.

The Woomera hunger strike was in its third day. Everyone was edgy. The temperature had hit forty. You could see the heat bouncing off the fences and razor wire. And the bushfires was going off again. The air was yellow and smoky and thick with ash like God be smoking a big cigar up there what be the flavour of eucalyptus. The guys in the queue grumbled and flicked the corners a them phone cards and kicked stones across the dirt and swore.

Nadia rushed past. She was pulling on her hair and muttering to herself.

'G'day, Nadia,' I said.

'Oh.' She stopped short, like she be braking. Her chassis wobbled. 'Oh. Oh. Zeki. Hellooo. Hellooo, Azad.'

'Where's the fire?'

She stared at me. I saw she had rings under her eyes. 'Everywhere. Everywhere.' She rushed off again.

I was about two people away from the front a the queue when Angel appeared. 'You see Hamid?' We hadn't. She told us she be worried about him. He had friends on the hunger strike. 'He thinking too much. Thinking, thinking, thinking. He get crazy.'

It was my turn for the phone.

I stuck the phone card in and pressed them buttons like I did every day, several times a day. *Binkbinkbinkbink binkbinkbinkbink*. Marlena answered.

'Hello, darl.'

'Stop calling, Zeki. I mean it.'

'Sweet —'

She Who Just Gotta Take Me Back Come Hills or High Water slammed down the receiver in me ear.

I was still working the redial when Azad tapped me on the shoulder. 'Zek, you mind? I have to call my lawyer.'

'No worries.' I sighed. 'All yours, mate.'

Azad patted me on the back like I was a good dog instead of the bad dog what I knew I was really.

I leaned up against the wall a the laundry and had a smoke, feeling sorry for meself. I was disconnected from the life like a telephone what hadn't got its bills paid. I tried to picture Marlena's face what was only eyes and fading away like some a Mum and Dad's photos a the Old Country. It wasn't just Marlena. All a me life on the Outside was slipping away.

'What do you mean?' Azad's voice caught me attention cuz it was loud. That was unusual with Azad, what is normally very soft-spoken like me aunt Elma, except me aunt Elma only been that way since she had them noodles removed from her vocal cords. 'When did this . . .' His face tightened up, like a fist. 'So what now?' The person what he was talking to jabbered in his ear for a few more minutes while Azad ate his lower lip. 'Okay, okay. I speak to you soon.' He hanged up and kicked the grass, what went flying up in a clomp. The Chinese guy behind him pounced on the phone like a cat on a rat.

'What's happening, bruvva?'

'I can't believe this.'

'What?'

'The barrister forgot to file some of my papers for court. The deadline passed. I'm stuffed, as they say here. How could he do that to me?'

'Muvvafucker!' I didn't say 'pardon me French' out loud cuz I was talking to another bloke. I lowered me voice and gave him a look a signification. 'Want me to get one a me old mates to pay your barrister a visit?'

Azad looked at me like he didn't know what I be getting at.

'You know, give him the old what-for. Make sure he doesn't forget next time?' I left-jabbed and right-hooked the air.

'No, no, no, Zek. Don't do that.' He looked at me like I farted or something.

I shrugged. 'Whatever. But if you change your mind . . .'

Azad put his head in his hands and, with his back against the wall, slid down to sit on the ground. I did the same except me own hands was cross me chest. We sat next to each other thinking about our own troubles, though I thought about Azad's troubles as well cuz I be sick a me own.

'You know, Zek, I was so innocent. I thought, only I reach this country, I can find justice, peace and protection.'

'That's what me mate be in — protection,' I go, but Azad didn't seem to be listening. He did take a ciggie, though.

He put his head in his hands again. I smoked me ciggie down to the butt and lit up another one. Azad took a second one from me and did the same.

'I've reached my limit,' he goes, real soft and then coughed for a while cuz he was only just getting used to smoking again.

'I know what you mean, bro,' I said and it was true. Even I was getting depressed and dark and untalkable. I what was naturally a bulient, what April told me be a word for a cheerful person. That made me realise she hadn't been back to visit for a while. 'April should be coming to see us again soon, eh.' Azad raised one corner of his mouth and jerked his head up, like maybe that way he'd get his lips to come down in a smile. It didn't work. 'Maybe she'll even bring her daughter with her next time.' Something like a smile lit up his face for half a second. I elbowed him in the ribs.

'Cut it out,' he said.

'Don't know about you,' I go, 'but women what have handcuffs on always does it for me.'

Azad almost laughed.

The sound of running footsteps made us look up. It was Hamid. He looked spun out, like he be at the end of his wash cycle.

'What's up, bro?' I asked.

'The hunger strike in Woomera,' he goes. 'They're sewing their lips together.' Me and Azad stood up. Hamid named some asylums what they both knew from Port Hedland. One guy what been in Detention four years swallowed painkillers and shampoo to try to top himself. They put him in hospital in Adelaide. He wasn't feeling too good and was apparently pissing streams a bubbles.

'At least his pubes'll be clean and shiny,' I go, but it was kinda lame for a joke what no one was in the mood for. So I didn't take it personal when they didn't laugh.

'They have to listen to us now,' Hamid goes. 'They have to give us visas.'

Me mobile vibrated in me pocket. There wasn't no blues in sight, so I sneaked a look at the number as I pressed the button, hoping it be Marlena. 'It's April,' I go. 'She must a heard me saying her name. I'm going back to me room to take the call. You guys wanna come and have a word with her?' They waved me off like they didn't even hear the question.

Nine

'Zek,' April goes, 'have you heard the news? About the lip-sewing?'

'Yeah. How are you, anyway?'

'Terrible. I can't think of anything but asylum seekers.'

'And me, of course.'

'Ha. Of course. But seriously, it's like . . . I'm not even living my life any more? I don't enjoy anything I used to. I've only played tennis twice in the last month. I can't focus on my work. I haven't . . . haven't even had a single Me Day. I go to dinner parties and all I can talk about is refugees? Even when I see people rolling their eyes? I'm having trouble sleeping, too. When I do sleep, I have this recurring dream. It starts out normally. Then suddenly something forces my mouth open and all this razor wire comes coiling out. I can't stop it. I can't breathe. It hurts. It's horrible. I wake up sweating, knowing it was a nightmare but convinced I'm in Villawood.'

'Me too. Then I look around and I really is.'

'I shouldn't . . . you know, I walked to the post office today to buy a stamp for a letter? I had forty-five cents exactly in my pocket. They told me that stamps had gone up to fifty cents. I burst out in tears. I was so embarrassed.'

A silence came up and sat between us, like Marlena's mum when we was younger and sitting on the sofa at them house.

'My problems must seem stupid and small to you,' she said.

They did, sometimes, I had to admit, specially when they was about crying over the price a stamps, or being boring at dinner parties or not having no Me Days, but I knew it wasn't really fair to say so. 'No, no, not at all. Everyone's problems are as big as them heads.' What is the truth.

'I'm sorry. Really, I called to ask about Azad . . . and Hamid and Thomas of course. They're not on the hunger strike, are they?'

'Nah. They're okay. When are you coming to visit?'

'Soon. I want to have some better news for Thomas first. I don't know when that'll be. I called Josh and apologised. He's coming over tomorrow. But I've got to go softly, softly. He said the whole issue of refugees gives him a headache.'

'He's a doctor,' I said. 'If he gets a headache, he can give himself a pill.' I searched in me stash for jelly snakes, what could be eaten on the phone without making any noise, unlike chips and biscuits, what get in people's ears.

'Ha. He also went on about how his relationship with the Minister was a professional one, and why it would be inappropriate for him to try to intervene in a case. I pointed out they were also friends who played golf and had philately in common too. They even go to Philately Society meetings together.'

I nearly choked on me jelly snake. I was horrorfied. 'You mean what does boys?'

'Sorry?'

Maybe she didn't know. 'Them meetings.'

'Yeah, philatelists, how boring would that be? A bunch of grown men getting together to talk about their stamp collections. Honestly.'

If that's what he told her, I spose it wasn't my place to say nuffin, but I reckoned she was definitely better off without a husband like that. I met too many a that sort in prison. Maybe if people knew that about the Minister they really would lock him up.

I flicked me tongue at the head a the jelly snake. 'How's Marley?'

'She's down in Tasmania saving the forests? She said . . . she said she was in touch with Azad . . . I don't know. She's got a different cause every week? Last year she was going to devote her life to organic farming. A few months ago she was going to become a deejay and rave organiser. It's easy to go on a protest, to demonstrate. But getting involved with asylum seekers requires real commitment. Azad is good-looking. He really is. But that's not the point.'

I was picking up on some subtextuals here.

'April, can I ask you something?'

'Yes, sure.'

'Do you reckon you'd be pushing harder on Josh if it was Azad you was trying to help and not Thomas?'

'What . . . oh, gee, Zeki. What are you saying?'

'I wasn't saying nuffin. I just be asking.'

There was a pausation. 'Of course not . . . no . . . not at all.'

After we hung up, I took the rest a me jelly snakes to find Azad and Hamid. When I got to the door of Hamid's room, I could hear Azad arguing with Hamid. 'Do you understand?' he said in a voice what was fully stressated. 'This country doesn't care if you live or die.' The door was open a crack. I peeked in.

Hamid was sitting on the bed with his skinny arms crossed over his chest. He was staring at a poster a the Great Barrier Reef what visitors gave him and what was on his wall. Azad was pacing up and down. 'It is not worth dying for something that doesn't care!'

'Yo,' I said, pushing the door open and coming in. 'What's going down?'

Hamid's green eyes kept staring at the wall. A fish what had yellow stripes and polka dots on stared back.

'Hamid is going on a hunger strike,' Azad said.

Ten

'Josh has agreed to think about it.' April gave Thomas a little smile, what he took his time giving back. 'I'll be speaking with him again tonight.'

'Thank you.'

On a count a Hamid hunger striking, he and Azad, what was looking after him, didn't come to Visits. 'I miss them,' April said, looking hard at the gate like she could vigilise them out. 'It feels really wrong to me, being here and not seeing them?'

Thomas frowned. 'It's not about you,' he said.

A big tear welled in her eye. I felt sorry for her then. She meaned well. And I knew it wasn't that easy for her neither.

She brung us some crystals that day what was sposed to crease our luck and help us chill. She gave Thomas one what was clear and me one what was pink. I asked her if I could have a blue one instead cuz I didn't want no one thinking I be a poofter, but she said it didn't work like that.

The good thing is that you're sposed to keep them in your pocket, so no one has to see them. She gave me ones for Azad and Hamid and Angel, and for Farshid and Reza too.

After April left, I went back into the compound to deliver the others' crystals. She'd said to send them kisses and hugs and love too. I reckoned I could get away with just handing over the rocks.

Farshid and Reza were on the path in front of their building, arguing with their mum. Nassrin was holding onto Reza's arm like it was a cricket bat.

'You can't stop us,' Reza said in English, jerking his arm free.

She was speaking them language, but you could tell she be pleading with them about something.

'Vy'd you bring us to this shit country?' Farshid shouted.

'Yeah,' Reza accused, his voice breaking into high bits and low bits. 'Ve're your kids. You let them treat us like animals.'

'Can't go to school.'

'Can't do anything.'

Nadia hurried over on her little feet. 'Hellooo. Anything you'd like to talk about, boys?'

'Fuck off,' Reza said.

'Reza! Apologise to Nadia.' Nassrin's cheeks was flushed.

Reza didn't say nuffin. Nassrin turned to Nadia. 'I'm sorry.'

'That's okaaaay,' Nadia said. 'I understand.'

'No, you don't,' Reza snapped like a rubber band. 'You can't understand, you stupid old bag. You go home every night to your own home. You have days off. You can't possibly understand vat we feel locked up in this shit place all day, all night for our whole lives.'

'Now, now, that's not fair, Reza.'

'Fair?' he screeched, his voice cracking. 'You talk about fair?'

Farshid kicked the ground. 'C'mon,' he said to Reza. The two of them stormed over to Hamid and Azad's flat.

Nassrin sat down hard on the ground, holding her big stomach. Nadia pursed her lips. 'How are *you* feeling, Nassrin?'

Nassrin gave her a look what said if she didn't know by then, she'd never know.

Nadia tried to smile but you could see she was feeling the stressation. 'I'm here if you want to talk,' she said. Nassrin stared at the ground and nodded.

After Nadia left, Nassrin pressed her palms into her eyes. 'You okay, Nassrin?' I asked. It was like she didn't even hear me.

Hamid was lying on his bed and Azad was slumped up against it. Hamid's lips was chapped and his eyes dull. His hair looked like it be painted matte instead of gloss, what it usually be. He was skinny again. He looked like one a them models for Bennelong clothes, what are from all different races and what are sometimes fucked up from war and shit too. I seen the ads in Marlena's fashion magazines and I reckon it be one sick muvvafucker what thought them up, pardon me French.

When they worked out what Farshid and Reza was there

for, Hamid sat up and put his face in his hands and Azad shook his head.

'It's not for kids,' Azad said.

'Ve aren't kids any more,' Farshid replied. 'Ve haven't been kids for a long time.'

'Yeah,' said Reza. 'Ve're prisoners.'

No one said nuffin for a long while.

'I got some crystals for you,' I go, opening me hands to show them. 'From April.'

They all looked at me like I'd just stepped outta me flying saucer.

I was fully stressed by the time I got back to me room. Sitting down on me bed, I scrounged in me pockets for a lolly. I sucked on that crystal for ages before I realised what it was and spat it out.

Eleven

'She still not taking your calls?'

'Oh, mate. Me dad always told me that in the Old Country they say, where there's beauty, there's strife. But it's been three weeks. If I could only just see her . . . It's fuh . . . torture being locked up. I can't just go round to her house with flowers or chocolates like in the past when I stuffed up.'

Anna's eyebrows, what were pale, lifted up like they be wings. 'So. This isn't the first time.'

'I'm a man. We got our needs what sometimes aren't our wants, what are to be good. But I seen the arrow of me ways, and it be sticking in me heart. And I haven't been unfaithful since Ching neither.'

Anna shot me a funny look and smiled that lopsided grin a hers, like she knew some secret. Maaan. This place be too small for secrets, I knew that, but some things oughta stay private. I wondered who told her. It wasn't even on her shift. Besides, that was fucken embarrassing —

pardon me French. I'll explain, but I don't want it going no further, so don't tell no one. The whole world don't need to know everything.

Over a week ago, before the hunger strike began, they brung in this chick from Thailand. A working girl, if you get my meaning. She was a babe. She had curly brown hair and big brown eyes and lips what be made for wrapping round stuff. She wore a short skirt low on her hips. Her legs were kinda muscly, but thin. She wore them platform shoes what She Who never wears cuz she be afraid a falling over in them. All of a sudden, the male detainees be shaving and shampooing and putting on them best clothes and swarming round her like flies, except she wasn't swatting them away. I reckoned I had Buckley's. Then for some reason everyone just gave up, and Clarence, what usually be such a muvvafucker, came up to me with a smile on his mug.

'She likes you, Togan,' he goes. 'Don't ask me why. But she's asking for you. She says she don't want no one else.'

'I knew she be a woman a taste,' I said.

'Clearly,' he goes.

So I spruced meself up real good. I put product in me hair, spritzed me pits, clasped on the gold chains, and put on me cleanest pair a daks. I soiréed over to where she was hanging out with some a the other girls. She winked at me. 'Hey, big boy,' she goes in this sexy voice what be all husky and cool like one a them sled dogs. We went for a walk, but everyone was watching us like we was TV, so she goes, without no further to-do, 'Let's go to your room.' Just like that. I thought I was in Lady Luck.

Oh maaan. It was the first time I ever got jiggy with a girl what had a bigger dick than me. I couldn't fucken believe it — pardon me French. The second I seen it I told the little poofter to get the fuck outta me crib before I decked him. When I came out a few minutes later, trying to look all suavée like nuffin happened, everyone was laughing. Turns out I was the only one what didn't know. I was so humeliorated. Clarence set me up, the muvvafucker. Just thinking about it makes me ears like whole beetroots what be attached to me head.

If Anna did know, she wasn't pushing on it, what made me relieved with a capital D. I held out me sandwich cremes. 'C'mon. Don't make me eat the whole pack.'

She got up and came over to the doorway. We wasn't allowed inside the Office on a count a the detainee files and other confidentials what be stored there. She picked the top off a one and scraped the cream with her teeth first, like a kid. 'At least you're not on the strike,' she said.

'You teasing me?' I looked down at me stomach and patted it. 'I'm just trying to keep up with Nassrin,' I joked. Nassrin was getting so big everyone was saying she was gonna have twins.

'You're getting close. Just don't go mute on us too.'

'Mate,' I go, 'fat chance a me shutting up.' It wasn't that funny, but. After Farshid and Reza been on the strike a few days, they sewed them lips shut. Maaan, that was gross. Blood everywhere. Their lips swole right up. Nassrin fainted. Finally, the boys agreed to the doctor cutting the stitches off. Hamid finally went off the strike then. Hamid said he wanted to be a doctor to save lives. He said that if he couldn't save himself he at least had a responsibility to them kids. Besides, it was upsetting Angel heaps. Azad, too.

Even though her boys wasn't on the strike no more, Nassrin hadn't spoke a word since. She was walking around like a ghost what be spooking the rest of us. She wouldn't even take calls from her husband over in Port Hedland, what was going spare according to Farshid, what talked to him every day. She and the other women didn't have nuffin to do neither since they took away the sewing machine on a count a the lip sewing what used needles.

'Poor Nassrin,' I go.

'If I had kids like that, I'd be half-mad too,' said Anna. She took another biscuit and sat back down at the desk.

'You can't blame them kids for being frustrated,' I said. 'They been locked up three years already. They just wanna have a normal life.'

'Then they should have stayed in their own country. Or joined the queue to come out here like real refugees.'

'They say the government's lying about that.'

She shrugged. 'All politicians lie. The point is, those boys are troublemakers. I'm not totally unsympathetic. But they act up and it's our necks on the block. The papers get hold of it, the government gets pissed off, and Immigration comes down on us like a load of bricks. You know, we've got to provide medical care, translation services, education, do this, do that. In the end, all DIMIA really cares about is that we stop stuff from happening that brings them bad publicity, like the hunger strike. And the Shit House management just wants to keep the shareholders happy. Whatever goes wrong, it's us, the staff, that get hauled over the coals. We don't have it easy either, you know.'

'Everyone's got them problems, I spose.' I ate another biscuit and mediterrated on this what have some truth. 'But still. You gotta feel for 'em, trapped in here. When I was Farshid's age,' I told Anna, 'they couldn't keep me in me room for one night even. Me dad was always grounding me but I just dove straight out the window. Maaan. Them were the days. Me and me mates, we was always stealing cars and taking 'em for joyrides, using fake IDs to get into the clubs. Later, I got me a fully-worked Val with subwoofers in. We used to race up and down the strip at Bondi, sometimes with the police on our tails. You know, if it weren't for me missus, what I known since Year Ten, I dunno what mighta happened. I coulda turned out pretty bad.' I suddenly remembered two crucial details — one, I didn't turn out too good in factuality, and two, me missus was me missus no longer, even if I had trouble believing it.

'What's wrong?' Her eyes was boring straight into me own like they had drill bits on.

'Nuffin. Must be something, a piece a biscuit or something . . .' I dug at me eye like I was looking for it. 'You know,' I said, what changed the subject, 'Nassrin was a professor in Iran.'

Anna shrugged like it didn't mean nuffin to her one way or the other.

'In factuality,' I go, thinking about it some more, 'there's a lotta talent in this place. Azad's real smart — he should be in uni.'

'Whatever.'

'Hamid too, he should be in medical school. And you ever seen Thomas's drawings? They're like, like Leonardo de Capria — no, you know, that old Italian dude. And Abeer's dad, Mohammed, he was a top chef. They ran away cuz first an Israeli soldier killed Abeer's little cousin what was carrying a kitten inside his shirt what the soldier thought was a bomb, and then the Israeli army flattened their house cuz they lived next door to someone in Hamas.'

'That's their story, anyway,' Anna said.

'The point is, Mohammed can cook fancy French food just like they do in Paris. And them two Russian chicks? They was croupiers in Vladivostok. And that other Afghani guy what just got his visa, he's a doctor. The Albanian chick what was here before, she could sing like Britney, I swear. And that Scottish visa overstayer what was here a few days last week? Dude was a real-live London deejay. Khalid — the Bedoon — he used to be the concierge in a fancy hotel in Kuwait. That Samoan overstayer, one with the big tattoo what says "Tuff girl", she's like a migration agent. She knows heaps about the law and helps everyone type their affy davids. The tall, skinny Chinese bloke with the taped-up glasses was a defence lawyer in Shanghai what defended someone the government didn't want defended. And Bhajan — he writes *wicked* songs, though they be heaps depressing, all about death and mountains and stuff. They say even crazy Bilal used to run a big company in Iraq before Saddam killed his wife and son. Mate, sometimes I wonder what I'm doing here among such illustrated company.'

Anna had a funny expression on her dial, like she'd gone somewhere without leaving her seat. 'Don't put yourself down, Zeki,' she goes. 'You've got your talents.'

'Well, I don't wanna brag, mate, but I was pretty well known in B 'n' E circles. They haven't made the window I can't get through.'

'Yeah, well, you know why you're here.'

'No, mate,' I protested. 'I've done the time already. I paid me dues. That's double jeopardy.'

'I'm no lawyer,' she goes, looking at her nails now instead a me. They was short and she didn't wear no polish, so there wasn't much to look at, but she took her time. 'Point is,' she goes, 'you all did something wrong or you wouldn't be here.'

I could feel meself getting hot under the collar, except I wasn't wearing one. Just me Snoop Dogg T-shirt and me trackies.

Another blue shoved by me to get into the office. He spoke to Anna in a low voice. I heard them say Angel's name. But I was too busy feeling sorry for meself and kinda righteous too to pay much attention.

'Yeah, well, I'll be seeing youse,' I said and left, what they didn't even notice.

I thought about calling April. But it was getting that depressing talking to her. Last time we spoke I told her she gotta try and enjoy her life cuz she got one in factuality, and she should leave the nightmares to us what is living them. She busted out in tears. Then she fessed up to her crush on Azad. She said she felt really stupid about it, and hoped he hadn't noticed — what I insured her he hadn't, cuz as far as I could tell he didn't notice nuffin having to do with chicks. That made her upset too, and she said something about women her age being invisible. I said I never noticed — but then again, I wouldn't if they was invisible. 'Oh, you make me laugh, Zeki,' she said.

Whatever.

Twelve

I thought I'd go see what Azad and them were up to. As I left the office, Tip came racing round the corner shouting into his walkie-talkie. From the other direction this Korean bloke, Kim, shot out onto the path followed by a pack a Chinamen. Noor was wandering round like she did every night looking for some mum to sleep with, cuz they still hadn't brung her own mum to Villawood like they said they would. I scooped her up so she wouldn't be run over. She was shaking all over, and buried her messy little head on me shoulder. That's when I noticed some a them Chinese had forks and knives in their hands. I thought they ate with chopsticks. But I didn't think they was rushing to dinner. One a them shouted in English that they was gonna kill the Korean if he didn't pay up. Just then the Korean tripped and fell on his face. The Chinamen was about to leap on top a him when Tip threw himself on the guy first. The Chinese knew they'd have to fight Tip to get to the Korean. They'd get into too much trouble if they did that, so they turned and peeled off, swearing under their breath '*tomato, tomato*', what one a them once told me means 'fuck your mother' in them language — pardon me Chinese. Tip stood up and pulled Kim to his feet what immediately bowed, thanking him for saving his life. Tip just told him to go easy on the gambling.

Kim hobbled over to Medical to get some sticking plasters for the cuts on his knees and hands. I put Noor down and she ran off towards the room what is for Abeer and her family. 'Thanks for looking after Noor, bro,' said Tip.

'No worries. Didn't want her to end up in the sweet and sour.'

He handed me a ciggie. Tip was a good man.

'Pity about Kim's nose, eh?' I said.

'What d'ya mean?'

'Got flattened.'

Tip rolled his eyes. 'You're bad, Zeki.' We weren't even halfway through our smokes when this cat-a-wailing began. Tip and I looked over to see this little Nepalese dude, an asylum what mostly kept to himself, curled up in a ball, sobbing and hitting his head against the paving. Tip chucked his ciggie on the ground and rushed off to get someone from Medical. An old Iraqi man hurried over and scooped up the butt, put it out by pinching it, stuck it in his shirt pocket and scurried off. The whole place was a fucken looney bin, pardon me French. At that minute, I felt that if I stayed in one more day I was gonna lose it meself big time.

But what were me chances a getting out now? I'd been devotioning a lotta thought to the problem. I had nine days left to organise me appeal. At first I'd thought a defending meself. But you gotta prove the AAT made a mistake a law. I knew lots about the wrong side a the law. Ask me anything about that. But I didn't know much about the right side. As for getting another lawyer, I learned that the free ones was just for asylums and chicks like Angel. What was fair enough, I spose, even if it didn't help me much. No one but them lawyers what charged lotsa money like Gubba was interested in helping five-oh-ones. The two and a half grand I had in me video wouldn't buy much a their time. And I owed Gubba four times that, what got me over a barrel like a poofter in a keg room. I'd have asked me brother Attila for help but he had a mortgage and kids, the full catastrophe, so he was bloody useless. Mum wanted to ask me uncle Baris if he could come up with the cash but I told her to forget it. She didn't know about that problem with the bookie over that dog what me mate swore was gonna pike. I already owed Baris about ten grand.

On the other hand, if the government thought they was gonna get away with deporting me to the Old Country, what wasn't my country like Australia was my country, they had another thing coming. I'd deport meself first — right over that fucken fence.

That's when it occurred to me.

The thing what was the thing what I hated the most, what scratched me eyeballs, what broke me world in half, what turned everybody and everything into In and Out, that might just be the thing what was me way out.

I went to me room. I had some thinking to do, and while I was at it I counted me money again. It weren't enough for

Gubba, but there are people what cost less than lawyers. Survival Rule Four: Know that there ain't no one what doesn't have his price.

I found some paper and made a list:

$

cutters

allies

I put a tick next to $ and thought about items two and three. Another of me best treats besides being a good listener is me ability to make mates and allies, though She Who don't always think this be one a me best treats cuz it sometimes get me into trouble when I make mates and allies what aren't from respectable people. This was different, but. Even if the government and the media always be dissing them like they was some disease what this whole country caught, the asylums was respectable people. Me time in here learned me that. Besides, you is born alone and you die alone, but it's fucken near impossible — pardon me French — to escape alone.

Thirteen

When I got to Azad's room, they was all there — Azad, Hamid and Thomas. Hamid was looking worser than usual and the others weren't too jolly neither. Hamid was rubbing his arms like he wanted to wipe the skin clear off. Azad was flicking his lighter and Thomas was digging his toes into the floor.

'Bastards,' said Hamid, what don't usually swear.

'They caught Angel in Hamid's room earlier,' Azad explained. 'They sent her back to Lima, and won't even let her come into Stage Two to be with Hamid any more.'

'My body is still weak from hunger strike. She just looking after me.' Like Azad, Hamid's a real gentleman. He never told us about him and Angel doing the thang, what we knew anyway cuz this place be too small for secrets.

'Shit, eh?' I go.

'What do I have to live for?' Hamid goes. 'When Taliban kill, at least they do it fast. Here, they kill us little bit each day, we die drop by drop. Why they separate us? Angel needs me. And I need her. It be different if she were Outside, if they gave her Bridging Visa. I'd be happy for her then. But she is Inside. Why can't we be together?' Hamid put his head in his hands and wept like a girl. I stood there, humeliorated for him and angry too, me hands in me pockets.

There was a knock on the door. This Sudanese dude popped his head in. 'Hear about Chaim?' Chaim was the Israeli bloke what got deported.

We shook our heads.

'You know that bus in Tel Aviv that got blown up?' It had been on the news. 'He was on it.'

'Dead?' Azad asked. His voice was shaking.

'Critical. Lost one arm. Burns and cuts everywhere. They don't know if he's going to survive. If he does, he'll be blind. The blast blew his eyes clear out of his sockets.'

I thought about Chaim's eyes, what was green. I thought about them not being in his head. I wanted to puke.

'How'd you hear?' Somehow even Thomas was looking pale, I swear.

'Abdullah.' Abdullah was a Palestinian nurse what was born in Israel and had an Israeli passport, what they called an Israeli Arab. He overstayed his visa and was in Detention for about three weeks at the same time Chaim was here. 'Abdullah was working at the hospital in Tel Aviv when they brought him in. He recognised him. He just called to tell me.'

Hamid's eyes was going red again. Thomas looked at the corner a the room like he was angry with it and Azad picked up a ruler and slapped it against his wrist like he wanted to break it. I just kept thinking a Chaim's green eyes not being in his head. We didn't even notice the Sudanese guy leave.

'I can't take it any more,' Azad goes after a while.

Thomas nodded, still staring at that corner.

'We've all had a gutful,' I go.

'I need freedom,' said Azad.

'Me too,' Hamid agreed.

'Me too,' Thomas said.

Like I just thought a something, I snapped me fingers. 'I got an idea.'

Fourteen

'But what about Angel? I can't leave without her.' This meant Hamid wasn't going. Even sneaking into Lima Dorm be like sneaking outta Alcatraz. Getting outta Lima — what Angel would have to do to come with — was impossible. 'She is my life.'

'Fair enough,' I said, what I believed to be true even if it didn't exactly suit me own purposes.

'You will never get away with it.' Thomas the Infernal Pessimist. 'Not after what happened six months ago.'

Thomas was talking about this mass escape what was already a legend. The camp mosque, what is in factuality a room for prayer and not a building with domes on, used to be at ground level and near to the fence. When people went to pray, what the strict ones do five times a day, they dug a hole, a little at a time, covering it up with a prayer rug and taking the dirt outside. A friendly guard gave them a map a the works, so they knew where the drainage pipes was.

More than twenty detainees got out through them pipes. Even though they went through the mosque, the escapees wasn't all Muslim. It was an ecological effort, with Christians and others in. There were some they still hadn't caught. Immigration punished the Shit House, fining them for every detainee what escaped. That meant the Shit House was looking sharp to make sure it didn't happen again. They moved the mosque to a room what was upstairs.

'They are watching closely these days,' Azad said, but he sounded interested.

'That's their job, mate. To watch,' I said. 'Ours is to escape. And I got a plan.'

Someone pushed open the door. We froze like peas.

It was only crazy Bilal coming for his coffee. When he left we breathed like we was blowing up balloons.

'So, say we skip,' goes Azad, what said 'skip' instead of 'escape' what is something they all said when they meaned 'escape'. It was part a the Villawood language. 'You need people to help on the Outside.'

'Easy peasie Japonesie. You all know heaps a people what wants to help asylums.' They looked at me like I just farted, what I didn't do in factuality for once. 'Wha?' I opened me hands. 'Wha?'

Thomas screwed up his mouth. 'So you're an asylum seeker now.'

'Nah, nah. I didn't say that. Anyway. How about April?'

'No, you're not asking April.' Thomas shook his head.

'What are you, her father?'

'Fuck off, Zeki. I've finally got a chance at a visa. But it's only because April has got her husband to help me. If she gets involved in something like that, I'm fucked, as you would say. Do what you like, but don't involve her.'

'You know,' Azad said, 'they asked me to sign a paper the other day. For voluntary deportation.'

We stared at him, horrorfied. He hadn't said nuffin about this before.

'But you know what the joke is?'

'What, mate?' I said, hoping it'd be funny. I didn't like me chances.

'They can't do it. See, because Kurds like me, called Fayli, are Shi'a, Saddam says we belong to Iran, but Iran doesn't want us either. No one will take a stateless man.' He flicked his lighter on and off. 'Some lawyers are talking about running a case for people like me — stateless people. That would include Palestinians from Gaza, and Bedoons from Kuwait. They say it can't be legal to keep us in Detention indefinitely. They say they can argue on the basis of something called habeas corpus. But it could take a long time. Who knows if they'll win. If they don't . . . I can't stand the thought of living inside a cage for the rest of my life. I'd kill myself first.' For some reason, I thought about all them feathers what Azad be collecting.

'Bruvva,' I said. 'So you're in?' Everyone was looking at Azad now.

'I don't know, Zek. I want real freedom. Papers. The right to work. Study. I feel like I've been running my whole life. I'm tired of running. I should to wait on this court case, this habeas corpus.'

'Looks like you're on your own, Zeki,' Thomas said.

'Fair enough,' I said, feeling da jection, what is da sadness you get when no one wants to play with you.

'But, Zek, good luck, eh?' Hamid said.

Fifteen

There was only one path left if I was gonna skip on me lonesome. The following afternoon, I approached Tip. 'A word in yer shell-like, mate?' I said.

A few minutes later, he came to me room. 'Whassup, Zek?' We did the bruvvas' handshake. 'How you going, bro?'

'Still breathing.' I was saying this now too, what be Villawood for 'good, thanks'.

'You're looking healthy.' He smiled and play-punched me gut.

'You too, mate.' I play-punched his. I gestated for him to sit down and passed over a handful a pistachios.

'Happy Australia Day,' he said, what it was. 'Did you hear? They named Pat Rafter Australian of the Year.'

'Pat Rafter? Tennis player?' I shook me head. 'Mate, I reckon Australian a the Year oughta be someone who plays a real sport — soccer or rugby league.'

'Oath.'

'So. How're the wife and kids?'

'Not bad,' he said, cracking a pistachio. 'Joey's starting Year Nine next year.'

'Smart kid, eh? Takes after him dad, I spose.'

'Flattery'll get you nowhere,' Tip goes. 'He's a smart luttle bugger, though.' He shook his head. 'But of a worry, to tell you the truth. School fees and all being what they are.'

I nodded. This was going better than expectorated. 'What'd be the fees for a good school?' I reached into the slot a me video and pulled out a neat stack a bills. 'One thou? Two thou?' I counted out two and a half. 'Take it, bro. For Joey's education. It's on me. What's a loser like me gonna use it for anyway?'

'Whoa, whoa, Togan.' Tip sat up straight and frowned, swatting the air like the money was flies what be bothering him. 'Let's just prutund I never saw that, okay? What's thus all about anyway?'

'Mate, I'm not gonna beat about the George W. I got a business proposal,' I said.

In the end he promised he'd 'thunk' about it. He said he was rostered off for a few days but he'd give me an answer when he got back. I knew he be a quiet person what didn't like trouble, but he also be a person what needed money — and a need for money could make people change their attitude to trouble.

Sixteen

That Monday was the twenty-eighth a January. I'd been Inside three and a half months. I'd lost me case. I'd lost me girl. I thought there was nuffin else to lose. I was wrong.

After lunch, I looked through me CDs but there wasn't nuffin I felt like listening to. I opened the journal what April gave me, thinking I might try writing a song, but I couldn't think of nuffin to say. Me room felt like a T-shirt what had grown tight and uncomfortable, what you had to take off even if people could see your man-boobs, what isn't a good look but was what I was getting in factuality.

I reminded meself a me Survival Rule Number One, what is that when times is tough and you can do bugger all about it, the best thing to do is to kick back.

I was feeling so stressed that I couldn't even remember how that worked, I swear.

At one-thirty, when visits started, I got Anna to let me out into the yard even though no one had called me. Not many visitors was in yet. Most a the chairs was still tipped forward over the tables, like they was so done in by the sadness in the place they had to put them heads down.

It was hot as buggery. I watched a Chinese gang, what they brung in the other day, file into the Yard from the Stage Three gate. Tip had told me they shoulda been put in Stage One but there wasn't enough beds. Waiting for them was a pack a visitors, about thirty in all. Funny thing was, both the gang members and them visitors was all wearing black T-shirts and black jeans. It seemed strange given the heat. And it made the Yard look like the set a one a them kung fu gangster flicks what has Chow Yun-Fat in. They had chicks with them too.

Angel and Hamid was already out and sitting with Sue, what was going through some papers with them, so I didn't wanna interrupt. I looked around for some detraction, and spotted Edward, another five-oh-one and a Leb what I met first when we was both doing time. He'd been brought into Villawood about two weeks earlier. His woman was visiting. She was sitting on his lap and they was doing big sloppy tongueys, what made Najah and some a the other women move their chairs so they didn't have to look. I didn't really wanna look either, cuz it was making me miss She Who something bad. It'd been more than three weeks since she last spoke to me.

I smoked the last ciggie in me pack. There was more in me room. But it was hot and I couldn't be stuffed getting me ID back from the blues, being let through the two locked gates, going to me room and then repeating the whole fucked-up routine to get back in, pardon me French. I thought about getting Bashir to do it in exchange for jelly snakes but he had his little head buried in his mum's lap and wasn't even looking up at a visitor what was waving a toy monkey at him. I never seen a kid so depressed. No one had seen him smile for days. I thought he was catching the depression from his dad, Mohammed, what hadn't come out of the room for a week. Najah looked like she was catching it too. Abeer was the last one standing in that family and she was only eight.

I glanced back at Edward and his woman. They was twined up like rope and she was sucking his face like it be a Chupa Chup. He was facing me and he had him eyes open, what is something you learn in prison, what is never close your eyes around other people. That and always sit with your back to the wall or the fence so no one can stab it when you're not looking.

I mouthed the word 'bruvva' and made the smokes signal to Edward, what took one hand off a his chick's back and pulled a packet a ciggies outta his back pocket, holding them out to me. I took two and winked me thanks at him. His woman never even noticed. She was working up a sweat what made dark circles in the fabrication under her arms. Women what sweat like that are fully sexy.

I thought about getting Edward in on the escape. Then I remembered he'd decided to go back to the Lebanon. His woman was going with him. Lucky him.

I was just stubbing out me second cigarette when this French dude, Jacques, came over. They brung in Jacques the day before. They took him from his office in the city cuz he was two days late renewing his work visa. He was wearing his suit and tie when they brung him in and he was still wearing it now. He sat down and pulled out a packet a them Gally-ose smokes. We'd barely lit up when he started bellyaching.

'I cannot believe I am ere, zees ees a travesty, a vee-o-lah-see-own of ooman rights, zees place ees a sheet–ole, *regards* ze razorwire, zees ole place ees a ooman rights problem.' Kvetch kvetch kvetch, what be a Jewish word for complain what April learned me. While he spoke, he blew air out of his lips, what he stuck out a lot, and he waved him hands round like he be from the Middle East. 'I am Franch!' he said like it be written with an A instead of an E what even I know is the right spelling. 'Franch! I am a citizen of France! I don't dees-erve to be ere!'

'Who fucken does, mate? Pardon me French,' I said, feeling grumpy.

'Pardon me . . . par-*done*?' He looked puzzled, like he be made up a five hundred pieces what hadn't been put together yet.

I explained how 'pardon me French' was just a trigger a speech. 'What do youse say in France when you swear in front a people and you wanna apologise for it, but not so much that you have to stop doing it?' He got even more confused then.

'Par-*done*?'

Fuck, maaan. I was just trying to be a conversationalist what passed the time. Eventually some people came into Visits from the *Franch* embassy and he went over to talk to them, what blew out more air and stuck out them lips, and waved them hands around a lot too. I reckoned he'd be outta Villawood in two days max.

After his woman left, Edward came over. He told me some news what got the hairs on the back a me neck doing a Mexican wave. Hadeon, the Hatchet — the meanest bastard I ever met in any prison, the muvvafucker I told you about what got that fella in the workshop in the back a the melon with a screwdriver — had been taken from the supermax at Goulburn to Stage One. They wanted to deport him back to the Ukraine, what was not far enough, but he was fighting the deportation. Thanks God, Stage One was separated from this place by two sets a double fences and gates and a road.

Apart from everything else, I was pretty sure he eventually figured out it was me what stole his drugs that time.

We was detracted by the appearance a Conchita, a South American babe what they brung in five days ago for overstaying her visa. Conchita was small and dark and pretty what everyone liked. Of all the guys she coulda chose to get with Inside, she got with crazy Bilal, what was so happy he forgot all about the coffee for two whole days. Now she was approaching the gate from the compound. She wore a red mini-dress and make-up and a big grin what be splitting her face like a slice a watermelon, except the juicy red bits was her lips what be on the outside. She pulled a suitcase with wheels what made a sound like thunder on the pitted concrete. Bilal followed, hauling another one of her suitcases. It looked like it be stuffed with bricks, or maybe it was just him what was heavy. He looked like all his Christmases had come at once and now was going away again. When she got to the gate what connects with the passage to Property and then Out, she sang

'I'm getting out! I'm getting out!' in her cute Spanish accent, and did a little dance. When the blue opened the gate for her, she was so excited she almost forgot to give Bilal a kiss goodbye and take her suitcase from him. About fifteen minutes later, we could see her walking down the exit road outside the fence with some Latino guy what was carrying her suitcases. She waved and jumped up and down and yelled, '*Buena suerta*, everybody! I'll miss you all!' We knew she wouldn't really.

'*Hasta la vista*, baby,' I said. It means 'catch youse later' in Spanish, what I learned from American movies what have Mexicans in.

'Fuck her,' Edward said, but not loud like she could hear. 'Fuck 'em all.' Then he went inside, tossing me another couple a ciggies first. I thought about how the ones what get Out after they been In for years and years never danced like Conchita did.

Bilal stood staring at the fence for a long time, but he didn't come into the Yard. I reckoned we'd be seeing him on his coffee rounds again that night. I was right.

At seven, the blues was getting everyone to leave. The Chinese gang and them mates all moved to the gate, a solid mass a black hair and black T-shirts. Some a the chicks started pashing gang members right in front a the gate. No one else could get past. Sue was looking at her watch and some a the other visitors was saying 'Excuse me, excuse me', but it was like them Chinamen's ears was painted on. They was blocking the road what good dogs don't do, and that be a Chinese proverbial what Ching learned me. The blue at the gate was clapping his hands and snapping his fingers at them.

Something about it got me criminal instincts going. Finally, the chicks let go a their men and went through with the others. When the last a the gang's visitors fronted up at the gate, he wasn't wearing his wristband. The stooge said he lost it, what was bullshit, and the guards knew it. In a spit they was ringing the alarms and running round, but by that time the gang leader was long gone. One a the blues what was himself a Chinaman told me that none a the officers twigged cuz they all looked alike. Fuck, maaan, I wish I all looked alike.

Par-*done* me Australian.

Two more days went by. Tip was nowhere to be seen. A blue what be a mate a Tip's came on duty. 'Seen Tip, mate?' I asked, all casual like it didn't matter much one way or the other.

'He's gone, mate,' he told me, and made his hand like a plane taking off.

I didn't wanna be hearing this. 'What d'ya talking about, mate?'

'They transferred him to Woomera. What with the hunger strike and all the shit going down over there, they needed reinforcements. He put his hand up. Said the hardship pay would help with his kids' school fees. Good man, Tip. We'll all miss him.'

He could say that again.

Seventeen

Feeling lower than a dachshund's balls, I dialled Marlena's number that evening outta habit more than hope. No answer. She mighta been at work, what was cool, but she mighta been out with some bloke, a friend a Pink-nuts maybe, what might be taller than me and better looking and have a steady job and smaller ears and maybe never even been Inside, but what could never give her sweet loving the way I did. Muvvafucker.

I played a game a poker with a new Bangladeshi dude and two Russians. I cleaned up and I hardly even cheated, I swear. I packed me winnings into the sock in the video player. I had a fresh stock a ciggies thanks to an old mate on the Outside what owed me a favour and brung me a couple a cartons the other day. I flogged some smokes to a new guy what told me he was from Innonesia. 'Where you from in Innonesia?' I asked, not cuz I been there or nuffin but I heard lots about Bali, what apparently be a good place to party.

'Aceh.'

'Bless you,' I said, even though it wasn't much of a sneeze. I asked him again about where he came from but he just shook his head and walked off. People can be so weird sometimes and they just get weirder when you lock them up, I swear.

I hung out in me room smoking a joint what Edward gave me. His woman was a real pro at getting the stuff in. I put on Public Enemy, what I was beginning to think I was, just like the asylums what was always complaining about being villainified in the media. It was past midnight. I didn't have no one to talk to. Ivan got released on a Bridging Visa two days ago. It was too depressing talking to Hamid and Azad, and Thomas was giving me the shits. I figured I'd hunt down some vids. I walked back to the fence with Stage Three and whistled for Edward.

'Whassup, bro?'

'Can't sleep, mate. Watcha got on vid?'

'*Texas Chainsaw Massacre*, *Pearl Harbor* and somefin else . . . *The Mummy Returns*. Want 'em?'

'Oh, mate.' I gave him the thumbs up.

'Wait there.'

He came back with the vids. Swinging one arm right back, he chucked *Pearl Harbor* straight over both fences to where I caught it. Not everyone throws that good. High up on the fence there was one shoe dangling by its laces, a baseball cap and a plastic bag snagged on the razor wire with some roast chicken in, what was beginning to smell. Then Edward let fly with *The Mummy Returns*. They shoulda had the Detention Double Fence Throw in the Sydney Olympics, I swear. He'd a been a gold medallionist for sure.

I was thinking we got a trifecta when *Texas Chainsaw Massacre* fell just short a the fence on my side and a blue appeared behind him.

I ducked behind a tree. Edward was shrugging like he didn't know nuffin. Good man. After the blue wandered off, I got me a broom from the laundry. Lying flat on the ground like a lizard what be drinking, I managed to extradite it by pushing it along the ground with the broom handle.

I was getting to me feet and brushing the dirt off me trackies when me heart stopped. Hadeon, the muvvafucker, was standing there on the Stage Three side, smoking and looking at me with them cold, dirty-ice eyes. He waved. His wrist had a tattoo like a bracelet a skulls on. They should never a moved him to Stage Three even. The man was an animal. 'Nice to see you, Bogan,' he goes, showing me every one a them skulls.

'Togan to youse,' I go, pretending to be tougher than I was in factuality. 'Nice to see youse too, Hatchet. Catch youse later.'

First Clarence, now him. Me past was tailgating me present. It was time to put the pedal to the metal.

I was heading back to me room, me head filled with thoughts about the highway to hell what I be on and where the exit be, when Angel whispered me name from the fence between Stage Two and Lima. 'Zek. Zeki.'

'Hey, Angel.'

'Zeki, please. Can you help me?'

'No worries, Angel. What's up?' I was thinking she wanted me to get Hamid to the fence to talk.

She looked around to make sure no one was watching and gestated like she was putting a needle in her arm.

'Whoa, whoa, you know I don't touch that shit. Besides, Hamid would have me balls for breakfast if I did that. You know that.'

'You know people, Zeki,' she said like she didn't hear nuffin I was saying. 'You get it for me. Please.'

A noise made me jump. 'What's goin' on 'ere?'

I turned to see Clarence's ugly mug what was in me own.

'Muvvafucker,' I go.

'Yeah, so? She loved it, your mum did. Moaned like a right ho.'

I saw red for a second. Like a kung fu master, like I was Jet Li or him cousin Bruce, like I was Zek Li, I smashed Clarence hard on the cheekbone with the corner a the *Texas Chainsaw Massacre.* Then I whacked him up the family jewels with *Pearl Harbor* and *The Mummy Returns*. I got him on his ugly knees with me hands round his thick neck. He was begging for mercy with them creepy girl's eyes.

That was all happening in me head, anyway. In factuality the joint I smoked earlier in me room had just kicked in. I realised I was just waving the videos at Clarence, what was pissing himself laughing and calling me a fuckwit.

I mighta been stoned but I got dignity. I turned and walked away.

Clarence headed up the walkway what passes by Medical and up towards Stage Three. That's when I realised how Hadeon got himself transferred outta Stage One when he be exactly the sort a person you need maximum security from. They was old friends, mates what was always doing favours.

Two days later, Clarence got him moved to Stage Two.

Eighteen

Farshid was in me room. He had his guitar. We was listening to the Eagles and singing along to 'Hotel California'. He put it on for the third time. We got to the bit about checking in any time you want, but never being able to leave.

'Just like us,' said Farshid.

'That's it, Farsh,' I go. 'That's what makes it worse than prison, and you know I speak with authority about prisons.'

'I should do something to get myself into prison,' he said darkly. Farshid wasn't in a top mood. The night before, Reza started pulling out his hair in clumps. Then he ate it, and then he vomited it up like furballs. Reza eating his own hair, what was gross as well as crazy, really flipped everyone out. The Shit House hauled him off in the middle a the night to some hospital what has a loony bin what is for children too. They told Nassrin she could visit Reza in hospital. But they wanted to put her in handcuffs. Everyone argued with them — it was too humeliorating and she wasn't gonna run nowhere with one son in the looney bin, the other in Villawood, and her husband still in Port Hedland. In the end they listened to Nadia the psych what said it would send Reza right off the deep end to see his mum in cuffs. We gave her heaps, but Nadia was all right, really.

I gave Farshid a ciggie for free.

The Eagles sang about how you could find them there any time a year.

'Fuck this shit,' Farshid said. 'I'm sick of it. Sick of it. Sick of it.'

I hit the eject button on the CD player.

'I got the new Eminem.'

'I don't mean the music. This shit.' Farshid swept his hand through the air. 'Villawood. Detention. I vant to be out. I vant to go to school. I vant to have a life. Detention is the opposite of life. Fuck this place and fuck everyvun in it.'

It occurred to me that I might still be able to buy some wire cutters with that two thou. Farshid would probably say yes to escaping. I could go back to me original plan. All I needed was two people in, besides two to keep a lookout. Farshid would be good. He was fast and strong and smart and young, only sixteen.

And he had a girlfriend now, what he'd be pretty keen to see outside the razor wire. Laura was from Chile. Her mum was being deported. Laura was fifteen and a babe, but she wasn't Inside cuz she and her brother had been in Australia long enough to get citizenship. Their little sisters, what were three and seven and nine and what were being deported with their mum, were Inside. The little ones was wetting them pants all the time with the stressation. Laura visited every day after school, and she and Farshid, they was spending a lotta time behind a particulate tree in the Visiting Yard what offered the only semi-privacy in the whole place, even though what was private to the rest a the Yard was open to the street beyond the fence. Plus they talked on the phone every night for hours.

'Vat're you looking at me like that for?'

'Mate, I was just thinking . . .' It then occurred to me that having him in on the escape meant I be abdicating a minor. And even if it'd make Laura one happy girl, it'd detonate Nassrin. I may have been a crim, but I had me family values. I couldn't do it. 'Nuffin,' I said. I gave him another smoke. He stuck it in his mouth, lit it, and attacked the strings on his guitar like they was something he wanted to hurt.

It took us a while to notice someone banging on the door. 'Farshid! You in there?' It was Tip's mate, that other Maori dude. 'Hey, Zek. Hey, Farshid. Yer ears painted on? They been calling both your names for half an hour. You got vusutors.'

Farshid looked at his watch. Laura would still be in school. 'Fuck visitors.'

The blue threw up his hands like it didn't mean nuffin to him one way or the nuther. 'I've seen her, though. She's a babe, bro.'

'Fuck visitors.'

'Total babe,' he goes. 'I'm talking ten outta ten?'

'Fuck visitors.'

'Up to you, bro.'

As soon as he was out the door, Farshid and I did a high-five. He went back to his room to change his shirt. I combed me hair and put in some product and changed into me Adidas shell suit, the black one with the blue trim. We wasn't really that interested. Just bored. Bored was the name a the game in that place, what I spose made it a bored game. What was a joke, what I wasn't making too many of at the time.

Nineteen

We saw her through the fence. She was seated on a chair. Her hair was long and curly and shiny. Every time it fell in front a her face, what was a lotta times, she threw it back with a move what stretched out her smooth, milky neck, what was long even when she wasn't stretching it. She wore one a them midriff tops and hipster jeans what revealed a lotta information, all good. Her tits was big and bouncy like her mum's, except perkier, what she was too. It was Marley, April's daughter, the handcuff protester babe. Azad was sitting facing her, his elbows on his knees and his head pulled forward like she had a rope through his nose. His face had a loopy smile on.

'So, Azad is a human being after all,' Farshid observed while we waited for the blue to let us through the gate.

April was there too. Thomas was talking in her ear, and she was nodding, but her eyes kept drifting to Azad and Marley.

'At least it looks like Azad's snapped outta his depression.' Azad hadn't come out for visits or even to meals in two days. Not since George W Bush, what is the most powerful man in the world and what our own Prime Minister be the deputy of, called Iraq and Iran part a the Axle of Evil, what meant they were the exact part a the Car of Evil what makes the wheels turn round. Azad hated Saddam but he didn't want to see the country bombed to buggery by the Yanks like Afghanistan. Even though he kinda foresaw it all on September Eleven, it still upset him.

The blue finally found the right key and the first padlock clunked open. In the short time we'd been waiting, a small crowd a male detainees had pulled up chairs and joined Marley's circle. More was collecting behind us.

Farshid made a face at me. 'Know vat's wrong with this place? Too little honey and too many bears.'

'Zeki! Farshid!' April gave us hugs and kisses. 'This is my daughter, Marley.'

Marley stood up to kiss us hello too. She smelled nice, like lemons and cinnamon with a faint pong a girl sweat, what is nicer than boy sweat. 'We were just talking about poetry,' she said. She looked at Azad again. 'Do you know Rumi?'

'I do,' said Azad, like he be tying the knot then and there. April bit her lip and I felt sorry for her.

'He vas Iranian poet,' Farshid said. 'From my country.'

'Poetry belongs to no country,' Azad said. 'It belongs to the world.'

'That's *so* true,' Marley said. She talked about all this stuff what I didn't know much about. I never heard anyone talk as fast as her. It was like she was filling in all the gaps what be in her mum's sentences and then some. She was a machine gun shooting out the syllabuses. Eventually, the subject shifted to her plans for next year. 'I'm gonna be a student at COFA next year, that's the College of Fine Arts, you know, You-En-Ess-Double-You? Doing conceptual art? We'll be, like, doing Chomsky and Klein as well as Barbara Kruger, who's so my hero. I'm trying to get my teeth into Chomsky but it's, like, pretty dense. I don't know if any of you know Chomsky?'

By now there were about twenty detainees, mostly asylums, all male, what had pulled chairs up. They nodded and shook their heads in lotsa different ways what didn't necessarily mean yes or no. Chomsky sounded like some kind a nougat and I wasn't sure what Calvin Kleins had to do with art. I kept me mouth shut in case I said something stupid.

'Your mum is very nice,' the Liberian guy said. It got April's dimples going. 'She comes to see us often. This is your first time to come Inside, Miss Marley?'

'Yeah. I can't believe Mum is doing this, it's so cool, but I'd never have guessed cuz compared to my bio-dad, she's so conservative. Mum probably told you guys I was living in Nimbin with my bio-dad. He's way cool, doesn't mind who I have to stay over, and we even do billies together.' She laughed. Her tits looked like they was making a bid for freedom from that tiny top.

I looked over at April what was making her lips thin. Another visitor came for Thomas, what went to sit with him, so April was fully concentrated on Marley. Then I looked at Azad, cuz I knew he didn't approve a drugs at all. I don't think he'd a understood even if she'd a used the word 'bong' instead of billy, what be Australian slang. He was just smiling like she was handing out choc tops, what in factuality woulda been a good thing in that heat. Maybe he was just listening to the sounds and not the words what I used to do sometimes when She Who be talking about stuff I wasn't interested in much. Marley's voice was pretty and clear like it had bells in, like it be one a them rivers what you see on TV what have wildlife in. Azad was on that river, and he wasn't swimming against the current neither.

She still hadn't stopped talking, what was amazing even for a woman, what talk more than men by nature. 'I'm heaps pissed off at the way this fascist government treats refugees. I've been in lots of marches and protests. But this is the first time I've ever been, like, actually *inside* a detention centre. I wasn't sure they'd let me in but they did and . . .' Then, like someone hit her pause button she stopped suddenly and looked round her. '*Fuck!*' Some a the guys exchanged looks what said they couldn't believe a young girl like that would swear, and in front of her mum, too. Azad winced cuz he didn't like it neither, I knew. 'It's terrible. All these gates and fences and razor wire and guards. It's like a concentration camp.'

'Oy. Marley,' said April.

'I know, I know, I know, I shouldn't say that. We're Jewish? Well, I consider myself kinda Hindu-Buddhist actually. But I know the concentration camps were a lot worse. I mean, they tortured and killed people . . .'

'Like your great-grandmother.'

'Like my great-grandmother.'

Everyone's heads be swivelling from one to the other, like we was watching one a them tennis matches at Wimpledown.

'But anyway,' Marley goes, 'whatever you compare it to, this is like . . . anyway, it's like a *crime*.'

'Maybe,' April suggested in a voice what was as thin as her smile, 'you should let other people have a chance to talk, darling.'

Marley clapped her hand over her mouth. 'Sorry, I'm so rude.' She turned to the detainee on her left. 'Where are you from?'

'Palestine.'

'Cool!' she exclaimed.

The bloke what was Palestinian looked like he didn't get what was so cool about coming from a place what was so fucked up and where people be dying all the time.

'I'm from Kashmir,' Bhajan said.

'Oh, wow, where they've got all those houseboats?'

'Yes. You are speaking of Srinagar and the Dal Lake, I think.'

'That's amazing,' goes Marley, turning her attention to Bhajan, what left Azad looking like someone just stole the cake off his plate. 'I've always wanted to go there. It sounds like such a romantic place. Really chilled.'

'Not always,' goes Bhajan, what had been tortured there.

'Huh.' Marley nodded. 'My bio-dad? He hung out there when he was travelling? When he was young? Said the hash was wicked.'

'Excuse me, Miss Marley? What is "bio-dad"?' The Afghani dude what asked just been transferred from Curtin in West Australia.

April's eyes met me own and did a tango. I raised me eyebrows, what is in factuality one eyebrow. I put me hand over me thigh and wiggled two a me fingers upside down, like they was walking. She gave me a look like I was her dad what just said it be okay to wag school, what dads never do in factual real life.

Twenty

I should explain about walks. Ching once told me that in Chinese there be no word for 'privacy', what makes it the same as in Villawood. Villawood was so locked up from the outside. You could always hear the sound a gates swinging shut and padlocks kachunking into place. But there wasn't no locks on our personal doors what was true in reality as well as met-oh-four.

And the Visiting Yard was just one big goldfish bowl what had lotsa big goldfish eyes in. If you was sitting down, you was a sitting duck, what is a duck what is waiting for the roast. Even if you was having a deep and meaningful with someone, another detainee was sure to come by and say hello. It was like a rule that you had to invite them to join you. They would, too. Cuz they had nuffin else to do. So in that goldfish bowl what had so many eyes and ducks in, there was only two ways to get some a that privacy what not be in the vocabulary.

One was to be doing something important with papers. The other was to go on a walk. In factuality there was nowhere to go, but so long as you kept moving, no one bothered you. A full circuit round the perimeter took approximately two hundred and seventy-three footsteps, though I reckoned it was more like two hundred and twenty steps, cuz most people avoided the shelter, where there was too much happening. Wherever you went, you couldn't get no more than a metre or two from other people, but it was the illusion a privacy that worked.

There was this Aussie chick what fell in love with a Somalian dude. They held hands and walked the perimeter from the second she got Inside till the blues ordered everyone out at seven. I tried to write a hip-hop song about it. The first lines went, *Let's get into motion, we be ships in the ocean, I'm the lover with emotion that is real, I'm the bruvva with the potion, make you feel* — but that's as far as I got. When I finished, I was gonna send it to Celine Dion what needed to upgrade into hip-hop. If she bought it I was gonna be rich and famous. Azad, what had a poster a Celine Dion on his wall, told me he was surprised that most a his Aussie visitors didn't like Celine Dion. I insured him that unless they was wogs, Australians didn't know nuffin about music unless it be rock 'n' roll.

We was just turning the corner round the playground when April sighed. 'I wish she'd shave under her arms.'

Twenty-One

'It's a hippy thing, eh? But it's not that important. She's your daughter, mate. So she gotta be beautiful and talented whatever she does with her pits. It's in the jeans, what you both look good in.'

April shook her head. 'Those jeans of hers couldn't get any lower. I swear they're only six centimetres from belt to crotch.'

I almost said 'six centimetres to paradise' but then I remembered who I was talking about and snapped me trap shut before me foot could make it all the way inside, what was for once.

'I was just telling Thomas that Josh has agreed to speak with the Minister this week? But I'm . . . I'm nervous nothing will come of it? There's no guarantee the Minister will listen. You know, I was asking Marley what she thought she was doing with that silly protest, and she said, "Well, what are *you* doing, Mum? Tea and biscuits isn't exactly setting them free either." It reminded me of something Sue said to me, after that first time I came, and I was telling her my doubts about talking to Josh. She said there were two kinds of people who visited detention — knitters and kayakers. I didn't really get it at first? But I see now. Sue's a real kayaker. Me, I don't know, Zeki. I feel like I'm a knitter trying to be a kayaker but I don't really have a clue how to do it? I'm using knitting needles for oars.' A look came onto April's face what reminded me a She Who Must Be Constantly Reinsured when she thinks her bum's too big in something.

I didn't know what to say. I never been in a kayak and I didn't know nuffin about knitting.

'Yo, Bogan.' Hadeon was sitting at a table near the playground with some other five-oh-ones and his skanky moll what was visiting. Since he got to Stage Two, I'd been avoiding him as much as possible, though it was like a sardine trying to ignore another sardine what be in the same tin. 'Introduce us to yer girlfriend, will ya?' The other guys laughed dumb laughs like huh-huh-huh-huh cuz that be what passes for wit in the five-oh-one world. Maaan. Gimme asylums any day. I glanced at April what was frowning like she wasn't sure if they was being insulting, what I knew they was on a count a her age.

We was close to the gate going into the compound when Angel came through.

'Hey, Angel.' Angel was looking round. I figured she was looking for Hamid. 'Hamid's over there, with Sue.' I pointed out where they be. Hamid was looking our way.

Angel nodded, but like she didn't care much. 'Thanks, Zek.' She kissed April hello. Then she headed in the opposite direction, what be to Hadeon's table. With a look a concern on his face, Hamid jumped up from the table and came hurrying across the yard towards Angel. Glancing back at Hadeon's table, I saw his moll quickly reach into her bra and palm something over to him.

Back in Marley's circle, Azad was sitting so far forward in his chair you coulda tipped him over by flicking his neck with two fingers, I swear. Marley was bent forward too, over one leg what was expended, and she was slowly rolling up the leg of her jeans. Every eye was on that leg as she showed it, inch by inch like in one a them peep shows in the Cross where you gotta keep putting in the money, except she were doing it for free.

'What the . . . ?' April picked up the pace.

By the time we got back to them, Marley had pulled her jeans clear over her knee. She was pointing at a bruise. 'See? That's what the pigs did when they pushed me the day I chained myself to the fence.'

All the guys was making noises like ooh and ahh. The Afghani guy what recently arrived, his cheeks was like two red apples, and Azad wasn't looking happy.

'People are looking,' he said like that be a bad thing, though he be one a them.

'Oh, it doesn't bother me,' Marley said, turning her leg this way and that and running her hand over the bare skin before she pulled the jeans back down again. She was wearing thongs and had silver rings on her toes what had nails what was painted blue and wore one a them hippy bracelets with silver bells around her ankle, what be slim.

'Azad, Azad.' Abeer, followed by Noor, pushed her way through to Azad. Her tiny hands was cupped round her pet gecko. 'Visa's sick.'

'Your gecko's called "Visa"?' Marley asked. 'That's *so* ironic.'

Abeer ignored her.

'What are you feeding him?' Azad asked her.

'Maltesers.'

Everyone laughed. Abeer stuck out her bottom lip. 'What's so funny?' she asked.

'I dunno,' I said, throwing me hands up. 'I live on Maltesers, and look at me — I'm fine.'

Azad shook his head. 'Maybe try mosquitoes or flies.'

'Yuck,' Abeer said, shaking her head. '*You* try mosquitoes and flies.'

'Yuck,' echoed Noor. She been a lot happier since her mum got transferred from Woomera to Villawood.

Marley turned to the others. 'How can they keep little children behind razor wire?' She looked back at the kids. 'What are your names?' she asked, opening her arms to them.

Abeer stared at her feet. Noor stared at Marley. They didn't move.

'What're your names?' Marley asked again.

Abeer mumbled her name, but added, 'I don't want you to say it cuz you'll say it wrong, like 'a beer'. Australians are stupid. You lock us up then ask how can we be here. We gotta go.' She stomped off like an elephant what was little, Noor following and stomping her feet too, like an elephant what was even littler.

Marley made a face. 'I don't think they liked me,' she said.

'No, no, no,' Azad said reinsuringly. 'They're just kids.'

'We better go, darling,' April said to break the Auckland Silence that settled round them after that. 'We've got dinner with Josh.'

Marley rolled her eyes. 'Did you guys hear? Mum's getting back together with Dr Rectum.'

'*Marley*.' April blushed. 'How many times have I told you not to . . .' She turned to us to explain. 'He's a proctologist.'

'Yeah,' Marley said. 'He treats arseholes like the Minister.'

I don't think everyone got what they was talking about, what was probably a good thing. People was picking up the empty cups and throwing them in the bin, looking round to make sure they didn't forget nuffin. Then we all walked them to the gate, Azad sticking right by Marley's side. I looked round at us — Iranians, Turks, Iraqis, Afghanis, Bangladeshis, Kashmiris, Palestinians, Sri Lankans and Africans, like a delegation from the United Fucken Nations a Misery, pardon me French.

Just before we got to the gate, Marley dropped her bomb. 'If you guys ever wanna escape, and I can do anything to help, I'm there. I'm so there.' This took everyone completely by surprise, including her mum, what blanched like an almond.

'She didn't mean that,' April said.

'Yes, I did. This place is fucked.' She raised her voice. 'Free the refugees! Free the refugees!'

Clarence looked over from his post at the gate. 'You were just leaving, were you, darling?'

After April and Marley passed through the vault door, everyone deflated and flew off in different directions like balloons what lost their air, except without those farting noises what balloons do.

'Zeki.' I turned. Azad was standing there with his hands in his pockets.

'Yeah, bruvva.'

'You still thinking about . . . you know?'

'You in, mate?'

'I don't know. Do you think . . .' He flicked him eyeballs at the gate.

'First offer we've had, and it's a good one, eh?'

He sighed. He shuffled over to the section a the fence facing the road, where he could wave goodbye at April and Marley when they'd come outta the office and gone through the last two gates.

I shoulda been feeling good, but I just felt tired. I missed She Who something wicked. If I skipped, that was gonna be the end for sure. I'd be on the run for the rest a me life. I'd never see her again. Then again, I was probably never gonna see her again as it was.

At that moment, something made me look up at the vault door. I couldn't believe me eyes.

It was me own Marlena, She Who Apparently Still Loved Me After All. She was looking mighty stern, I had to admit. Her mouth was all pinched up into a line. But them eyes were like big brown pools, pools what not be brown for any bad reason but cuz a tea tree or something else what makes pools brown in a nice way. Them eyes never lied and they was saying she missed me. It was all I could do from jumping up and punching the air.

'Hey,' she said, soft as pillows. She was still on the other side a the gate.

'Hey,' I said, raising up me chin, me hands in me pockets.

While I waited for Clarence to open the gate, Hadeon came towards the gate with his moll.

'Ya promised ya was gonna marry me,' the moll whinged in one a them voices what is spoked through the nose.

'Sweetheart,' Hadeon answered, 'the only way you're getting my ring on your finger is if I sit on your hand.'

Clarence snickered.

The moll busted into tears.

For some reason, me own Marlena did the same.

Women. I swear if I live to a hundred and fifty I'll never understand them.

Clarence opened the gate. Hadeon's moll went out and She Who came in.

Even though I hates it when women cry, I was so happy to see her I almost bawled meself.

Twenty-Two

Turned out it was Reza and him furballs what brought She Who back to me. She was working in the hospital when they wheeled him in. She recognised him from Visits.

'I'm sorry,' I said to her cuz I believe in apologising when you be wrong, what I sorta was, and also when it means you can get something you want out of it. Like me woman back, what I wanted pretty badly.

She wiped her eyes, what had eyeliner on. The black smudged, making her look like one a them Chinese panda bears what, in factuality, are very cute. She'd put lip gloss on too, making them sweet lips all shiny and wet like me Celica when it be raining, what is so sexy. Her hair was clean and shining like the gold on the little chain around her neck, what I got from the same place them earrings came from. She'd made herself up to look good for me, what was her man. 'I'm so glad you're back, babydoll.'

'I didn't say I'm coming back to you.'

Me heart shrunk like a T-shirt in the dryer. The words to Britney's 'From the Bottom a Me Broken Heart' floated up in me head instead a me own words. I know it's a girl song, but to be truthful I wasn't feeling too much like a man.

'C'mon, darl, let's sit down,' I said finally. All me other words was piling up behind them like a ten-car smash on the Pacific Highway. It took all me emergency services to get that one sentence out.

Some people was leaving so we took their table. It was sticky with spilled soda and bits a rice and Korean food, what smelled a garlic and cabbage. She Who Likes a Clean Home stared at a tiny scrap a cooked meat like it was gonna jump up and bite her. I went to borrow a serviette from Abeer's family, what was sitting with some Palestinians from the community what was visiting. Her dad had come out of their room, what was for once and a good thing to see. He invited me to join them, but I told him I had a visitor. Najah, Abeer's mum, sent me back with a plastic plate heaped full a falafels and pickles and Leb bread and hummus. I wiped the table with me sleeve, cuz I forgot to get the serviette, and placed the food down in the middle. I gestated at She Who to help herself, but she sat staring down at her hands in her lap. That's when I noticed she'd got thinner. She was wearing a new T-shirt with sparkles on.

This was making me nervous. I wrapped a falafel in some Leb bread with hummus and salad and offered it to her. She shook her head what proved that she was looking at me even if she was pretending not to. I tore it in half and put half on the plate, where it be pointing at her. I started to eat the other half meself outta stressation.

'I wanted to see how you were,' she said. 'It sounds . . . you know, just from seeing Reza, like things here have been pretty full-on.' She Who Wasn't Gonna Make This Easy had a treble in her voice, like one a them opera singers.

I nodded. Sweat was trickling down me face. I wiped it with me sleeve before I remembered I already wiped the table with the same one. I could feel Korean food bits stick to me cheeks. I pretended I was scratching me face and picked them off.

'Your nose,' she said, pointing to the tip of her own. 'Cabbage.'

Sometimes I think how the hell did a clown like me get a girl like Marlena? Then the Infernal Optimist kicks in and I think, who else could make her laugh the way I do?

'Hello, Marlena. Nice to see you.' Azad came over and shook Marlena's hand.

'Nice to see you too, Azad,' Marlena said, turning on a smile for him what she wasn't giving me. 'How are you?'

'Still breathing,' he said.

'No news?'

'Is good news. Anyway, I only came over to say hello. Enjoy your visit. I will see you later.' Azad wandered off to join some other visitors.

'He's really nice,' Marlena said. She gazed after him like she be thinking how nice he was compared to yours truly.

'You too,' I said with a grin, trying on some a me old

charm. 'You're really nice.' She gave me a look what said it wasn't working. I took another tack. 'You look great, darl.'

Nada. It was one a them all-care-no-response situations.

'I brought you some cigarettes and bickies and stuff,' Marlena said, picking up one a the bags in her hands to show me. There was a box a Tiny Teddies, what I figured be a good sign. But what really jump-started me heart was the sight of a pile a videos in the other bag, cuz they was rented. She'd have to come back to pick them up. There was mostly weeklies but a couple was three-day hire. I knew she knew I knew what that meant, cuz when I looked up our eyes met and she smiled. Then she caught herself, like she be her own lady cop for a change, and put on a expression of accusation.

'How's your girlfriend?' she asked.

'I dunno,' I said. 'I ain't seen her for weeks, what feels like years.'

'Why not? Where's she been?'

'I was about to ask her that meself.'

Her bottom lip stuck out. 'Well, go on then. I'm sure she's here somewhere.'

'Where you been, babydoll?' I asked, looking straight at her.

'Me? You talking about me, then?'

I said I was.

She Who said that if she was gonna stay with me, there was gonna be some new rules. She talked about fidelity, what she said was not about the quality of sound in a home entertainment system. I knew that, of course. I was just stirring her when I made her explain. She talked about respect, what she said was not just an Aretha Franklin song. And she talked about commitment, what was exactly what it sounded like — long.

Women is the most difficult thing, I swear. I'm coming back a monk in the next life. Or a nun what gets it on with other nuns, cuz that'd be all right. Women gotta be easier if you're one a them yourself. And lezzos always look like they be having fun on those websites what is devotioned to them.

Twenty-Three

After Visits I did some business what lifted me cash pile to match me spirits. Then I went to see Azad and them.

'So, Marlena's back.' Thomas gave me the bruvvas' handshake.

'Careful she doesn't hear about Sunny,' said Hamid.

'Mate.' Everyone knows everything about everybody here. 'I didn't know she was coming back, did I?'

I wanna make one thing perfectly clear. Sunny is a girl and not a man like what that other one was, and what I didn't know until he dropped him pants. As you know, I like lesbians as much as any other red-blooded male, but that's where me homogeneity stops. Anyway, I insured Thomas that Sunny was being deported back to Thailand before the three-day hire on the videos was up. No worries there.

A commotion had us all running outside to see what was going on. Abeer's dad was arguing with Clarence, but his

English wasn't too fluid. He repeated 'No good, no good!' while the women shouted and pointed at Hadeon, what was leaning up against the wall a the laundry, whistling to himself and checking him nails.

The mums and kids was all there. Bashir was holding on to Najah's leg like he be scared to let go, but Abeer was standing in front a her, back straight, her little fists clenched like she was gonna beat up anyone what even be thinking a coming near to her mum. Noor was hiding under her mum's long dress what I knew cuz her little feets was sticking out the bottom. Nassrin was holding onto her big stomach and standing next to Najah.

'Where's Farshid?' I asked, cuz with Reza in hospital it looked like Nassrin could use some support.

Bhajan put his hand to his ear like it be a phone. 'Laura,' he whispered.

'No good!' Mohammed shouted again, waving his hands. Then suddenly he stopped. His shoulders fell and his head drooped and his eyes closed for a moment.

Azad stepped forward and said something to Mohammed in Arabic.

'Hey, hey. I don't speak monkey,' Clarence said. 'Share.' Hadeon busted into laughter what was as ugly as him melon.

Azad turned to Clarence. He pointed at Hadeon. 'That man should not be here. He is bothering the women and the children.'

'Awww,' Clarence said. 'And you're bothering me. So what.'

'What is this shit country that locks up women and children and other people who have committed no crime?'

Thomas stepped forward. 'And locks them up together with real criminals?'

This didn't make me feel too good though I knew it wasn't aimed at me in particulate.

'You calling Australia a shit country?' Clarence sneered. 'Who invited you here anyway? Why don't you go home? Your country is obviously a great place to be, judging from the number of youse who couldn't wait to get your black arses onto the first boat here.'

'I didn't come by boat,' Thomas snapped. 'I came by plane.'

'You could've come by space shuttle for all I care. The point is, you're illegal. Like the rest of these cretins.'

'Better a black arse than a red one like a baboon.' I never heard Thomas dish it out like that before. Respect.

'What did you say, boy?' Clarence was moving in on Thomas.

'Oi,' I said, stepping forward and inserting meself into the situation. 'Fuck off outta his face.'

'Oh, it's Bogan.' Clarence put his hands up. 'I'm scared.'

'Muvvafucker.'

By now lotsa people had come outta their rooms and everyone was shouting in English and every other language. Flora, the Operations Manager, what had been escorting Bilal to Medical when this started, raced onto the scene. Bilal was close on her heels. She pushed past Thomas and shoved me aside. She eyeballed Clarence. He looked away. 'Everyone shut up!' she shouted, raising her hands and patting down the air with her palms. 'Shut up!'

She looked from the women to Clarence and then to Hadeon and back. She planted her feet on the ground like they was two trees, and put her hands on her big hips, what took up a lotta room and got people's full attention. Bilal peeped out from behind her with him big eyes round like he be a character in a cartoon, what made some people laugh. After Conchita *hasta-la-vista*-ed, he'd gone back to his crazy old ways big time.

'Now, will somebody tell me what's going on?' goes Flora.

Everyone started to talk and shout at once except Hadeon, what kept on whistling to himself.

'Shut up!' she yelled louder than anyone. 'Shut up! All of youse! Now. One at a time.' She looked around. The only sound then was Noor's soft little hiccups, and the *whootwhootwhoot AIYA whootwhoot HAI whootwhoot* what be the soundtrack from a Chinese sword-fight film playing in the video room next to the laundry. 'Okay, Nassrin, you look like you've got something to say.'

Nassrin said that since Hadeon had been transferred to Stage Two, he'd been sneaking round the dorms what got women and families in. She said she'd seen him there late at night. They was afraid a him. I reckoned they was right to be scared a him cuz back in prison we was too, and we was men.

Flora — what was not to be fooled with, what even the likes a Hadeon would know — then looked to the Hatchet himself. She still had her hands on her hips. He shrugged, like he didn't know what Nassrin be talking about. When Flora turned away, Hadeon did this thing where he grabbed his crotch and licked him lips while looking straight at Nassrin. He was slime.

Anna approached. She was walking fast. She whispered something to Flora. 'Yeah,' said Flora. 'I can handle it. You take her.'

Anna turned to Nassrin. 'Sorry, Nassrin, I've come to tell you to get ready to go to the hospital.' Nassrin turned pale. 'It's okay,' Anna said, and she was trying to smile. 'They want you to visit Reza. He's still not eating, that's all.' All the shit that had been going down was finally getting to Anna. The night before, she told me that while she still didn't think people should be allowed to come to this country any which way they wanted, she was starting to think it wasn't such a good idea to lock up asylums, specially women and children, for years and years. She touched Nassrin's shoulder. 'Let's get you a jacket or something. You might be there a while.' Then she led her off.

'Show's over,' Flora goes, clapping her hands. 'Back to your rooms. That means you.' She pointed to Hamid, what wasn't doing nuffin but looking. 'And you and you and you.' That be me and Azad and Thomas. 'Clarence, escort Mr Vitrenko to Management and then come to the office to write an incident report.' Vitrenko was Hadeon's last name. Clarence made like a salute what be sarcastic but what she couldn't see cuz she was speaking to Najah and them. 'Ladies, I understand you have some complaints.'

'Azad, he translate, okay?' Najah looked to Azad and then to Flora. Mohammed looked at the ground like he be fully humeliorated.

Azad stepped forward. Flora sighed and flapped her hand at him to say he should come with them. We watched them go.

'Hamid! Hamid!' The Lima girls was at the fence. They'd heard all the shouting but couldn't see what was going down. I went over to the fence with Hamid and Thomas. What was weird was that it was the Malaysian chick Lili what was calling Hamid's name, not Angel, so at first I thought Angel wasn't there. As we got closer we could see Angel was there all right but she was pinned off her nut. She was sitting on a chair staring ahead and scratching her face with her long pink nails. Her eyes looked like they had no pupils at all, I swear.

'Angel,' Hamid said. 'What have you done, my Angel?' Her head slowly turned. 'Who got it for you?' Hamid's voice was cracking so loud I knew his heart must be too. 'Tell me.'

Angel smiled like she be far away. I thought I knew the answer.

Hamid punched the fence, what wasn't a good idea cuz it be made a steel. 'Let's go,' he said to me and Thomas.

Thomas pulled a tissue outta his pocket and handed it to Hamid. 'Your hand,' he said. Hamid didn't even know his knuckles were bleeding.

I looked back. Angel was still smiling that zombie smile and scratching her neck.

It was turning out to be a pretty fucked night, pardon me French. What was a shame cuz the day had such good moments, like the return a She Who Still Loves Me After All.

We went back to Thomas's room. He was still in his high dungeon what be an expression what the counsellor at Silverwater used to use and what means when your anger be like a tall prison what is locking you up.

'Fucking racist fucking country,' Thomas said. For once, I didn't feel like defending it.

Hadeon got moved back to Stage Three the next day. Everyone reckoned that was the end a his bad influence on things.

Twenty-Four

Maybe we shoulda seen it coming, but we was all preoccupied with our own shit.

Me, I'd run outta time for that appeal. I didn't dare ask She Who if she wanted to go back to the Old Country with me cuz I knew how she didn't even like leaving Fairfield half the time. Parramatta was the limits of her comforting zone. She had her job, and her parents, and her mates like My Le. She loved going for a steak at the RSL or Chinese at the Leagues Club, what I didn't think they had over in the Old Country. Couldn't even say for sure if they had Leagues.

Marlena's reappearance had put a damper on the escape plan, too. I didn't have to ask to know that no way was she gonna be the girlfriend a some escapee what was living life on the underground, what not be a train in London.

What was a shame, cuz between you and me and the fence, I'd worked out all the details by then, cased out the route and everything. It came to me a few days earlier, when

I had to go to Medical. I don't wanna go into it, but Sunny left me a little gift when she left, what was in factuality a lotta little gifts, what moved into me pubes and what had a fancy Latino name, but I won't try and bamboozle you with it cuz they was just crabs. Apparently they love body hair, what I got a lot of. I had to shave from me knees to me man-boobs. The point is, I had to be in Medical a few nights in a row getting creams and whatnot, and I began to check out me surrounds.

See Medical was a demountable. A caravan really. It backed onto the fence on the left side a Stage Two, not too far from Stage Three. It had one window what looked out on the fence, but the blind was usually pulled down. There was two consulting rooms, and a waiting room. At night there'd be maybe seven or eight detainees waiting on them medication. If you had a pair a wire cutters and slipped round the back a Medical when no one was looking, it'd take two guys no more than five minutes to cut through the inner fence, then the razor wire — what needed more care — then the outer fence. Then it was about a five, six-hundred-metre dash to the road. We'd need a blue to get us the wire cutters and someone to drive the getaway car, and two mates to sit lookout on the Stage Two and Stage Three approaches to Medical. It would be like something outta *Escape from Alcatraz*, except it would be me, the Zekster, what would be doing it instead a watching it on the small screen.

Me other options, as I just explained, wasn't what you'd call a lot. And none a them was for a movie starring Nicole

Kidman. In case you was wondering, Nic wasn't really an old girlfriend a mine, in spite a what I told the others that time. I wouldn't a kicked her outta bed if I had the chance but life never handed me that particulate opportunity.

Me dad was still barracking for me to go back to the Old Country. Mrs Kunt told me that if I bought me own ticket, it wouldn't count as a deportation neither. What meant that if I was able to cover the cost a me four-star accommodation in the Villawood Ritz — three and a half months at $127.60 a night for the privilege, room service included — I might possibly be able to return one day to the country where I belonged in the first.

Dad came to visit with me brother Attila one rainy day early in February to try and convince me to do it.

'It'll make a man of you.'

'Wha, wha? I'm not a man in Australia?' I hated these conversationals.

'I'm talking about the army.'

'What are you talking about, the army?'

'*Piew piew*,' he said, what was supposed to be the sound a guns. He explained that cuz I was a citizen a the Old Country, and a man — what I apparently was for these particulate purposes, even if I still had to be made one for others — I was gonna have to serve in the Turkish army. Eighteen months a compulsory service, sergeants barking orders at you like in the movies except not in American, waking up at all hours, marching, running, climbing over them nets what they got for climbing over. Just thinking about it made me wanna curl up under me doona with a bar a chocolate.

Dad grinned, showing me all him big teeth. He joined the Turkish army when he was eighteen, in time to go to fight in Korea with the Yanks. Me Old Country was the first to follow the US into Korea. It was probably gonna keep following the US into lotsa other great trouble spots as well. Another possibility would be that it has a revolution or something and becomes a trouble spot itself. The possibilities was endless, none a them good. When we was young, we used to have to listen to Dad's war stories, what we didn't much appreciate then, and what I wasn't particulately appreciating at that moment neither. 'The experience didn't hurt me none,' Dad said.

I'm like, 'Dad. You lost your left hand.'

'It'd be cool, Zek,' Attila said. He could say that. He was an Australian citizen what had both him hands and didn't have to go into the Turkish army himself.

Rain pounded the tin roof a the shelter. It was like the soundtrack to Dad's war movie, *ratatatat ratatatat*, with a coupla thunderbolts what be like the bombs.

I munched down one a Mum's *eraiyes* what they brung. 'So, can we talk about something else?' I asked, picking the spinach outta me teeth with a fingernail. 'How's this weather, eh?'

'Parts of Sydney are flooding,' Attila said. 'Trees are down and some houses have been crushed.'

That was me. A crushed house with all me trees down.

'It's all experience,' Dad said, though I didn't know if he be talking about losing his hand or about people what had them houses crushed or about me going to the Old Country and into the army.

Me dad didn't visit as often as Mum, and when he did it was usually on rainy days, cuz he was a builder what took rainy days off. It was always to tell me to pull up me socks, what was an expression Mum liked as well in reference to me what didn't always wear them.

Me brother Attila, he had his socks pulled up since he been a boy. Shoelaces tied and everything. When Dad talked some more about me going back to the Old Country, all the while gestating forcefully with him stump, Attila nodded.

'It's good in the Old Country, Zek,' Attila said. He only been there on holidays. Of course it was good. 'The food's awesome. Like Mum's but to the max.'

'Great. But what am I sposed to do there besides eat when I finish the army, assuming the army don't finish me? Sell carpets?'

'What is wrong with selling carpets?' Dad asked. 'You could do worse. You have done worse.' Oh maaan. 'You know, your old uncle Abi has a kilim shop. He is looking for someone to take it over when he retires.'

Luckily, me brother had to get back to his own shop before they could start talking about how I could marry me first cousin, the Lady Ninja, and have lotsa little retards while I was at it.

Twenty-Five

The war in Afghanistan kinda ended and they got a new president. He was called Hamid too. He told our Prime Minister that the Afghani asylums was welcome to come back. The Taliban what prosecuted them was gone, though it wasn't clear exactly where they'd gone. But that was good enough for the Australian Government, what froze all Afghani applications for asylum. They told the Afghanis what had been in Detention, some for three years or more, that they'd give them plane tickets and resettlement money if they'd go home. His case officer was putting the pressurisers on our own Hamid, what wasn't the President a nuffin but Misery, to accept the offer. They told him that other Afghani asylums had already accepted the package. In factuality, they was all ones what had wives and kids back there and was more worried about them families than themselves.

Hamid was normally a very quiet and gentle bloke. But he hadn't slept for days. He was worried about Angel, what he was trying to keep an eye on, talking to her every night through the fence and trying to get her to come out to Visits, what she didn't do every day any more. And he still hadn't got any news of his family what he was waiting for from the Red Cross. He went off at his case officer. I was next door with Mrs Kunt, talking about the possibility a me own repatriotism, so I heard the whole thing. 'First you don't accept me as refugee because you say I not from Afghanistan,' he shouted. 'So you keep me here for years while I try to prove I am from Afghanistan. Now you say, okay, you really are Afghani then — now go home. Do you understand how cruel this is? I need to know what happened to my family. I need to know if the people who went after my family, who wanted to go after me, are still around. You think Americans won the war and it's all over, it's that easy? That the Taliban are all gone? Then you don't know my country. And if you don't know my country, you have no right to tell me what to do.' We heard a bang. Me and Mrs Kunt ran to the door and looked. Hamid and his case officer, they was both staring at his chair, what was on the ground. 'I'm scared, don't you understand? Do you even care?' he shouted. Then he kicked the wall a the office. 'Do you even listen?'

The noise got the attention a the blues. Anna raced in and pulled Hamid's arm up sharp behind his back. 'Sorry,' she whispered as she did it.

'Sorry?' Hamid yelled. 'Say sorry after you do something wrong you didn't know was wrong at the time. Like keeping refugees inside razor wire. Or something you later believe is wrong. Like keeping us there for years and years. But don't do wrong thing and say sorry at the same time. Doesn't work!' He struggled. But before he knew what was going down, the nurse ran over and gave him an injection.

'Shall we talk later, then, Zeki?' Mrs Kunt called out. I was already halfway to the compound gate.

When Hamid came to, in his room, his eyelids like they had weights on, we was all sitting there. Azad took his hand. Thomas was pacing. I held out the bag a bite-sized chocolate bars I was eating, one after the other on a count a the stress. I offered them round, but no one was interested.

Thomas was getting worse migraines, and more often. 'How long does it take the Minister to read a letter?' he grumbled. Now that he knew Josh was gonna speak to the Minister, he was even more tense.

'At least you got a connection,' Bhajan said. 'April's the only visitor we know who knows someone who knows someone in the government.' Bhajan and Thomas and I was sitting outside Shoalhaven having a smoke. Azad joined us. 'Hamid's asleep,' he told us.

'You know,' Bhajan continued, 'the visitors always say, if the other Party was in we'd be able to help, no worries. They all tell you who they know in the Opposition, like it matters. They make themselves sound important saying it, but it's useless.' Bhajan also had an application in with the Minister, his second one. It was his last chance. This visitor had helped him write the first one. She was full a confidence, saying she knew this person and that person. They all turned out to be in the Greens, what is even more useless than the Opposition. One a the ladies from the Uniting Church, what helps people, looked at his first application when it got turned down and shook her head. She wrote a better one what got some good support from the community, but she warned Bhajan that it was nearly impossible to get the Minister to look twice at an application from the same person. We all remembered what happened to Babak.

The loudspeaker went off. They was saying Bhajan's name. '. . . Come to DIMIA . . . come to DIMIA.' We gave him the thumbs up for luck. 'Good luck, bruvva,' I said. No one said nuffin after that.

Azad closed his eyes. '*La ilaha ilallah. La ilaha ilallah*,' he said.

Bhajan returned, his face blank like it'd been erased. 'I am a dead man,' he said. We followed him into his room.

We'd only just sat ourselves on the bed and floor when there was a cheerful 'Knock knock!' A head with a buffet hairdo peered in the door. It was Nadia.

'Hellooo. Hellooo.' She saw us all in there and stopped. 'Can I come in?'

Bhajan gestated with his hand.

She stepped inside, smiling and nodding the whole time. 'Azad. Zeki. Thomas. How are you all?'

Thomas spoke for us all. 'Still breathing.'

'True,' she said. 'True.' She scrunched up her mouth like she was trying hard to get it closer to her nose. She tapped one little foot, and rubbed her hands together like she was washing them.

We waited for her to say something. 'Well. Bhajan. Can we have a little talk?' she finally asked.

'Any time,' he said. She looked at us and lowered her chin, what then became two chins, and raised her eyebrows. Them eyebrows suggested we get a move on. We started to get up, but Bhajan put a hand out to tell us not to go. 'They are my friends,' Bhajan said. 'You can say anything in front of them.'

'O-kaaay,' she went, dragging the word along the ground for a while. 'So. How do you feel?' It was a stupid question.

'Great,' Bhajan answered. 'Terrific.'

'Do you understand what they told you?' she asked. 'You understand you've been rejected? That your application failed?'

'Yes, of course,' said Bhajan, grinning.

'And you're feeling okay.' She frowned like she knew this wasn't possible.

'I feel great,' said Bhajan nodding and shaking his head. 'On top of the world.'

She put her head to one side and then to the other, like she be checking her hinges. 'You sure?'

'Yes, why not?'

'You're not thinking of . . . you won't do anything. . .' She was trying hard to can the frown. Them feet were stomping all up and down her forehead.

'Ohhhhhh,' Bhajan said, like he just got her meaning. 'You mean like *this*?' He sliced at his wrist with the edge a his hand. 'Or *this*?' He made like his hands was a noose what be strangulating his face.

She looked horrorfied. 'Yes. Actually.'

'No,' he said. 'Don't worry. I'm fine.'

It took a while to persuade Nadia to leave after that, but when she finally did we laughed, for about five seconds.

Nadia was a busy lady that day. Reza, what was back from the loony bin, tried to top himself again and crazy Bilal, what had been growing a mad mullah beard, shaved half of it off. The right half.

Twenty-Six

The next day, the Red Cross delivered a letter to Hamid. There was a form on the front what said the letter was from his dad. His hands shook so bad I thought he wasn't gonna be able to open the letter at all. Azad and me, we was almost as nervous as he was. When Hamid finished reading the letter, his hands went slack. The letter fluttered to the ground. His eyes closed and a tear squeezed out. More tears fell but he still wasn't making no noise, like he be holding him breath. I felt a chill crawl up me spine and neck and all over me skull like ants. I picked up the letter but it was in his language. Azad shook his head at me, but I wasn't sure if he be telling me to put it back down or that he couldn't read it neither.

It turned out his dad said that after Hamid's mum's arrest, he had gone into hiding with Hamid's little sister and brother. His sister, what was only six, got dysentery and died. When the Taliban fell, his dad rushed back and went straight to the prison to find his wife. He was two days too late. Just before they took to the hills, the Taliban guards killed all their prisoners, including Hamid's mum. Hamid's dad, what loved her very much, went crazy for a while. The authorities told Hamid's dad he could open his school for girls again. But he didn't know where he'd be getting teachers, or even books or desks or chairs, cuz the old ones had all been burned for firewood. Mostly, he didn't know how he was gonna do it without Hamid's mum, what he missed too much. He worked hard to do it anyways, cuz he knew she'd want him to. Then someone burned the new school down cuz they was like the Taliban and didn't think girls should get education, even though the new government said they could.

Hamid's dad told him he hoped he would continue with his medical degree, what he guessed Hamid nearly be through with by now. He said Hamid should stay till it was safe to return, what it still wasn't.

His dad didn't know nuffin about Hamid being in Detention.

Hamid hadn't opened his eyes the whole time he was telling us this. 'I'm sorry about your mum,' I said. He began to shake all over his body.

The next day Azad said his lawyers told him something he didn't know about that Habee's corpse business, what was that even if he got it, he wouldn't be able to work or study. 'All I want is to be able to support myself and make a new life in this country, Zeki. I'm young and healthy. I want to work and I want to study. I want to write poetry again. I just want the chance. It is not a lot to ask.'

'Could you get the dole, mate?'

'No. I'd have to rely on charity. I don't want charity, and even if they gave me the dole, I would not want it. I am not a beggar.'

'You know,' I said, 'if you skipped, you could work illegal. It wouldn't be much different from getting Habee's corpse, really.'

'I don't know. It is not my dream.'

'Is this, mate?' I gestated at the razor wire.

He put head in his hands. 'No.'

Twenty-Seven

Some a the people what was for the refugees started organising concerts in the Detention Centre. After that time on Boxing Day when those musos came into Visits with them instruments, the Shit House decided that if there was gonna be music, they had to organise it. The concerts could only take place at lunchtime, under the shelter in the Visiting Yard. They had to finish before Visits started. A group a belly dancers once came from the Blue Mountains, what was specially good cuz some a them was babes. There was a rock band what I liked, though Azad said it be too noisy for him, and a gypsy cabaret band what had some a the kids dancing and everyone clapping them hands.

On this particulate day, what was Monday the eleventh a February, we was getting a choir. I didn't specially like choirs, not that I ever heard one before except at She Who's church when I went with her one Sunday. But I didn't have nuffin else to do so I went out with Azad and Thomas and we got

Hamid to come out too, though he said he didn't feel like it much. Pretty much everyone went out that day, even Reza, what was back from hospital and starting to come good again. At least he wasn't sewing his lips or eating his hair. The blues stuck rows a chairs under the shelter. There was about thirty kids in detention and they all ran in soon as the blues opened the gate. They sat in the front rows swinging their feets back and forth. Abeer and Noor was holding hands, and on Abeer's other side Bashir pushed his face into her shoulder.

The choir had both men and women in. They was all wearing matching yellow T-shirts with the word 'Peace' and doves on, and they arranged themselves into two rows what had short and tall people in. Smiling like they was nervous, some a them wiped tears from them eyes, what made me scared that they was gonna break down and we was gonna have to comfort them. Some younger members a the choir went round shaking people's hands, and then stepped back into line.

The leader a the choir stepped forward and told us they was a World Music choir. World Music is a word for all the music what be from countries what don't got mostly white people in, what is a lotta music. They said they was very honoured to be there and jawed on about how terrible the policy a detaining asylums was. I tuned out cuz I don't like speeches, but it didn't go on too long, thanks God. The Program Manager coughed and pointed at his watch to tell them they should start. They began the concert with a sad song about refugees, what made everyone sadder. Then they sang a song what was sposed to be Arabic but wasn't exactly, and another what was sposed to be about the depressed people a the Amazon or something like that. I was glad we was sitting towards the back cuz I was already working out me escape routes. Hamid kept looking round for Angel, what said she was gonna come. The choir said they wrote the next song specially for this concert. 'Oh the refugees, locked up for years and years, nothing but tears and fears . . . tears and fears!' they sang with two-bit harmony. Everyone sank further down into their seats.

'Remember Tears for Fears?' I asked Azad, what didn't and was looking glazed like a window.

Some a the choir had hair stylings what looked like they been locked up since the seventies and not allowed to look at TV what was made after. 'If there was ever a reason for skipping, this singing got to be it, mate,' I whispered to Azad, what smiled. 'It's no Dire Straits, innit? It's just the Dire Choir.'

'They are good people,' he whispered back.

I thought I'd check out what was happening inside the compound.

Azad leaned over close. 'Take this back inside,' he whispered and dropped a small plastic camera outta his sleeve and into me hands. I quickly stuck it in the waistband a me trackies.

I couldn't believe it. 'Where . . . ?'

With his chin he pointed to one a the young choir guys had come round shaking hands earlier.
ect.'

'What, aren't you enjoying it?' Anna asked as she handed back me ID and let me through the first gate.

'Mate,' I said. 'Maybe when I's ninety I be into it.'

'I know what you mean,' she said. She slid the second padlock into place behind me.

It was quiet in the compound. Some Chinaman was standing on the phone arguing with someone in his own language, and crazy Bilal was walking back and forth having a conversation with himself and stroking the beard what covered only half his face. I went to me room and wrote down a few lines for a hip-hop song what came to me while listening to the Dire Choir. I got stuck trying to find words what rhyme with 'asylums'. But it wasn't like I was gonna be heading into the studio with Dr Dre any time soon. I tore up the paper into pieces and threw them away. I thought a stashing the camera, but sometimes they did room searches and I didn't have no hiding places what wasn't already in use, so I tucked it back in me waistband.

Outside again, I glanced over at the fence between me own building and Lima Dorm to see if I could see Angel, but no one was around except this lady from Vietnam what was nutso. She called out to me in her language. She was pointing and gestating at the building. I waved back at her and wandered out past the empty school and the playground and hung a left at the path, but then I remembered me smokes so I turned back. As I was exiting me room the second time I noticed Clarence walking real fast outta Lima Dorm. That was strange cuz in normality male officers didn't go into Lima, and when they did they had to sign in and out and explain what they be doing there and shit. Me criminal instincts told me something was up. I took out the camera and got a quick snap. To tell you the truth, I didn't think that much about it cuz I was thinking about meself and I was pissed off with the world and bored. And I didn't wanna waste the film cuz I thought a telling Azad that Nassrin might wanna take a few snaps a the kids with it too.

I checked out what was going down in the Rec Room. I wouldn't a minded a game a billiards but these Islander dudes was already playing. A few a the guys what is strict with the religion and don't go out to hear no music was sitting on chairs between the children's play room and the building what held the mosque. They nodded to me and I nodded back but I walked fast cuz I wasn't sure if they heard me making this joke the other day. See, Hamid was telling us that in his country, the Taliban went around checking the length a your beard and if you couldn't make a fist a the beard they'd beat the crap outta you. Hamid's one a them boys what don't grow much beard anyway, so it was particulately hard on him. Once, after he got a warning, he cut off some a the hair off his head and glued it onto him face, but the glue weren't too hot and the fake beard fell off as he was walking out the door. Lucky for him, there weren't none a them Talibs round to see. 'It's stupid,' he said, 'judging people to be good or bad on the basis of the length of their beards and not the way they behave before God and the people. This is not Islam.'

'In me Old Country,' I told him, 'we got a saying — "If beards were a sign a wisdom, we'd all be looking up to goats".' Hamid laughed. Only then did I realise that them strict dudes, what had long beards, was right there. Dunno if they heard or not. I didn't mean nuffin personal, but it was hard to explain, so I'd been avoiding them ever since.

I thought about doing some exercise, running round the soccer yard or something, but I only had to think about exercising and I felt puffed. I used chocolate as a constellation after She Who Had Every Right dumped me, and when She Who Loved Me After All came back, I had a good appetite on a count a being happy. Besides, it was midday and hot.

Before I knew it I was at the fence with Stage Three. After all that shit went down the other day, Hadeon got moved back to Stage Three. Sure enough, there he was, sitting and smoking a cigarette with a look a pure evil on his peach. He was staring into space. He hadn't seen me so I ducked into one a the doorways a Manning Dorm, what is by the fence. I flattened meself against the wall, what wasn't easy considering me stomach be the opposite a flatten. I was waiting for an opportunity to sneak away again when Clarence busted into view, walking real fast and looking round him like he didn't wanna be seen. Hadeon looked up with a smarmy grin and said something to him like he be asking him a question. Though they wasn't far, I couldn't hear on a count a them talking real low. Clarence said something what made the Hatchet stand up. I knew something heavy was going down cuz when another blue walked by they looked real stiff and uncomfortable till the other blue was outta sight again. Then Clarence handed something to Hadeon. I got the camera out again and pressed the shutter.

Hadeon looked around sharp at the sound but didn't see me. Then he said something else to Clarence, turned and pissed off. Clarence stood looking broken, what I never seen him look. He rubbed his face with his hands, swore, and then spun on him heel and he pissed off too. Once they was both outta sight I made like a scuttlefish. I went into Azad and Hamid's room and stashed the camera, what was small, inside the hollow rod what was for the shower curtain. I tried to guess what was going down, but nuffin made sense. Soon I was back at the gate to the Visiting Yard.

'Back for more punishment?' Anna asked as she opened the first gate.

'Yeah, mate. Punishment's me middle name.' As I went out into the Yard, Lili and her kid, what was crying, were heading back inside.

'She no like the music, I think,' Lili said like she be apologising. 'Stupid girl.'

'A girl a taste,' I said. Lili handed her over and I gave her a peck on the cheek. She sniffed and looked at me with sad eyes. She'd never known nuffin but what be inside the razor wire. I picked up her shirt and blew a raspberry on her tummy, what made her laugh. Lili smiled.

'You should have kids, Zek,' she said. 'You good with kids.'

'I can't hardly look after meself, mate,' I said. 'Anyway, who's gonna have me kids?' Her words gave me a pang. She Who In Factuality Wants to Have Me Children is back but it's not like I can do nuffin about it. Some people gets it on in

Visits under them tablecloths but Marlena got too much self-steam, what is a good thing even if it means we can never get jiggy.

The choir was singing something about tyrants and soldiers and cannibals what got me attention, specially the cannibals. One a me favourite movies is *Cannibal Apocalypse* what is about Vietnam Vets what get a cannibal virus and eat people. 'They soon shall hear the bullets flying. We'll shoot the generals on our own side.' Now, I had to admit this song was kinda interesting. Catchy too. Some a the detainees was nodding and tapping their thighs like they knew it. I slipped back into the chair next to Azad.

'Last song,' Azad whispered. I gave him the thumbs up.

The choir's voices rose in a thundering finale. 'So comrades, come rally, and the last fight let us face! The Internationale unites the human race!'

It was like everyone was zombies what suddenly came back to life. 'More! More!' The detainees was applauding, and whistling and stamping them feet. I stuck two fingers in me gob and whistled too.

Cuz a all the noise we was making, we didn't notice right away that the blues was talking into them walkie-talkies and some a the ones what was in the Yard was running towards the gate. Then we heard Lili screaming from the other side a the fence. 'Hamid! Hamid!' Lili was waving her hands and jumping up and down. 'It's Angel!'

Hamid turned pale. He was off like a flash and we followed. We got to the gate but the blues was so detracted they weren't letting no one through for the moment. They was also busy hurrying the choir out the other gate. Some a them choir people was protesting that they was sposed to be able to visit with us after the concert but the blues kept shoving them towards the gate. 'Let me in,' yelled Hamid what was desperate. 'Please. Please.'

We saw Anna through the fence. She was running towards Lima Dorm. 'Anna, what's going on?' I yelled. She ignored us and kept running.

Twenty-Eight

Later that afternoon, Hamid climbed up onto the fence and threw himself on the razor wire. He did it so quick none of us was in time to stop him. Abeer and Noor, what was playing by the fence, saw it first and screamed. Their mums came running over and grabbed the kids, covering their eyes with their hands, but they were screaming too. I wanted to scream meself when I seen him, blood coming outta everywhere, his face white and his brown eyes like someone switched off the light in them.

You know, when I was in the nick, I once heard someone talking about the history a razor wire. It's not like barbed wire, what was invented for to keep sheep and cows in paddocks. They don't use razor wire for animals cuz sheep and cows be considered too valuable and they can really hurt themselves on it. They only use it on people what they don't care if they hurt themselves on. The Germans invented razor wire in World War I cuz they didn't have enough wire to make barbed wire for them trenches and fortifications. So they punched thin strips outta sheets a steel, making steel tape what had upside-down triangles on what be the razor parts. But the enemy soldiers worked out they could cut through the tape with shears. In the seventies the Yanks started using it to enforce the perimeter fences in them prisons. Being Yanks, what always invents new things and what got plenty a wire, they figured out that if they wrapped the steel tape round strong wire every place except for those triangles what be the razors, then it would be strong enough to stop anyone who wanted to keep their hands and skin on. According to this prisoner what told me all this and what read books sometimes so he knew what he was talking about, in the eighties there was two brand names for the stuff — Man Barrier and Razor Ribbon. I reckon Man Barrier sounded too much like Man Bra what George's father had to wear in that episode a *Seinfeld*. And ribbon is a girly word. So it ended up getting called razor wire.

There's another thing you gotta understand about the razor wire. The shape a the razor part makes it like hooks. So if you do what Reza did on him birthday — hit it and pull away in one straight line — you can end up with a clean cut. But there wasn't nuffin about what Hamid did to himself what was clean.

The next thing I knew, more alarms was ringing, more people was screaming, and I was puking me guts up. By the time the ambulance came to take Hamid away, I what haven't really cried since I be ten was weeping like a girl. Then I got thinking and then I got angry.

See, Angel was dead.

Twenty-Nine

I gotta explain something about what I'm gonna tell you next. I can figure out crimes what other people can't cuz I been around crims so much a me life. That's what I been calling me criminal instincts. Once, I had this job in a petrol station what had a mechanic in. It was before everything went to self-service. One day we was very busy — pumps, lube jobs, tyre changes, the works. We was tidying up that evening when I noticed paint peeling off the wall a the garage, near where the tins a brake fluid was stacked. 'We been ripped off, mate,' I told the mechanic.

'What are you talking about?' Joe goes, scratching his head. He was getting bald and was doing the comb-over. When he scratched, he sent the long bits flopping down below his ears.

'We just painted in here, yeah?'

'Yeah,' he said like he wasn't so sure, even though we did it together.

'Okay, so what's this about?' I pointed to the part a the wall what was peeling like an onion.

He shrugged. 'I dunno. What're ya getting at?'

'Watch your uncle Zek.' I picked up the tins at the top a the stack one at a time, checking their weight. Sure enough, there was one what was a lot lighter. Someone had opened it. I splashed some on the wall, what peeled. 'Some stooge came in and stole some brake fluid, dumping it into another container and splashing some on the wall by accident. And by the way . . .' I made a motion like I be slicking me hair back over the top a me head. He pulled a comb outta his back pocket and fixed the hair back over the shiny bit, giving me the thumbs up and a rise at the same time.

That was a good job and Joe was a good boss. If I hadn't had to go and sublimate me income all a time, I might not a gone to prison the second time, what was the time before the last time what was the time before I got here.

Like that day with Joe, this time I was gonna use me powers for good and not for evil. Of course I never use them for evil, really, just not always for the best what I could use them for.

Thirty

'I'm busy, Zek,' Anna said. Her voice was tense.

'I know,' I said. 'But I got some information you might want.'

She studied me face for a minute. 'Your room in five,' she said.

I boiled the jug for tea and offered her some bickies. 'No, thanks,' she said. In factuality, even I didn't feel like eating anything, what was for once. 'I can't stay long.'

'Okay, I won't beat round the George W,' I said.

As I explained me theory, I saw the colour drain outta her face like there be a plughole in her collar. 'What d'ya reckon?'

She pointed to her arm. All the hairs was standing up. Then Anna — me mate, a blue, a tough chick what once took another five-oh-one down to his knees in a second and had him singing for mercy — began to cry.

'I can't take it any more,' she said. She wiped her eyes and then her nose on the back a her sleeve.

I gave her a tissue. 'You looks like you need a hug,' I said, what she did and what I gave her.

'You know,' she said after a while, straightening up and wiping her eyes, 'she was one of the most beautiful girls I've ever seen. Even dead. You wouldn't have known about the . . . the other thing just looking at her face. Her expression was so peaceful.'

'That's the smack,' I said.

'But there's no question about it. It's true. And they want the whole thing covered up.'

Me phone vibrated in me pocket. I forgot where I was for a second. I pulled it out and looked at the number what was calling before I remembered about Anna being a blue, what was sposed to confiscate mobiles.

Anna put her hands over her eyes, then her ears and then her mouth, what be saying she was a monkey what didn't talk.

It was a private number what come up.

'Hello?'

'Hi, Zeki? It's Marley. April's daughter.'

'Oh, hi.'

'Azad told me what was happening and told me to call you. That's so fucked. So so fucked. I wanna talk to you about helping you. What I said in the Visiting Yard. I meant it. Just don't tell my mum. I'll never get the car keys off her.'

'Oh, mate. We need to talk. But not now,' I told her. 'There's officers around and I don't wanna get caught with me mobile.' I winked at Anna, what sorta smiled. 'Can I call you back?'

'Sure.' She said Azad had her number. Sly bugger. 'Just let me know if and when and what. I'm so there.'

'You know all that stuff I said?' Anna asked after I hanged up.

'What stuff?'

'About asylum seekers.' She winced.

I nodded. 'Don't worry about it,' I said. 'It's a free country. Everyone be entitled to their opinions.'

A knock at the door made us both jump. It was Thomas.

Anna was on her feet by the time he pushed open the door.

He spoke so quiet we almost didn't hear him. 'They just gave me a letter,' he said. 'The Minister. He gave me a visa.' It took a few seconds for the factuality of it to sink in.

'My man!' We embraced.

Anna shook his hand. 'Congratulations, Thomas,' she said in a voice warm as fresh pide. 'I'm really happy for you.'

'I wish . . . it just doesn't feel like the best time. I wish there was good news for everyone.'

'We'll miss you, mate,' I said.

'You too, Zek. I've given you a lot of shit, haven't I?'

'We're used to it, mate.'

'I'm going to call April and thank her. I haven't been very nice to her. I feel really bad about that.'

Later, Azad came to me room. 'Did Marley call you?'

'Sure did, mate.'

'I have reached my limit,' he said.

'You in, then, mate?'

He nodded. We did the bruvvas' handshake. He could do it good by then.

The next day, Hamid came back from hospital with bandages on. The doctors at the hospital told him he shoulda stayed there a few more days. But the Shit House was paying for it and like I told you before they was cheap as a two-dollar shop, except cheaper. We was glad to see Hamid again, though it be like getting a shadow back instead a the man, I swear.

Thirty-One

'Bogan.'

'That's Togan,' I said, standing in the doorway a the office. 'I wanna word.'

'And what's in it for me?' Clarence scratched his belly and leaned back further in his chair. 'My words ain't cheap. Not like your mother.' He licked him ugly lips.

'My mother runs the place where your mother spreads hers. Anyway, I think you'll find there's something in it for you.'

'Like what?'

'Like maybe you won't get what you deserve to get. What is life.'

'That's what it feels like I got when I have to look at your fugly face every day, Bogan.'

'Togan to youse, mate. And you'll be seeing a lot more a the likes a me when they send you up the proverbial.'

'Why don't you fuck off outta my face, Bogan-ville. I got real work to do.'

'Like writing incident reports, mate? There been a few incidents lately, eh, mate. You gonna be writing about how you fucked her for the smack what you been getting through Hadeon?' I pulled some jellybeans outta me pocket and popped them into me mouth.

A shadow passed over Clarence's creepy girl eyes.

'You really do have an arsehole for a mouth. Shit just pours out of it.'

I chewed and swallowed, taking me time. 'I have evidence. Photos, mate.'

Clarence stared hard at me. I stared hard back.

He snorted. 'No way . . .'

'I'm not joking. I got you coming outta Lima Dorm at the time a the crime, and I happens to know you didn't exactly sign in neither.' Thank you, Anna, I thought. 'And I got another happy snap of you handing something to your mate Hadeon right afterwards. Anyway, as me mum likes to say, it'll all come out in the wash. What be a met-oh-four.'

'What the fuck are you talking about, Bogan?'

'A met-oh-four be when —'

'Cut to the fucken chase, Bogan.'

'Well. Sometimes you put a red T-shirt in together with white socks and undies. And then, when all them colours come out in the wash, well, it ain't so good in factuality.' About halfway through me explanation I began to wonder if I'd picked the right met-oh-four after all, but I forged on like I knew where I be going with it.

'If you're fucking with me . . . Show me these photos.'

'They're already Outside. With a friend. Undeveloped. All I need to do is say the word.'

I had time to eat a few more jellybeans while I waited for him to say something.

'Who else . . . who else have you told this bullshit to?'

I shrugged.

'What do you want from me exactly, Bogan?'

'Now we's talking business. Jellybean?'

Thirty-Two

There was plenty a things what Anna could do to help what didn't put her at any risk. Providing the wire cutters was a bigger deal. If a blue got caught doing that, they could be charged with aiding and abetting. It was a big risk for a blue. The risk went two ways, of course — you couldn't be sure that they wasn't gonna double-cross you at the last minute. What was good about getting Clarence in on the story was that he knew that if he stuffed us around, he'd be the one what be going down big-time. And I wouldn't have to pay him, neither, like I was ready to do with Tip. I reckon I coulda almost got him to pay me, but I wasn't gonna try and push it that far.

Besides, in factuality, I wasn't planning to let him off the hook for what he done to Angel. Anna had the photos and she was fully ready to take them to the cops after we'd cleared outta there. She knew it be him what was giving us the wire cutters too, what be just another nail in his coffin. Muvvafucker.

There was just one more loose end, but it was me big one. She Who. She heard about the trouble on the news, that someone had OD'ed, and someone else had thrown himself on the razor wire. The Minister said it was 'attention-seeking behaviour', but there wasn't no names mentioned. When I told her, she was shattered like glass. She came to visit.

'Let's go to Turkey, Zek,' she said. 'You'll do your army service. I'll meet you there. We'll get by somehow.'

'Babydoll, you do love me, don't you?'

She straightened up. 'Don't think that means you can get away with anything.'

'Wha?' I said, holding up me palms like I was showing her I had nuffin in them. 'Wha? What d'you think I'm wanting to get away with besides you?'

I didn't tell her about the escape plan. Didn't want her to worry her pretty little head about it. But I had it worked out. She'd come round in the end. She always did. I'd sort out some fake papers for meself and we'd go start a new life over in Perth, what be far from all this shit. I wouldn't do nuffin illegal no more. It'd be sweet. Everyone was gonna be happy when the Zekster finished doing what the Zekster had to do.

Finally, everything was set up. Clarence, what was looking haunted like ghosts moved in, got me two good pairs a wire cutters. He was still calling me Bogan, but I think we both knew who be the boss. Anna, what was gonna be on duty, told me when the other blues was likely to be busy.

Thomas, what was still waiting on his health and security checks, was gonna sit lookout on the Stage Two side, what couldn't never be proved cuz lotsa people sat there all the time, and Edward the Leb five-oh-one was gonna sit lookout on the Stage Three side. Marley was gonna borrow April's car and wait on the road outside. She didn't tell her mum what she wanted the car for. April had asked her if she was going to have a licensed driver with her, cuz Marley only had her Ls. Marley insured her she did, but didn't say it was gonna be me.

April was busy helping Thomas through the final stages of his security checks. Also, the Minister had said that for Thomas to get out, someone had to sign up to support him financially for two years. That was causing some stressation cuz Thomas didn't wanna be relying on nobody. But April insisted it was no problem, and Josh was being really good about it, and he even came to Detention to meet Thomas. They was sorting it all out, anyway. She was so busy getting back together with Josh and with the paperwork for Thomas that she didn't even notice Marley was spending a lotta time on the phone.

All the pieces was falling into place. Hamid told us he signed that paper to go home, but it was gonna take a few weeks to organise. He offered to make a detraction what would occupy the attention a the blues. And Azad and Bhajan and me, we was going to Medical with headaches what we didn't really have, if you didn't count Detention. Then the three of us, we was gonna get outta that hellhole for once and for all. We was gonna do it at nine-thirty pee-em, what was the time Anna recommended. I was eating chocolates to kill the butterflies in me stomach, what was big as horses. The others said they couldn't eat a thing, what I never understood. We was all in me room, watching the evening news.

First item on the news was about some bloke what sneaked into the baggage area in Melbourne Airport causing a panic about security. Second item was how Our Nicole — My Nic — and Our Russ was the bookies' favourites to win the Oscars what was in March. And people, including in the Navy, was saying the Prime Minister lied when he said that stuff about refugees throwing them children overboard. The Senate was looking into it.

'Maybe the Prime Minister will go to jail,' said Azad.

'If he does,' I said, 'I'll get me mates what is still Inside to find him a boyfriend.'

Bhajan shook his head. 'Please say you'll always be my friend, Zeki.'

'You're me *mate*,' I said, 'what is more than friends. It's Australian.'

Thirty-Three

I looked at me watch. It took Azad and Bhajan only four minutes to cut through the first fence, the razor wire and the second fence. Being the leader, I was going last. Bhajan, what was wearing the heavy gloves what Clarence got for us too, was holding open the coil a razor wire for me when suddenly Edward whistled. The whistle was an alarm what said there be danger. It spooked Bhajan, what let the wire go for a second. It snagged on me clothes, what I was wearing a lotta for that very reason. 'C'mon,' he said, his whole body shaking like his voice.

But I couldn't move. Where skinny Azad and Bhajan had just slipped through, me and me big stomach was caught in the wire. A pitcher a that currawong what I once rescued popped into me head, but there wasn't any trail a seeds leading outta this mess. I tried to flap me wings and cut me hand. 'Go,' I said. 'Get outta here.'

A minute later, couldn't have been much more than that, I heard two car doors slam and a squeal a tyres. I glanced over at where Thomas had been sitting, but he wasn't there no more.

Survival Rule Number Five: You gotta laugh. And so I did, what only made the razor bits stick in me clothes even more. I was still laughing when Anna ran over with some other blues, looking pale and grim in the face. They extradited me from the wire, and slapped me in cuffs. That's when I learned that Hamid had created a top-rate detraction all right.

Stupid bugger had gone and topped himself.

Epilogue

I got a philosophy a life. When times be tough and you can do bugger all about it, me Rule a Survival is to kick back. The bad times were pretty bad. I still felt sick and sad and angry whenever I thought about Angel and Hamid. And I always wondered what happened to Azad and Marley and Bhajan, and how April and Thomas was getting on. I hoped Abeer and Bashir and Noor got out and got to be kids again, and that all the others got their freedom too. Me, I did all right in the end. See, I did me military service, and though it wasn't much fun, She Who reckons it really did make a man outta me. Times were good. And when times are good, kicking back is even sweeter. And kicking back was exactly what I was doing, puffing on me hookah, working on me smoke rings, when I saw this lady coming through the door a the shop. I reckoned she was a bit of all right. She glanced around at the carpets and stuff.

'G'day,' I said. She looked up from the rugs.

'G'day,' she said. But her tone be real surprised. 'You speak like an Australian.'

I smiled and shrugged.

'You been to Australia?'

'You could say that. Where are you from?'

'Sydney, but —'

'Where in Sydney?'

She was looking at me like she was having trouble putting two and two together, what be an expression what means four. 'You know Sydney?'

I gave her me best International Man a Mystery smile.

'Do you know Rushcutters Bay?' She said it like she was testing me.

'Bayswater Road. Picolo Bar, Barrons, Candy's Apartment and that joint up on the corner what have the chicken and pizza. Big park round the bay what has yachts in. And Dancers. You know Dancers?'

She laughed. 'I've been past it. I don't think I'm exactly their target audience. How the —' She paused and wiped her forehead, what was perspiring, with a tissue.

'Hot as buggery, innit — pardon me French.'

'You *are* Australian, aren't you?' The lady had cute dimples what reminded me of April.

'Sort of. Not really.'

She looked a million hard pointy question marks at me.

'It's a long story,' I said. 'It's got both really sad and really funny bits in.'

'I'm just travelling. I've got time,' she said, smiling. 'If I'm not interrupting.'

I gestated round the shop. There was a few other customers at the moment but they seemed happy enough just looking.

Just then, She Who Followed Me to the Ends a the Earth came in from the back room with a tray with glasses a mint tea. Our son what was only little but had big ears and one eyebrow like his dad, followed close behind with a plate a sweets. I swear She Who is a witch what knows every time a pretty woman be in the shop. She offered tea to all the customers, including the lady, and then to me own good self. 'Thanks, darl,' I said.

'I'm Marlena,' goes She Who. She put down the tray and held out her hand to the woman, giving me a tiny look a accusation.

'I'm Penny,' said the woman.

'I was just gonna introduce youse,' I said. 'Anyway, I'm Zeki. Zek for short, what I is as you can see. And this little one what has inherited all me good looks and charm is Babar, what means lion.'

The woman laughed and shook Babar's hand. He offered her a sweet what she took and thanked him for. 'What a lovely boy you are.'

'You too,' Babar replied, smooth as cream. 'Lady, that is.'

One a the customers came to the counter holding a small kilim. 'Do. You. Speak. English?' he asked She Who, who winked at me.

'Yes, of course,' she said. 'And I must say, that's a *very* good choice. You don't find many like that these days.' Except out the back where we keep them, but she wasn't gonna tell him that. Marlena learned heaps about rugs and shit when she first came. I was in the army, so me rellies, including me

Uncle Abi, showed her the ropes and taught her to speak some Turkish, too. She can sound real authoritative.

Penny, what was sitting down now, and me, we watched Marlena sell the Yank the kilim, plus another rug what was bigger, plus a set a tea glasses, and two evil-eye keychains. The next customers, a couple from England, was fingering another kilim what they liked but they was complaining about the price. 'There is an old Turkish proverb,' She Who quoted to them. 'That which is cheap is cheap for a reason; when you pay money, you get value.' The woman looked to her husband. He nodded and handed over the plastic.

As she wrapped up the deal, I glanced at me watch. 'Looks like time for more tea, darl,' I said.

'Nice watch,' Penny said.

'It's got what they call sentimental value,' I said.

'Keep an eye on your dad,' Marlena said to Babar. She went into the back to make more tea and bring out another kilim like the one the Yank bought cuz it be our most popular.

'She's a good saleswoman, your wife,' Penny said after they left. I got all puffed up like she be talking about meself.

'I always told her she was a natural born businesswoman.' It turned out to be true. She Who told me that if she hadn't a taken the leap and come with me when I was deported, she probably woulda ended up emptying bedpans and sweeping hospital corridors the rest of her life.

Penny turned back to me. 'So, Zeki. What's this long story of yours?'

Acknowledgments

The author gratefully acknowledges a generous New Work grant for *The Infernal Optimist* from the Australia Council. I also thank the U-Committee of the University of New South Wales for making me UNSW Literary Fellow for 2004, a fellowship which provided not only invaluable financial assistance, but also an office on the friendly campus of the College of Fine Arts, where I wrote much of the second draft of the book. The Tasmanian Writers' Centre, with the support of the City of Hobart and Arts Tasmania, gave me a home in the Hobart Writers' Cottage in April 2005 as part of their 2005 Island of Residencies Program, where I pushed the work to completion. Thank you all.

My agent Lesley McFadzean and her predecessors Rose Creswell and Annette Hughes believed in the *Optimist* from the beginning. Lesley helped me find an ideal publisher in Linda Funnell of Fourth Estate and I have been delighted by the enthusiasm for this novel on the part of Linda and all her colleagues at HarperCollins Australia, especially my editor Sophie Hamley.

Others who have supported and helped me include Peter Bishop of Varuna, A Writer's House; refugee activist and fellow Villawood visitor Judy McLallen, who contributed the notion of 'knitters and kayakers', and Jonathan Cohen, who gave me the delightful malapropism 'for all intensive purposes'. Most of all, and from the bottom of my heart, I thank former detainees Morteza Poorvadi and Amir Mesrinejad, who took the time to read the entire draft and offer many useful suggestions, as well as Mahmoud Mohammed Ali and other Palestinian, Kurdish, Iraqi, Bedoon, Afghani and African refugees, many of whom were also 'Villawood alumni', and even some Villawood guards, who asked to remain nameless but were generous with both their time and knowledge. I am, of course, 'infernally grateful' to Attila, a former Villawood 'five-oh-one', for inspiration, encouragement, stories and insights. My partner, Tim Smith, was his usual supportive and wonderful self; it is to him that this book is, as Zeki might say, lovingly devotioned.